ALSO BY FREIDA MCFADDEN

Ward D
Never Lie
The Coworker
The Housemaid
The Housemaid's Secret
Do You Remember?
Do Not Disturb
The Locked Door
Want to Know a Secret?
One by One
The Wife Upstairs
The Perfect Son
The Ex
The Surrogate Mother
Brain Damage
Baby City
Suicide Med
The Devil Wears Scrubs
The Devil You Know

THE INMATE

FREIDA McFADDEN

Published by Poisoned Pen Press, an imprint of Sourcebooks
P.O. Box 4410, Naperville, Illinois 60567-4410
(630) 961-3900
sourcebooks.com

Originally self-published in 2022 by Freida McFadden.

Library of Congress Cataloging-in-Publication Data

Names: McFadden, Freida, author.
Title: The inmate / Freida McFadden.
Description: Naperville, Illinois : Poisoned Pen Press, 2024.
Identifiers: LCCN 2023028433 | (trade paperback)
Subjects: LCGFT: Prison fiction. | Thrillers (Fiction) | Novels.
Classification: LCC PS3613.C4365 I56 2024 | DDC 813/.6--dc23/eng/20230626
LC record available at https://lccn.loc.gov/2023028433

Printed and bound in the United States of America.
VP 12 11 10 9 8

To my family

CHAPTER 1

PRESENT DAY

As the prison doors slam shut behind me, I question every decision I've ever made in my life.

This is not where I want to be right now. At *all.* Who wants to be in a maximum-security penitentiary? I'm going to wager nobody wants that. If you are within these walls, you may have made some poor life choices along the way.

I sure have.

"Name?"

A woman in a blue correctional officer's uniform is looking up at me from behind the glass partition just inside the entrance to the prison. Her eyes are dull and glassy, and she looks like she doesn't want to be here any more than I do.

"Brooke Sullivan." I clear my throat. "I'm supposed to meet with Dorothy Kuntz?"

The woman looks down at a clipboard of papers in front of her. She scans the list, not acknowledging that she heard me or that she knows anything about why I'm here. I glance behind me into the small waiting area, which is empty except for a wrinkled old man sitting in one of the plastic chairs, reading a newspaper like he's sitting on the bus. Like there isn't a barbed wire fence surrounding us, dotted with hulking guard towers.

After what feels like several minutes, a buzzing sound echoes through the room—loud enough that I jump and take a step back. A door to my right with red vertical bars slowly slides open, revealing a long, dimly lit hallway.

I stare down the hallway, my feet frozen to the floor. "Should…should I go in?"

The woman looks up at me with her dull eyes. "Yes, go. You pass through the security check down the hall."

She nods in the direction of the dark hallway, and a chill goes through me as I walk tentatively through the barred door, which slides closed again and locks with a resounding thud. I've never been here before. My job interview was over the phone, and the warden was so desperate to hire me, he didn't even feel compelled to meet me first—my résumé and letters of recommendation were enough. I signed a one-year contract and faxed it over last week.

And now I'm here. For the next year of my life.

This is a mistake. I never should have come here.

I look behind me at the red metal bars that have already slammed shut. It's not too late. Even though I signed a contract, I'm sure I could get out of it. I could still turn around and leave this place. Unlike the residents of this prison, I don't have to be here.

I didn't want this job. I wanted any other job but this one. But I applied to every single job within a sixty-minute commute of the town of Raker in upstate New York, and this prison was the only place that called me back for an interview. It was my last choice, and I felt lucky to get it.

So I keep walking.

There's a man at the security check-in all the way down the hall, guarding a second barred door. He's in his forties with a short, military-style haircut and wearing the same crisp blue uniform as the dead-eyed woman at the front desk. I looked down at the ID badge clipped to his breast pocket: Correctional Officer Steven Benton.

"Hi!" I say, in a voice that I realize is a little too chirpy, but I can't help myself. "My name is Brooke Sullivan, and it's my first day working here."

Benton's expression doesn't shift as his dark eyes rake over me. I squirm as I rethink all the fashion choices I made this morning. Working in a men's maximum-security prison, I figured it was better not to dress in a way that might be construed as suggestive. So I'm wearing a pair of boot-cut black dress pants, paired with a black button-up long-sleeved shirt. It's almost eighty degrees out, one of the last hot days of the summer, and I'm regretting all the black, but it seemed like the way to call the least attention to myself. My dark hair is pinned back in a simple ponytail. The only makeup I have on is some concealer to hide the dark circles under my eyes and a scrap of lipstick that's almost the same color as my lips.

"Next time," he says, "no high heels."

"Oh!" I look down at my black pumps. Nobody gave me any guidance whatsoever on the dress code, much less the *shoe* code. "Well, they're not very high. And they're *chunky*—not sharp or anything. I really don't think..."

My protests die on my lips as Benton stares at me. No high heels. Got it.

Benton runs my purse through a metal detector, and then I walk through a much larger one myself. I make a nervous joke about how it feels like I'm at the airport, but I'm getting the sense that this guy doesn't like jokes too much. Next time, no high heels, no jokes.

"I'm supposed to meet Dorothy Kuntz," I tell him. "She's a nurse here."

Benton grunts. "You a nurse too?"

"Nurse practitioner," I correct him. "I'm going to be working at the clinic here."

He raises an eyebrow at me. "Good luck with that."

I'm not sure what that means exactly.

Benton presses a button, and again, that ear-shattering buzzing sound goes off, just before the second set of barred doors slides open. He directs me down a hallway to the medical ward of the prison. There's a strange chemical smell in the hallway, and the fluorescent lights overhead keep flickering. With every step I take, I'm terrified that some prisoner will appear out of nowhere and bludgeon me to death with one of my high-heeled shoes.

When I turn left at the end of the hallway, a woman is waiting for me. She is roughly in her sixties, with close-cropped gray hair and a sturdy build. There's something vaguely familiar about her, but I can't put my finger on what it is. Unlike the guards, she's dressed in a pair of navy-blue scrubs. Like everyone else I've met so far at this prison, she isn't smiling. I wonder if it's against the rules here. I should check my contract. *Employees may be terminated for smiling.*

"Brooke Sullivan?" she asks in a clipped voice that's deeper than I would have expected.

"That's right. You're Dorothy?"

Much like the guard at the front, she looks me up and down. And much like him, she looks utterly disappointed by what she sees. "No high heels," she tells me.

"I know. I—"

"If you know, why did you wear them?"

"I mean…" My face burns. "I know *now*."

She reluctantly accepts this answer and decides not to force me to spend my orientation barefoot. She waves a hand, and I obediently trot after her down the hallway. The whole outside of the medical ward has the same chemical smell as the rest of the prison and the same flickering fluorescent lights. There's a set of plastic chairs lined up against the wall, but they're empty. She wrenches open the door of one of the rooms.

"This will be your exam room," she tells me.

I peer inside. The room is about half the size of the ones at the urgent care clinic where I used to work in Queens. But other than that, it looks the same. An examining table in the center of the room, a stool for me to sit on, and a small desk.

"Will I have an office?" I ask.

Dorothy shakes her head. "No, but you've got a perfectly good desk in there. Don't you see it?"

So I'm supposed to document with the patients looking over my shoulder? "What about a computer?"

"Medical records are all on paper."

I am stunned to hear that. I've never worked in a place with paper medical records. I didn't even know it was allowed anymore. But I suppose the rules are a little different in prison.

She points to a room next to the examining room. "That's the records room. Your ID badge will open it up. We'll get you one of those before you leave."

She holds her ID badge up to the scanner on the wall, and there's a loud click. She throws open the door to reveal a small dusty room filled with file cabinets. Tons and tons of file cabinets. This is going to be agony.

"Is there a doctor here supervising?" I ask.

She hesitates. "Dr. Wittenburg covers about half a dozen prisons. You won't see him much, but he's available by phone."

That makes me uneasy. At the urgent care, I was never alone. But I suppose the issues there were more acute than what I'll see here. At least that's what I'm hoping.

Our next stop on the tour is the supply room. It's about the same as the room at the urgent care clinic, but of course smaller—also with ID badge access. There are bandages, suture materials, and various bins and tubes and chemicals.

"Only I can dispense medications," Dorothy tells me. "You write the order, and I'll dispense the medication to the patient. If there's something we don't have, we can put it on order."

I rub my sweaty hands against my black dress pants. "Right, okay."

Dorothy gives me a long look. "I know you're anxious working in a maximum-security prison, but you have to know that a lot of these men will be grateful for your care. As long as you're professional, you won't have any problems."

"Right."

"Do *not* share any personal information." Her lips set into a straight line. "Do *not* tell them where you live. Don't tell them *anything* about your life. Don't put up any photos. Do you have children?"

"I have a son."

Dorothy regards me in surprise. She expected me to say no. Most people are surprised when I tell them I have a child. Even though I'm twenty-eight, I look much younger. Although I feel a lot older.

I look like I'm in college, and I feel like I'm fifty. Story of my life.

"Well," Dorothy says, "don't talk about your kid. Keep it professional. Always. I don't know what you're used to in your old job, but these men are not your friends. These are criminals who have committed extremely serious offenses, and a lot of them are here for life."

"I know." Boy, do I know.

"And most of all..." Dorothy's icy-blue eyes bore into me. "You need to remember that while most of these men will see you for legitimate reasons, some of them are here to get drugs. We have a small quantity of narcotics in the pharmacy, but those are reserved for rare occasions. Do not let these men trick you into prescribing narcotics for them to abuse or sell."

"Of course."

"Also," she adds, "never accept any sort of payment in exchange for narcotics. If anyone makes an offer like that to you, you come straight to me."

I suck in a breath. "I would *never* do that."

Dorothy gives me a pointed look. "Yes, well, that's what the last one said. Now she's gonna end up in a place like this herself."

For a moment, I am speechless. When the warden interviewed me, I asked about the last person working here, and he said that she left for "personal reasons." He didn't happen to mention that she was arrested for selling narcotics to prisoners.

It's sobering to think that the last person who had this job before me is now incarcerated. I've heard that once you're in the prison system, it's hard to get out of it. Maybe the same is true for people who work here.

Dorothy notices the look on my face, and her expression softens just the tiniest bit. "Don't worry," she says. "It's not as scary as you think. Really, it's just like any other medical job. You see patients, you make them better, then you send them back to their lives."

"Yes..." I rub the back of my neck. "I was just wondering...am I going to be responsible for seeing *all* the prisoners in the penitentiary? Like, do I just cover a segment or...?"

Her lips curl. "No, you're it, girlie. You're seeing everyone. Any problem with that?"

"No, not at all," I say.

But that's a lie.

The real reason I was reluctant to take this job isn't that I'm scared a prisoner will murder me with my own shoe. It's because of one of the inmates in this prison. Someone I knew a long time ago, who I am not eager to see ever again.

But I can't tell that to Dorothy. I can't reveal to her that the man who was my very first boyfriend is an inmate at Raker Maximum Security Penitentiary, currently serving life without the possibility of parole.

And I'm the one who put him here.

CHAPTER 2

When I pull onto the street of my parents' house in my old blue Toyota, I've got a laminated ID badge for Raker Penitentiary in my handbag. Dorothy gave me an ominous warning about not letting it fall into the wrong hands, but based on my access privileges, I'm pretty sure the only thing somebody could do with it is steal some Band-Aids and use the employee toilet. Still, I'll guard it with my life.

Despite the sour note on which I left town over a decade ago, I loved growing up in Raker. It's a beautiful town, with trees on every corner, picturesque old houses, and neighbors who won't automatically avert their eyes when they pass you on the street like in Queens. And when you look at the sky at night, you can make out the individual constellations instead of just a few random dots of light that are probably airplanes.

This is exactly the sort of place where a child should grow up. This is exactly what my little family needed.

I park outside the two-car garage, which is a holdover to the old days, when my parents would park in the garage and I had to park outside or on the street. Old habits die hard. I still think of this as their house, even though it's not anymore. It's mine—all mine.

After all, they're both dead now.

When I unlock the front door, the sound of the TV wafts into the foyer, along with the smell of cooking meat. I close my eyes, and for a moment, I let myself fantasize about some alternate universe in which I'm coming home to my family and my partner is in the kitchen, cooking dinner.

But of course, it's nothing but a fantasy. There's never been a partner in my life who has been around enough to cook dinner. I'm beginning to wonder if there ever will be. The delicious smell is courtesy of the babysitter, who was kind enough to get dinner started.

"Hello?" I call out. "I'm home!"

I wait for a moment, wondering if Josh will come out to greet me. There was an age when Mommy coming home was followed by the scrambling of little feet and a warm body hurling itself at my knees. Those kinds of greetings are less common now that Josh has turned ten years old. He still loves me, don't get me wrong, just not quite so *emphatically*.

Sure enough, a second later, Josh stumbles into the foyer in his bare feet. This is the last week before school starts, and he's taking advantage of it by spending 90 percent of his time on the sofa, either watching television or playing Nintendo. I shouldn't let him do it, but soon enough, there will be school and homework and sports teams. His big thing is Little League, and that doesn't start till the spring, but when it gets closer, he'll want me to take him to the park to practice.

"Hi, Mom!"

I hold out my arms, and he falls into them, not entirely reluctantly. "Hey, kiddo. How was your day?"

"Okay."

"Did you do anything besides sit on the couch?"

He grins at me. "Why would I?"

Josh brushes his brown hair out of his eyes. He needs a haircut, which, if history is any indication, will be done in the bathroom over the sink. But he's definitely getting a haircut before school starts. Every day, the kid looks a bit more like his father, and with his hair shaggy like that, the resemblance is enough to make my chest ache.

A timer goes off in the kitchen, and I head in that direction as the smell of baking chicken intensifies. God, I miss home-cooked meals. My mother used to cook most nights, but I hadn't lived under her roof for a long time before I moved here for good last month, following her death.

I approach the kitchen just as Margie is pulling a tray out of the oven. Margie is a local grandma who is going to be watching Josh when I am working. He tried to protest that he didn't need a babysitter, but I'm not comfortable with him being alone for hours while I am forty-five minutes away—at a *prison*. Besides, Josh is only ten years old. And he's not exactly a *mature* ten.

"That smells incredible, Margie," I say.

Margie beams at me and tucks an errant strand of gray hair behind one ear. "Oh, it's nothing. Just roast chicken pieces with garlic butter sauce. And of course, rice and asparagus on the side. You can't *just* eat chicken."

Hmm, you can't? Because I am pretty sure that over the last ten years, there have been plenty of nights when Josh and I have eaten nothing but chicken. From a bucket with a smiling colonel on the side of it.

But that's in the past. Things are going to be different now. This is a fresh start for both of us.

Josh takes an overly exaggerated whiff of air. "It smells too *saucy*."

I stare at him. "What does that mean? You can't smell too much sauce."

Margie winks. "I think he's smelling the butter and garlic."

He crinkles his nose. "I don't like garlic. Can't we just go to McDonald's?"

I don't quite understand how you can love somebody so much yet so frequently want to throttle them.

"First of all," I say, "there's no McDonald's in Raker, so no, we *can't* go to McDonald's. And second, Margie made us a delicious home-cooked meal. If you don't want it, you can make your own dinner."

Margie laughs. "You sound like my daughter."

I'm hoping that's a compliment. "Thank you so much for coming today, Margie. You'll be here to meet Josh after school on Monday? The school bus is supposed to be here around three."

"It's a date!" she confirms.

I walk Margie to the door, even though she's got her own key. Just before I bid her goodbye, she hesitates, a groove between her gray eyebrows. "Listen, Brooke..."

If she tells me she's quitting, I am going to curl up in a ball and cry. She was the only available sitter even remotely in my price range, and I can barely afford her as is. "Yes?"

"Josh seems really nervous about starting school," she says. "I know it's hard being in a new town and all, especially at his age. But he seemed even more anxious than I would expect."

"Oh…"

"I don't want to worry you, dear," she says. "I just wanted to let you know."

My heart goes out to my ten-year-old son. I can't blame him for missing McDonald's. McDonald's is familiar. Raker is not familiar, and neither is this house. In his entire life, my parents would never let us visit—they always came out to us in the city, until I told them they couldn't anymore. This town is home to me, but to Josh, it's a town full of strangers.

And I can think of a few other reasons why he would be scared about starting school after what happened back in Queens.

"I'll take care of it," I say. "Thanks again, Margie."

I come back into the kitchen, where Josh is sitting at the kitchen table, playing with the salt and pepper shakers. He's making a little pile of salt and pepper, which I've told him repeatedly not to do, but I'm not angry about it right now. I slide into the seat across from him.

"Hey, buddy," I say. "You okay?"

Josh traces his first initial, *J*, in the pile of condiments on the table. "Yeah."

"Feeling nervous about school?"

He lifts one of his skinny shoulders.

"I heard the kids are really nice here," I say. "It won't be like back home."

He lifts his brown eyes. "How could you know that?"

I flinch, experiencing his pain like it's my own. Last

year at school, Josh got bullied. *Badly*. I didn't even know that it was happening because he didn't talk about it at home. He just started getting quieter and quieter. I couldn't figure out why until the day he came home with a black eye.

Even with the shiner, Josh tried to deny anything was going on. He was so ashamed to tell me why the other kids were bullying him. I had no idea what happened. My son is a little on the quiet side, but there's nothing about him that stands out—I didn't have a clue what made him a target. Until I found out the name all the other kids were calling him:

Bastard.

It was a knife in my heart that the other kids were bullying him because of *me*. Because of *my* history and the fact that my son never had a father. I had some dark thoughts after that, believe me.

The school had a no-tolerance bullying policy, but apparently, that was just something they said to sound like they were doing the right thing. Nobody seemed to have any compulsion to do anything to help my son. And it didn't help that the principal had judgment in his eyes when he noted that the other kids were simply pointing out an unfortunate reality about my *situation*.

When you are a single mom who is barely keeping it together as it is, it's hard to deal with a school that pretends nothing is wrong. And a bunch of other parents twenty years older than you are and who have a lot more money. I even consulted with a lawyer, which wiped out most of my checking account, but the upshot was that they recommended moving Josh to a new school.

So after a car wreck killed both my parents at the end

of the school year, I decided not to sell the house where I grew up. This was the fresh start Josh and I needed.

"You are going to make friends," I say to my son.

"Maybe," he says.

"You will," I insist. "I *promise*."

The problem with your kid getting older is they know there are some things you can't promise.

Josh doesn't look up from the little pile of salt and pepper. This time, he writes an *S* in it for his last name. "Mom?"

"Yes, sweetie?"

"Now that we're living here, am I going to meet my dad?"

I almost choke on my own saliva. Wow, I did not know that thought was going through his head. As much as I have tried my best to be two parents for this kid, there have been times in Josh's life when he has seemed obsessed with who his father is. When he was five, I couldn't get him to stop talking about it. Every day, he would come home with a new drawing of his father and what he imagined that father would look like. An astronaut. A police officer. A veterinarian. But he hasn't mentioned his father in a while.

"Josh," I begin.

"Because he lives here?" He raises his eyes from the table. "Right?"

Every word is like a little tiny dagger in my heart. I should've just told him that his father was dead. That would've made things so much easier. I could have made up some wonderful story about how his father was a hero who died, I don't know, trying to save a puppy from a fire. He would've been happy with that. Maybe if I told him the puppy fire story, the kids wouldn't have bullied him last year.

"Honey," I say, "your dad used to live here, but now he doesn't. Not anymore."

I can't quite read the expression on Josh's face. The other problem with your kid getting older is that they can tell when you're lying.

CHAPTER 3

The man in front of me has exactly one tooth.

Okay, that's not entirely true. Mr. Henderson has a couple of teeth in the back that are black and in need of serious dental care, but when he smiles, all I can see is that one yellow tooth on the top row of his mouth.

"You're a lifesaver, Doc," Mr. Henderson tells me as he flashes ol' Chomper at me one more time. I've told him twice now that I'm not a doctor, but he seems to like to call me that. "I can't tell you how much I appreciate this."

"Happy to help," I say.

I have done practically nothing for Mr. Henderson. All I have done is give him a prescription for a new inhaler for his emphysema, which seems to have worsened in the last few months. The prisoners have to fill out a kite form, which is a requisition to come see me if it's not a regularly scheduled visit, and the form Mr. Henderson filled out just says, "Can't breathe."

All the patients I have seen on my first day have been like this. I don't know what these men did to end up in the maximum-security prison, but they are all so incredibly polite and grateful for the care I provide. I don't know what terrible crime this sixty-three-year-old man committed, and I don't want to know. Right now, I like the guy.

"I've been coughing and wheezing ever since the other girl left," Mr. Henderson tells me. As if to demonstrate his point, Mr. Henderson gives a loud, wet, hacking cough. I'd love to get a chest X-ray, but the technician isn't here today, so it will have to wait until tomorrow.

The staffing here is terrible. One day into the job, and that much is painfully obvious. Before I came aboard, Dr. Wittenburg was stopping by occasionally, and other than that, they were sending inmates to the ER or urgent care for basic medical care—at enormous cost to the prison. No wonder they seemed so desperate to hire me.

Desperate enough to overlook my intimate connection to one of the inmates.

"What about Dorothy?" I ask. "Did you tell her about your breathing problems?"

He waves a hand. "She just says stop being such a baby."

While the men are polite enough, I've heard my fair share of whining about Dorothy today. None of them seem to like her much.

"You're great though, Doc," Mr. Henderson says.

"Thank you." I smile at him. "Do you have any other questions or concerns?"

"Yeah, I got a question." He scratches at the rat's nest of gray hair on his head. "Are you married?"

Dorothy's warning about not giving out personal information to any of the patients is still ringing in my ears. But this seems like a rather harmless question. And he can clearly see that I'm not wearing a wedding band.

"No," I say. "Not married."

"Well, I'm sure you'll find somebody soon, Doc," he says. "You're real young and pretty. You don't need to worry."

Great.

Mr. Henderson hops off the examining table, and I lead him out of the room, making a few last-minute quick notes on his paper chart. The documentation requirements here are pretty limited from what I've seen. The last nurse practitioner, Elise, just made a few notes in her large loopy handwriting for each of her visits. Whatever else Elise is guilty of, I'm grateful she had good handwriting.

Correctional Officer Marcus Hunt is waiting outside the exam room. Hunt is the officer assigned to the medical unit, which means he brings the patients to the waiting area (i.e., the plastic chairs lined up outside the examining room), and he stands at attention right outside the room while I'm with the patients.

Hunt is tall, and while he's not exactly broad, he looks strong under his blue guard's uniform. He's maybe in his early thirties with a shaved skull and a few days' growth of a beard on his chin. There are no windows on the doors, so it's comforting to leave the door to the exam room open and know Hunt is right outside. I've noticed sometimes Hunt leaves the door wide open, and other times, like with Mr. Henderson, he just cracks it slightly. I figure he knows more about the inmates than I do, so I leave it to his discretion.

About a third of the men today came in with their wrists shackled. A couple of them had their ankles shackled as well. I didn't ask how they determine who gets shackled and who doesn't.

I deliver Mr. Henderson to Officer Hunt, and he nods at me without expression. Like Dorothy, he doesn't smile much, or at all. The only people who have smiled at me since I've been here have been the prisoners.

"I'll take him back to his cell," Hunt tells me.

I check the plastic chairs outside the examining room. "Nobody else is waiting?"

"No, you get a break."

I watch Hunt disappear down a hallway with Mr. Henderson, leaving me alone. Not that I'm not glad to have a break, but there's not much to do around here. The Wi-Fi signal is practically nonexistent, and there's nobody around to talk to. I should start bringing a book to read if there's a break in the schedule.

The medical records room is located on the left. I've been in there a couple of times today to locate charts, since nobody does it for me. I look down at my watch—still another hour before quitting time. Then I look both ways down the hallway.

There's nobody here but me.

I creep over to the medical records room and use my ID badge to unlock the door. It's a painfully claustrophobic room packed with as many file cabinets as can be squeezed into this amount of space, lit by a single naked bulb on the ceiling. There's also a stack of files dumped in the corner of the room, the pages spilling out. Dorothy told me those are from inmates who are no longer here. Since most of these men are serving life sentences, I'm guessing that means they're dead.

I don't have much time here before Hunt returns. Fortunately, I know exactly what I'm looking for.

I make a beeline for the drawer marked *N.* I pull it open, exposing a thick stack of charts packed tightly into the drawer. I thumb through the names. Nash. Nabb. Napier. Neil.

Nelson.

I pull out the chart, my hands shaking slightly. The name scribbled on the tab is Shane Nelson. It's *him*. He's still here. Not that I should be surprised, since the last time I saw him, he was being sentenced to spend the rest of his life here.

I close my eyes, and I can still see his ruggedly handsome face. His eyes looking into mine. *I love you, Brooke.*

That was what he said to me just a few hours before he tried to kill me.

And that's not even the worst thing he did.

I stare down at the paper chart, wanting to open it and look inside but knowing I shouldn't. Morally, I definitely shouldn't. Legally…it's a gray area. Technically, as a prisoner of this facility, he's one of my patients. But if I open this chart, I won't be looking at it as a practitioner.

I've only been here a day. It's a bit early to be breaking the rules.

When I applied for this job, I didn't think I would get it, given my connection to one of the inmates. But I was a minor at the time of Shane's trial, and my parents worked hard to keep my name out of public records. Still, I had believed a background check would give me away. But I was wrong.

Or else the warden knew about the connection, but they were so desperate to hire somebody, they let it slide.

I hear a click, and I realize somebody has used their ID badge to unlock the door to medical records. Panicked, I stuff Shane's chart back into the file cabinet and slam the drawer shut just as the door swings open. Officer Hunt is standing there, his tall silhouette filling the doorway.

"We have another patient for you." In the dim light of the room, his eyes look like two dark sockets. "What are you doing in here?"

"I…uh…" I glance back at the file cabinet. "There was just something I thought of on a patient from this morning that I wanted to make a note of."

I have every right to be in this file room. There's no way for him to know that what I was doing in this room was far from kosher, although I suspect my burning cheeks are giving me away.

Hunt narrows his eyes at me. "I laid out all the charts for the scheduled visits. If you need any other charts, I can bring them to you."

"Oh!" I force a smile. "Well, thank you then. I sure appreciate it."

He doesn't return the smile.

Well, great. I've been here less than a day, and the guard already thinks I'm a problem. But it sounds like they need me more than I need them, so my job is safe. For now.

As long as Shane Nelson doesn't need to be seen in the medical ward anytime soon.

CHAPTER 4

ELEVEN YEARS EARLIER

My parents would kill me if they knew what I'm doing right now.

They think I'm studying after school with my best friend Chelsea. They think Chelsea is giving me a ride home, then I'm going to pick up a change of clothes and have a sleepover at her house.

If they knew I was sitting in a car a block away from my house with Shane Nelson, it would be bad. And if they knew it will actually be *Shane's* house where I'll be spending the night tonight…well, I don't even want to know what they would do. For starters, I would be grounded. And not the kind of grounded where I don't get to play video games or I'm deprived of an extra serving of dessert. I would be yanked out of high school, probably homeschooled, and never allowed to leave my bedroom ever again. *That* kind of grounded.

So that's why when Shane drives me home, he always parks a block or two away. Even that is a risk, but when it comes to Shane, I'm all about taking stupid risks. I've always been a good girl—straight As, honor society, debate club. I've never met a guy who has made me want to break all my rules before. And when Shane looks at me from the driver's seat of his Chevy, I realize there's not much I wouldn't do for him.

"I'm really looking forward to tonight," I tell him in a voice that I hope sounds mature and sexy but more likely sounds squeaky and nervous. I can't help it—I've never spent the night at a boy's house before.

"Me too." He traces the curve of the gold snowflake necklace I always wear around my throat. "So much."

Shane's vivid brown eyes meet mine. I've known Shane since middle school, and I swear he gets better looking every year. Shaggy dark hair, a dangerous grin, and now all those damn muscles. Back when we were twelve, he was just a punk who couldn't quit getting in trouble at school. Then in high school, he joined the football team and became the star quarterback. I watch him every day as Chelsea and I cheer from the stands, and he is *really* talented. Still not good enough for my parents though.

"You know," Shane says, "it could just be us at my house tonight. You say the word..."

When Chelsea found out that Shane's mother was going to be out of town visiting his grandmother for the weekend, it was her brilliant idea to have a little party at his house tonight. She quickly invited herself and her own football-star boyfriend, Brandon. Brandon is particularly skilled at always having a bottle of something alcoholic at every party.

"I don't know if that's a good idea," I say. "If Chelsea doesn't get to come, she'll rat me out to my parents."

Shane makes a face. "She's your best friend. You really think she would do that?"

Oh, she absolutely would. Chelsea might be my best friend, but she is always looking out for number one. But for once, I'm sort of glad. Shane and I have been together for three months, and I'm nervous about being all alone with him. I don't think he even knows I'm still a virgin. He isn't one—he hasn't said so, but I'm sure of it. It's not possible.

"It's fine," I say. "It'll be fun to hang out with Chelsea and Brandon."

Shane doesn't protest because Brandon is one of his good friends. But *he's* not nervous about being alone with me. He seems excited about any time he gets to spend with me. It's flattering how much he seems to like me. I dated a few guys before, but Shane is my first real *boyfriend*. He doesn't even seem to mind that we have to sneak around because my parents don't approve of him.

I glance at my watch—I told my mother I would be home by five. "I better go."

"Just another five minutes?"

"Better not."

I don't want to give my parents any excuse to tell me I can't go out tonight. It's only recently that they have eased up on the restrictions from this summer, when a teenage girl named Tracy Gifford from a neighboring town was found murdered in the woods. For a good month after that, everyone was absolutely terrified. But now it's four months later, and it's almost like it never happened. Tracy Gifford was such a big deal, and now it's like she never existed.

"Okay, fine." He grabs my shoulder and pulls me close

to him. I kiss him, deep and hungry, like we're in a competition to see who will swallow the other one first. We can't seem to get enough of each other. "I'll see you tonight."

"See ya."

I start to open the car door, and then I feel his hand on my shoulder. "Brooke?"

I turn to look back at him. "Yes?"

"Brooke, I lope you."

I can't help but grin at him. That's a private joke between the two of us. I was texting him once that I love ice cream, but I mistyped it and wrote *I lope ice cream.* You would think my phone would autocorrect that, but it didn't. And then it became a joke. *I lope french fries. I lope foot rubs.* And then a couple of weeks ago, he blurted out,

I lope you, Brooke.

He doesn't *love* me. Obviously not. I mean, we're only seventeen, and we've only been dating for three months. But he *lopes* me. And that's almost better than love.

"I lope you too," I say.

Shane laughs, and he releases my shoulder to let me leave the car. As I slam the door to the Chevy, the whole car shakes. Shane's car is a piece of junk. He literally got it at the junkyard and used his skills from auto mechanics class to rebuild the engine and get the damn thing running. He painted it, and it looks halfway decent now, but I'm always a little worried it's just going to die in the middle of the road and I'll have to walk back to civilization in what will almost certainly be incredibly uncomfortable shoes because that's just my luck.

But Shane can't afford a new car. Or even a used car. Even though he works every weekend at the pizza parlor, the only car he can afford is one that he bought from the junkyard.

And now you know why my parents will never approve of him. Because according to them, much like his car, Shane is "trash."

Shane rolls down the passenger-side window of the car. "See you tonight, Brooke! Seven thirty!"

"Seven thirty," I repeat obediently.

After that confirmation, Shane's car zooms away, making a lot more noise than a car rightfully should because his muffler is also from the junkyard. I watch the Chevy disappear around the corner because I'm just that kind of infatuated with him. The kind where I have to watch him disappear into the distance. It's sickening, I know.

"So what are you doing at seven thirty, Brooke?"

I come toppling down from my cloud of love (I mean *lope*) at the sound of the voice from behind me. I didn't notice that Shane had parked dangerously close to the Reese household, which he's usually careful not to do. Tim Reese is standing on the front lawn, raking up the last of the leaves from the fall.

Tim. Damn.

"Nothing," I say.

Tim arches an eyebrow at me as I look up at him. I am still not used to looking up at Tim. I've known him since we were both in diapers, when he went by Timmy and had a face full of freckles, like a freckle bomb had exploded in his face. He was always a couple of inches shorter than me, then he suddenly shot up about a year ago.

"Are you meeting Shane at seven thirty?" Tim presses me.

I avert my eyes. Chelsea might be my best friend, but Tim knows me better than anybody in the world. "Maybe…"

Tim's blue eyes darken. "I can't believe you're still dating that jerk."

My parents hate Shane, but Tim hates him even more. He hates him with a strange passion that I don't entirely understand. Tim isn't the kind of guy who would judge somebody because they drive a thirdhand car and live in an old farmhouse that's one loose shingle away from being condemned. There are other reasons he hates Shane.

"Tim," I mutter, "stop it."

He rubs his chin. The freckles have mostly faded in the last few years, partially because he's careful to stay out of the sun. But I miss Tim's freckles. The freckles were adorable. Without them and now half a head taller than I am, he's become handsome, but he's not adorable anymore. Moreover, he seems like a different person. A different kid from the one I spent the summers with, running and screaming through the sprinklers in his backyard.

"Shane's a jerk," he declares.

"Oh, come on."

"He is," Tim snaps. "He and all his football buddies are a bunch of bullies. I can't believe you don't see it, Brooke."

I shift between my feet in Tim's yard, which is muddy from the moisture in the air. The air is heavy and damp, and I can feel my hair starting to curl. The forecast called for heavy rain and thunderstorms tonight, and Chelsea and I are intending to reach the farmhouse before it begins. So I should get a move on, but I hate the judgment on Tim's face, and I'm desperate to prove him wrong. He doesn't know Shane the way I do. I used to think Shane was a jerk, but he's not. He's a good guy, and I really like him. I *lope* him. Tim just can't see it. I wish he could.

"If you got to know Shane," I say, "I bet you'd like him."

Tim snorts and shakes his head.

"Listen," I say, "you should come tonight."

He narrows his eyes. "Come where?"

The words spill out before I can overthink them. "We're meeting at Shane's house tonight. His mom is going to be out of town. It's going to be me and Shane and Chelsea and Brandon." I raise an eyebrow hopefully. "And you?"

"Sorry, I'm going to pass."

"Come on, it'll be fun! Just tell your parents you went to Jordan's house—they'll never check. We're all going to spend the night."

Tim tilts his head to the side, considering it. He used to make that same expression when we were little kids. It used to be so easy back then. I would go over to Tim's house, and there was no discussion about boyfriends or bullies or any of that. We would *play*. And back then, I felt like it would always be that way. It felt like Tim and I would always be friends that way.

Tim was the one who bought me the snowflake necklace I always wear. He got it for me for my tenth birthday because one of our favorite things to do together was play in the snow—sledding, building snowmen, having snowball fights. Whenever it snowed, the first thing I would do was tug on my boots and snowsuit and head over to Tim's house. The necklace was the first genuine piece of jewelry anyone had ever gotten for me. Considering I've had it on every day since then and it hasn't turned my neck green, I suspect he must have spent a fortune on it. He was probably saving all year to buy it for me.

"Fine," he says. "Why not?"

Vaguely, I'm aware of the fact that Tim never, ever says no to me. But I try not to think about it. There are certain aspects of my relationship with the boy next door that are better not to analyze too deeply.

"That's great!" I clap my hands together. "Chelsea is picking me up at a quarter after seven. We'll swing by to get you after."

Tim could not possibly look less excited about this. "Fine."

Tim thinks the whole thing is a mistake, but he's wrong. He's going to have a great time tonight, and I'll prove to him that Shane is a good guy. And I'll tell Chelsea to bring along a girl for him as well. After all, may as well show him a good time.

CHAPTER 5

PRESENT DAY

If it were socially acceptable, Josh would hide between my legs.

But he's ten years old, so instead, he is standing close to me, his fingers clinging to my shirt sleeve, still reluctant to join the crowd of kids who will be in his fifth-grade class. His teacher, Mrs. Conway, shoots me a sympathetic look. She seems nice enough—a seasoned teacher in her forties who looks like she's skilled at keeping the class in line. She wasn't around when I was a student at the school, but I suspect she must have started soon after.

"He'll be fine, Ms. Sullivan," she assures me. "I promise I'll keep a close eye on him."

"Thank you," I say.

It doesn't escape me that she called me *Ms.* Sullivan rather than *Mrs.* Sullivan. Does she know I'm a single parent? Does she know Josh doesn't have a father in the picture? Does she know the whole sordid story? People do talk in towns like this, even though my parents did everything they could to conceal my pregnancy.

And if she knows, then maybe all the other parents know. And then the kids will know. And then the name-calling will start all over again.

No, I'm being paranoid. Josh will be fine.

The excited buzz of children is interrupted by the shrill sound of a bell ringing through the air. The first day of school has officially begun. It takes all my self-restraint to keep from crushing Josh in an embarrassing bear hug. He's a bit small for his age, just up to the level of my shoulder, and he still sometimes seems painfully young. Too young to face something scary like a classroom of strangers who all know each other from the last five years of school.

"Good luck," I whisper in his ear. "Remember—everyone likes the cool new kid."

Josh's chin trembles slightly—he's trying not to cry. When he was two, he used to unabashedly bawl his eyes out, but it's even more painful to watch him as a big kid, struggling to hold back those tears. I plant a kiss on the top of his head and give his back a gentle push. He walks off to follow his classmates into the school like he's being led to his execution.

He's going to be fine. The other children will love him, even if he was born out of wedlock. It was absolutely the right decision to move here.

Keep telling yourself that, Brooke.

I watch until Josh's green backpack is no longer visible. I would love to plant myself outside his classroom so I could be available if he needs me during the day. But I couldn't do that when he was in kindergarten, and it certainly is not acceptable now. I'm just going to trust that everything will be okay. He'll get through this.

"Brooke? Brooke Sullivan?"

My jaw tightens at the sound of my name. The worst thing about moving back to the town where I grew up is that people occasionally recognize me. Thankfully, it's a big enough town that it doesn't happen too often, but I suppose I should expect it when I'm standing in front of the elementary school that I attended back when I was Josh's age.

I turn to greet the teacher who recognized me. But before I can say hello, my mouth falls open.

"Tim?" I manage.

It's Tim. Tim Reese. Who lived down the block from me during my entire childhood. My best friend.

Well, until I left town without saying a word to him about it.

"Brooke!" His face lights up. "It's really you!"

As Tim sprints across the grass surrounding the school, I get a better look at him. And...well, wow. When we were little, Tim was a cute kid. Lots of freckles and a smile that made all the adults love him. And then near the end of high school, he shot up six inches practically overnight, and he became a little less cute and a little more handsome but still too skinny and gangly. But now he's filled in completely, gained the weight he needed and some muscle on top of that. The freckles are long gone.

Tim Reese is *hot.*

I self-consciously run a hand over my dark hair, which I pulled back into a messy ponytail before I left the house. I'm also wearing an oversize T-shirt and yoga pants. This is not what I would have liked to be wearing to run into Tim Reese for the first time in ten years. But it is what it is.

"Hey," he says when he gets closer to me. "This is so wild. I saw you across the lawn, and I was thinking to myself, 'That can't be Brooke Sullivan. I'm imagining things.' But it's you. It's really you."

"It's me," I say stiffly.

He grins. "I can see that."

And then we just stand there awkwardly. Well, I'm feeling awkward. Tim can't seem to stop smiling. I don't get what he's so happy about, and it's irking me.

"So." I scratch at my elbow. "Are you a teacher here or...?"

He rakes a hand through his hair, which always reminded me of the color of a maple tree. "Well, actually, I'm the assistant principal."

"Oh!" I fix my lips into a smile. My lips feel like putty. "That's awesome. Congratulations."

"Uh, thanks." He rubs his chin, and I can't help but notice there's no ring on his left fourth finger. "How about you?"

"Me? I'm a nurse practitioner."

His eyes light up. "You're our new nurse?"

"No, I'm not," I say quickly. "I work...somewhere else." I'm sure as hell not telling him I've got a job at the maximum-security prison forty-five minutes away from here.

He frowns. "Oh."

It takes a second to figure out why he looks so confused. He doesn't know why I'm here. I'm going to have to tell him.

"I was just here dropping my son off," I explain. "It's his first day of school, so, you know, he's pretty nervous."

"Oh!" He smiles again, but it looks slightly more forced this time. "Well, the first day of kindergarten is always scary for kids. I'm sure he'll do great."

When I told him it was Josh's first day of school, he assumed I meant he was starting kindergarten. He doesn't realize my son is ten years old. He's going to find out eventually, and I'm dreading it. I don't want him to do the math.

After all, he was there that night too. He has the scars to prove it.

"I heard about your parents' accident, Brooke. I'm so sorry. I was out of the country, or else I would've come to the funeral."

"I'm okay," I mumble. "We weren't exactly close. They weren't the best parents in the world." I don't mention that I hadn't seen or spoken to my parents in five years. No need to get into the details.

"It...it was a car accident, wasn't it?"

I nod. "They died together, which is ironic because I always felt like they couldn't stand each other. My dad used to cheat on my mom all the time."

"Still." He shoves his hands into his pockets. "It must have been hard on you. Are you staying at their house?"

"Yes. Easier than selling it in this market, you know?"

"Oh, sure." He bobs his head. "I'm staying at my parents' old place too. They moved to Florida two years ago, so officially, I'm house-sitting. But I think at this point, I need to stop kidding myself and admit that I live there."

"I always liked your old house."

"Yeah." He shrugs. "It's fine. It's just big. You know, for just me."

As if I need another clue that he's single. He's making absolutely sure that I know.

"So, um…" His eyes dart around the slowly emptying lawn around the school, which has been trampled by little footprints. "Does your husband have a job around here too?"

"I'm not married."

"Really?"

"That's right."

We stare at each other for another few seconds, then Tim's face breaks into a sheepish grin. "Pretty smooth how I found out you're still single, huh? You impressed with those skills?"

Despite everything, I have to laugh. Tim always knew how to make me smile. "Extremely impressive. You must be quite the player."

"All elementary school assistant principals are."

"I'd assume as much."

His smile widens. "Look, I have to get inside, but we really do need to catch up. Could we get coffee sometime?"

The last thing I want is to catch up with someone from my old life—especially someone I was as close with as Tim. "I'm pretty busy."

"Well, coffee doesn't take long, does it? Twenty minutes—tops."

This can't lead to anything good. I don't have any room in my life for whatever Tim wants. Plus, I have a feeling when he finds out the truth about Josh, he's going to feel differently about me. But I want to end this conversation, so I've got to throw him a bone.

"Maybe," I finally say, "after I get settled in."

"Well..." His face is still glowing. God, I forgot how he used to look at me. "It was really great seeing you again, Brooke. *Really* great. And I'm going to hold you to that *maybe*."

There's an extra skip in his step as he sprints back toward the elementary school. Tim Reese. Wow. I really never believed I'd see him again.

CHAPTER 6

I am outraged.

The patient I'm seeing right now is Mr. Carpenter. He is in his late twenties, and he was shot in the spine while doing…well, whatever got him sent to a maximum-security prison for life. It was bad, I'm sure. I don't want to know.

But none of that is my concern. What is my concern is that Mr. Carpenter is a paraplegic and uses a wheelchair. So he's sitting on his bottom all day, and then he's lying on a mattress at night that is paper-thin, and now he has a rather impressive sore on his coccyx that has not been addressed in God knows how long.

"What do you think, Brooke?" Mr. Carpenter asks me. He's lying on the examining table on his side with his pants pulled down, waiting for my assessment. Unfortunately, I don't have anything good to say.

"It's a pressure wound," I say. "We can put a dressing

on it, but it's never going to heal if you don't keep pressure off it."

"Yeah, well, how am I supposed to do that? The cushion on my chair is halfway decent, but the mattress in my bed is terrible. I'm basically lying directly on metal springs."

"So you need a better mattress."

Mr. Carpenter snorts. "How long have you worked here? Nobody's getting me a new mattress."

"They have to get it for you if I prescribe it."

"Whatever you say."

Despite Mr. Carpenter's skepticism, he's going to get that mattress. It's medical neglect not to give a paraplegic a decent mattress with pressure relief. It might involve a stack of paperwork, but I'm going to make it happen.

As soon as I'm done with Mr. Carpenter, I confirm nobody is waiting to be seen and head down the hall to Dorothy's office. Yes, she has an *office*, and I have a desk in my examining room. But I recognize she has seniority, so I'm not going to say anything. Hopefully, I won't be working here long enough to get an office.

I knock on the door to Dorothy's office and wait to hear her say to come in. After what seems like five minutes, she calls for me to come inside. When I enter the office, she's sitting at her desk, a pair of half-moon glasses balanced on the bridge of her bulbous nose.

"I'm very busy, Brooke," she says.

"This won't take long," I say. "I just need to find out how I can get a pressure-relief mattress for Malcolm Carpenter."

She peers at me over the rim of her glasses. "A *pressure-relief mattress*?"

She says it like I was speaking in an unfamiliar language. She knows very well what I'm talking about. "He's a paraplegic, and he's developed a pressure sore on his coccyx. He needs a decent mattress or it won't heal."

"Brooke," she says flatly, "this is not the Ritz-Carlton. We can't get dream mattresses for all the inmates."

A muscle twitches under my eye. "I'm not asking for a luxury item. This is medically indicated."

"I'm afraid it isn't."

"Of course it is!" I burst out. "He can't move or feel the lower half of his body. The sore is just going to get worse if we don't relieve pressure on it. Getting him a decent mattress is the least we can do."

"I'm afraid a new mattress just isn't in the budget. You'll have to come up with a more creative solution." She shakes her head. "Don't you have any problem-solving skills?"

I stare at her, too stunned to respond. The problem is that the man has a pressure ulcer. The simple solution is a decent mattress. What is *wrong* with this woman? Doesn't she care about these prisoners at all? They're human beings after all.

The phone rings on Dorothy's desk. She picks it up without saying another word to me. I stand there while she listens to the other person speaking. Finally, she says, "Yes, I'll send her right over."

Damn. She probably means me.

Sure enough, when Dorothy hangs up the phone, she raises her eyes to look at me over the rims of her glasses. "There was an incident out on the yard. Officer Hunt is bringing one of the inmates over to see you for an injury."

Great.

My shoulders sag in defeat as I march back to my examining room / office. I haven't given up though. I'm going to figure out a way to get Mr. Carpenter that mattress if it's the last thing I do. But first, I have to treat this guy who got injured in the yard.

I wonder how he got hurt. Was it a lock in a sock? Is that a real thing they do in prison?

Just as I reach my office, I catch sight of Officer Hunt coming down the hallway with one of the prisoners. It must be the guy who got injured in the yard. The inmate is wearing the standard prison khaki jumpsuit, and unlike most of the prisoners, both his wrists and his ankles are shackled, so he's shuffling along slowly next to Hunt.

As he gets closer, I can see the bandage taped to his forehead, which is saturated with bright-red blood. Whatever is under there, it's almost certainly going to need stitches. Then my eyes drop to the prisoner's face.

Oh. Oh no. No, no, no...

It's Shane.

CHAPTER 7

ELEVEN YEARS EARLIER

Somehow it's not possible for Chelsea to pull up in front of my house without leaning all her weight on her car horn. I come racing out the front door, my backpack slung on my right shoulder, and sprint down the walkway, swearing under my breath. She doesn't let up on the horn until I've wrenched open the passenger-side door of the car and plopped myself down next to her.

"Oh my God!" I smack Chelsea in the arm. "I heard you. You're disturbing the whole neighborhood!"

Chelsea rolls her eyes dramatically. She's wearing so much mascara around her dark-brown eyes, her eyelashes are at least three times as long as they would be otherwise. Chelsea wears a ton of makeup. My parents would never allow me to leave the house looking like that. If I even want a darker shade of lipstick than nude, I have to put it on in the bathroom at school.

"Can I help it if you're slow?" Chelsea says.

I glance at the back seat for support. Chelsea texted

me she was bringing along Kayla Olivera as a sixth for Tim. Kayla is another cheerleader—dark and petite and very pretty. When I crane my neck, I feel perturbed by the fact that she is texting on her phone, oblivious to the volume of Chelsea's horn.

"Hey, Kayla," I say.

"Hey," she says without looking up.

I clear my throat. "Thanks for coming."

Kayla finally rips her eyes away from the screen of her phone. "Chelsea said Tim Reese is going to be there, right?"

I feel a jolt of surprise. I had figured that Chelsea had recruited some unsuspecting girl to our party to be foisted on Tim. But that isn't the case at all. Kayla *wants* to be here. She's interested in Tim. Apparently, when Tim sprouted up those six extra inches, he also became the kind of guy who girls take an interest in. I never noticed it before, but now I see it written all over Kayla's face. Tim is *hot* now.

The idea of it doesn't quite sit well with me.

I'm not sure why though. I've got Shane after all.

"So is Shane's mom gone?" Chelsea asks me. "Can we go over there?"

I reach into my purse and pull out my phone. Sure enough, there's a text from Shane that came in about a minute ago: *Just picked up Brandon, and my mom is already on the road. Come on over!*

I text back: *Be there soon! Lope you!*

His reply comes instantly: *Lope you too.*

Chelsea drives the extra block over to Tim's house. I can see her getting ready to lean on the horn, but she doesn't have to. Tim is already sitting on the front steps of his house, and he leaps to his feet when he sees Chelsea's Beetle. Kayla watches him through the window, a smile playing on her lips.

Tim hops into the back seat of the car next to Kayla. She scooches toward him as much as her seat belt will allow. "Hey, Tim," she says.

"Hey..." He frowns, obviously struggling to come up with her name. I turn and mouth "Kayla" as emphatically as I can, but he can't understand me. Finally, he takes a stab at it: "Kara?"

Kayla's cheeks turn slightly pink. "*Kayla*."

"Right. Sorry." But he doesn't sound sorry. He doesn't sound like he cares at all. Tim has never liked cheerleaders. I could see him holding his tongue when I told him I was trying out.

"Where's your bag?" Kayla asks him.

He frowns. "Bag?"

"We're spending the night." Kayla looks at Chelsea for confirmation. "Right?"

"That's right, *Timothy*," Chelsea says. "This is an *overnight* party. Didn't Brooke tell you?"

"Yes." He shrugs. "It's fine. I don't need anything."

Kayla looks scandalized. "What about a change of clothes?"

Tim glances down at his jacket, which is hanging open to reveal a gray T-shirt and blue jeans. "I don't know. I'll just wear this tomorrow."

"*Boys*." Chelsea shoots me a look. "Sometimes I wonder what we see in them."

I laugh along with Chelsea, but when I look back at Tim, there's something in his expression that makes me a little uneasy. I told him we were spending the night.

Back when we were much younger and such things were allowed, Tim used to come to my house for sleepovers, and he always brought along everything but the kitchen sink. Yes, a lot of time has passed since then, but it still seems strange that he would come to a sleepover at Shane's house and not bring anything but himself. It doesn't seem like Tim at all.

Maybe I don't know Tim anymore.

Or maybe he doesn't plan on staying.

CHAPTER 8

PRESENT DAY

I had hoped it would be months before I ran into Shane Nelson—if ever. But here I am, only on my second week, and here he is. Live and in the flesh.

The man who tried to kill me.

For a moment, I feel a tightening in my neck. The necklace he tried to choke me with cutting off my windpipe. I can't breathe. I grab on to the doorframe, taking deep breaths. I can't let this get to me. I have to be a professional.

I'm okay. *I'm okay.* He can't hurt me anymore.

Shane notices me a split second after I recognize him. He looks about as shocked as I felt. Maybe more, because he had no idea I was working here. He had been shuffling in the shackles, but when he sees me, he stops short, his mouth falling open.

"Come on." Hunt gives him a shove to get him moving again. "We don't have all day, Nelson. Move it."

They keep walking until they reach the examining

room, where they come to an abrupt halt. Shane's brown eyes are filled with pain when they meet mine.

"Hi, I'm Brooke," I say stiffly. I feel a little ridiculous introducing myself to the man I lost my virginity to, but here we are.

Before Shane can open his mouth, Hunt barks out, "This is Shane Nelson. Injury on the yard to his forehead."

"Okay." My voice sounds oddly calm considering my heart is doing jumping jacks. "Come on in, Mr. Nelson."

Shane again seems frozen in place. Hunt has to give him another shove to get him moving again.

Climbing onto the examining table is tricky given he's got his wrists and his ankles shackled. I've seen Hunt help other men in this position before, but he does nothing to help Shane. It takes him a few tries, but Shane manages to get up on the table.

Once Shane is situated, Hunt leaves the exam room. I start to close the door behind him, but he puts up a hand to keep the door from closing.

"You should keep the door open with this one," Hunt says.

I glance over at Shane, who is sitting on my examining table, his head hanging down, his wrists and his ankles bound together. I have felt twinges of fear around some of the inmates, but I don't feel it right now. Despite what I know he's capable of.

"I'll be fine," I say, hoping I don't regret my words.

Hunt keeps his hand on the door, still preventing me from closing it. Our eyes lock, and for a moment, I'm sure he's going to push his way in. But then he releases his hold on the door. "I'll be right outside," he tells me. "You have any problems, you give me a yell."

"I'll be fine," I say again. But I don't close the door completely. I keep it cracked just the slightest bit.

Now Shane and I are alone in the examining room. It's the first time we've been alone together since he… well, we don't need to relive that night. He looks different from the way he did when he was seventeen. Different and the same. His hair is much shorter, clipped barely an inch from his skull, and there's a hardness to his face that wasn't there before.

I hate that he's still every bit as handsome as he was back then.

I hate even more how much he looks like my son.

For a moment, the two of us just stare at each other. Glaring, more like—his eyes are dripping with venom. I don't know what *he's* so upset about. I should be the angry one—if it were up to him, I would be dead. I suppose he's mad that I told the truth in that courtroom.

"Hello," I say in the flattest, most emotionless voice I can muster.

Shane doesn't break his gaze. "Hi."

I square my shoulders. This was what I had been dreading when I took this job in the first place. And now here I am, and I just have to deal with it. I'll get his injury taken care of like a professional, and I'll send him on his way.

"How are you?" I say.

At my question, he whips his head up and stares at me. "Well, Brooke, I'm spending my life in prison for something I didn't do, so how the hell do you think I am? I'm not great."

I return his seething gaze. "I meant your *head*."

"Oh." He lifts a shackled hand to touch the bandage on his forehead. "That's not great either."

I slip my hands into a pair of blue latex gloves. I cross the small room to take a look at his forehead. This is the closest I've been to him in a long time—except in my nightmares. A decade ago, the thought of being this close to him would have made my skin crawl. But I can handle it now. I'm stronger than I used to be. This monster won't get the better of me.

The last time I was near Shane like this, he was wearing an aftershave that smelled like sandalwood. If I close my eyes, I can still almost imagine that deep, woody but floral aroma. I can't stand the smell of it anymore. I once went on a date with a guy who was wearing a sandalwood cologne, and I wouldn't go out with him ever again. I dodged his phone calls rather than explaining why.

I peel back the tape from the wound on his forehead, not bothering to be as gentle as I normally would be. It looks pretty bad. Despite the bandage, it's still bleeding significantly. It definitely needs stitches. He also has what looks like the start of a black eye forming on the same side.

"How did this happen?" I ask.

"I ran into the fence."

I raise my eyebrows. "Really?"

He stares at me, challenging me to question him further. "That's right."

"Because it looks like somebody did this to you."

"If somebody *had* done this to me," he says, "and I ratted them out to you, the next time, whatever they did to me would be worse. So, you know, good thing this just happened from walking into the fence."

I notice now that he has other scars on his face. He's got a scar splitting his other eyebrow and one running along the curve of his jaw, almost concealed by the stubble on his chin. There's also a long white scar just on the base of his throat.

For some reason, I think of Josh. About the other kids bullying him at school and giving him a black eye like Shane has right now. Shane, who also grew up without a father. And I feel the tiniest twinge of…

Well, not sympathy. I would never feel sympathy for a monster like this. Somebody capable of doing what he did.

"Shane," I say, "if someone is beating up on you…"

"Stop it, Brooke." His voice is firm. "Whatever you think you're trying to do, just stop. Just stitch me up and let me go back to my cell, okay?"

"Fine."

He's right. I can't do anything to help him, even if I wanted to, and I *don't*. My job is to get him stitched up and back to his cell, like he said. And that is all I'm going to do.

I can handle it.

I leave Shane alone in the room while I go to grab some suture material. Everything I need is in the supply room except for the lidocaine to numb him up. Since that's a medication, I'll need Dorothy to dispense it. So I return to her office, where she again takes her sweet time telling me to come in.

"Done already?" she asks me.

I press my lips together. "I need to stitch up a forehead laceration. I need some lidocaine."

"We're all out."

I blink at her. "Excuse me?"

She shrugs. "We carry a small amount of anesthetic, but at the moment, we're out of stock."

"So what am I supposed to do?"

"Stitch him up without it."

My jaw tightens. What is wrong with this woman? These men are *human beings*. How could she be so cavalier about their health? I have more reason to hate Shane Nelson than anyone else here, and maybe I should be happy for a chance to torture him a bit after what he did to me, but even I think he deserves to be treated with dignity. "It's inhumane."

Dorothy lifts her eyes skyward. "Don't be so dramatic, Brooke. It's a few needle sticks. I'm sure he won't mind. Or you can glue it if you want."

This laceration is too messy for glue, but Dorothy doesn't care about my protests. And if she tells me I need to problem solve again, I'm going to scream. Even though that's apparently what I have to do.

I return to the examining room, where Shane is still sitting on the table with his open head wound. He looks up when I come in, and a lot of the anger that I saw in his face when we first locked eyes has now dissipated. Maybe he isn't as furious with me as I had thought, even though it was my testimony that put him in here. All these years, I imagined he was sitting in a prison cell, tattooing death threats against me on his body, but he doesn't seem all that angry. Just…well, kind of sad. Beaten down.

"So here's the situation," I tell him. "I have the suture material, but we're all out of lidocaine. So—"

"It's fine," Shane interrupts me before I can tell him his options. "Stitch me up without it."

"Are you sure? Because—"

"Yeah, it's fine. They're always out of lidocaine."

He does not seem at all fazed by this. I wonder how it felt to have that long jagged scar at the base of his throat sutured without lidocaine.

"All right," I say. Let's get this over with. "I'm going to need you to lie down."

He tries to lean backward, but it's hard for him with his wrists bound. He starts to slip on the table, and instinctively, I reach out and put a hand on his back to help guide him down.

I touched him. After all these years, I touched Shane Nelson again.

I wait for the wave of revulsion. I hate this man—I had nightmares about him for years after. It would not be an exaggeration to say he ruined my life, and if it were up to him, I wouldn't even have a life.

But the revulsion doesn't come. Touching Shane's shoulder doesn't feel any different than touching anyone else. I guess I really have gotten over it, all these years later.

It's about time. I'm proud of myself.

I draw up the suture material while Shane watches me. He doesn't look that nervous about the fact that I'm going to sew his forehead together with no anesthetic. I sure would be. I've never even had stitches before, except for the ones I got after childbirth.

"This must be your dream, huh?" he says. "Getting to stick a needle in me without anesthetic."

"I tried to get it," I say defensively.

"I'm sure."

"I *did*." I turn to glare at him. "I'm not like you. I don't *enjoy* hurting people."

"Well," he says, "it's not like I could blame you after what you think I did to you."

There is something in his eyes I can't quite interpret. It's enough to make me look away.

"So you're a nurse practitioner now, huh?" he says. "Good for you."

"Thanks," I say stiffly.

"I…uh…" One corner of his lips quirks up. "I got my GED while I've been in here. And I've been tutoring other inmates so they could do the same."

He says it almost like he's trying to impress me, the way he used to when he would throw a pass across the football field and look in my direction to make sure I saw it.

"Oh," I say, because I'm not sure what else to say.

"Never mind," he mumbles. "I don't know why I thought you'd want to know that."

I clean off the laceration with some sterile water before sewing it up. It's got to be painful, but Shane barely flinches. I get my needle ready to make the first stitch. "Going to be a little poke," I warn him.

"Go for it."

I've stitched up many people during my tenure in urgent care. I've seen grown men cry, even with the lidocaine to numb the area. Shane winces slightly when the needle goes in, but nobody could say he's not taking it like a champ.

"So," he says as I tie off the first stitch, "you're not married, huh?"

My fingers freeze on the needle. "*Excuse* me?"

He starts to shrug but then thinks better of it with the needle still in his skin. "No ring. And I heard some of the guys talking about the cute new nurse practitioner who's also single."

"That's really none of their business."

"Hey, you were the one who must've told one of them you're not married."

He's right, of course. The first thing Dorothy warned me was not to share any personal information, but I got careless. To be fair, a lot of these men don't look like criminals. They just look like harmless old men.

"And you have a kid," he adds.

Now I'm really going to be sick. I'm *such* an idiot. What am I supposed to say when a patient asks me if I have a child? *None of your damn business?* Well, that probably is the right answer, but it's hard not to talk about my son when I'm away from him the whole day. I'm learning this lesson the hard way.

"Anyway, congratulations," Shane says. There's no bitterness or anger in his voice, which is a relief. "How old is he?"

I cringe at this question. Like Tim, he's not stupid. If I tell him I have a ten-year-old son, he will figure it out. But unlike Tim, he has no way of finding out the truth on his own. "He's five."

He flinches slightly as the needle passes through his skin again. "I always wanted kids. Guess that's never going to happen."

I don't reply to that. I just quietly tie off the suture.

"I can't believe you're living out here again," he comments. "I figured you would be gone for good. Except maybe to visit your parents."

"My parents died in a car accident," I blurt out. I shouldn't have given him any more information, but this seems like the most innocuous thing I've told him. I want him to know that I've had other tragedies in the last decade that have not involved him. That what he did hasn't defined my existence.

He frowns. "I'm so sorry, Brooke."

"It's okay," I mutter. "We weren't close."

I can't explain to him why my relationship with my parents fell apart. Partially, they were angry that I had defied them and dated Shane in the first place. That I had lied and gone to his house, which almost resulted in the end of my life. But what they were furious about—what they could never forgive me for—was that when I found out I was pregnant, I decided I wanted to keep it. I have no regrets about doing that, but my parents' love for Josh was always reserved. Even when Josh was part of the family, they still made it clear that they thought I made a mistake. My son was a mistake and an embarrassment—the child of a monster.

And that was what I couldn't forgive them for. It was the reason I eventually cut them out of my life.

"My mother died a couple of years ago too," Shane says.

I tie off another suture. "I'm sorry to hear that."

I mean it. Shane was close with his mother—after his father took off, it was just the two of them. If she's gone, that means he has nobody.

He holds my gaze for a moment. "She died believing that I had killed those people."

My hand gripping the needle trembles, nearly missing his skin. *But you* did *kill those people.* I want to say it, but it would be unprofessional. And there's no point.

Despite all the evidence, Shane would never own up to what he did that night.

But it doesn't matter. Shane is guilty. I was *there* that night. If it were up to him, I would be dead right now.

I can never forget that. And I will never forgive him.

CHAPTER 9

ELEVEN YEARS EARLIER

The farmhouse where the Nelsons live is about a mile off the main road.

It's on a dirt road. One that you would miss if you didn't know exactly where it was. Shane told me that when he was in elementary school, the school bus wouldn't travel that extra mile up the dirt road to the farmhouse. He used to have to walk that mile every morning to get to the bus stop, then another mile back home in the afternoon. Even if there was a foot of snow on the ground.

It made me feel guilty when Shane told me about it. After all, the school bus used to stop right outside my door. I walked exactly fifteen feet to get from my door to the bus in the morning, and I still used to whine about it. And Shane walked a *mile*. But he didn't tell me to make me feel bad. He just said it in that matter-of-fact way he always tells me things about his life.

"You sure Shane's mom is gone?" Chelsea asks as the tires of her Beetle slip on the dirt road. The rain hasn't quite started, but the air outside has turned into a fine mist.

"Yep. He texted me that she left."

Mrs. Nelson is nice. The times I've been to her house, she's always been kind to me in a way that my parents would never be kind to Shane. But she's not nice enough that she would be okay with five random teenagers spending the night in her house. Especially since Brandon surely brought alcohol.

The farmhouse where Shane lives looks like it has seen better days. It might have once been a brilliant red, but now the paint has worn away to practically white in some places and just bare wood in others. The roof is crooked and covered in moss, and it looks like one powerful storm could easily rip it right off. The window frames all look a little crooked as well, like whoever built the farmhouse wasn't quite sure how to put everything together properly but they were giving it their best college try.

As Chelsea pulls up beside Shane's Chevy, the door to the farmhouse swings open. Shane appears in the doorway, and his eyes light up. He waves vigorously. "Come on! Before the rain starts!"

I grab my backpack and climb out of the car, slamming the door behind me. I look up at the sky, and the clouds look heavy—they're about to break open at any second. I pick my way through the dirt pathway to the front door, my backpack on my shoulder. Shane grabs it from me when I reach the door.

"Let me take that, Brooke," he says with a grin.

"What a gentleman!" Chelsea declares. She gives Tim a pointed look, and he dutifully holds out his arm to Kayla, who dumps her gigantic duffel bag in his arms. I swear to God, that girl has packed enough stuff for a month.

After we're inside the house, I shut the screen door

behind us. Even though I've watched Shane fix that screen door with my own eyes, it always seems to hang off the hinges. I suspect the entire door needs to be replaced, but he doesn't have the money for it. Mrs. Nelson already works two minimum-wage jobs, and they need Shane's salary at the pizza parlor just to pay for rent and food.

As I turn the lock on the front door, Shane grabs me and pulls me in for a kiss. I melt like I always do. And he smells nice tonight. Not that he doesn't always smell good, but he smells extra nice tonight. It's that aftershave he sometimes uses.

"I love your aftershave," I murmur.

"It's sandalwood scented."

I frown. "What's sandalwood?"

"I don't know. The wood you make sandals from?"

"So basically, you smell like feet?"

He laughs. "Hey, you're the weirdo who likes it."

Shane kisses me again, but when I pull away, I get an uneasy feeling. A prickly sensation on the back of my neck. Like somebody's watching me.

I jerk my head around. Tim is standing across the room, staring at us, an unreadable expression on his face. But when our eyes meet, he quickly looks away. Good thing because I wouldn't want Shane to know he was staring at us that way.

"So," Shane says, "you brought Tim, huh?"

There's disapproval in Shane's dark eyes. Tim hates Shane, but it's not like Shane is any big fan of Tim's either. I need to change that.

"He's a good guy," I say, a touch defensively.

"Hmm."

"Also, Chelsea brought Kayla along for him. For, you know..."

Shane is quiet for a moment. "Okay," he says. "That's fine. We have three bedrooms anyway."

I let out a sigh of relief. Shane doesn't usually get too worked up over stuff, but you never know. After all, I've only been dating him for three months. There's still plenty of time for his dark side to come out. But so far, I haven't seen it. Despite Tim's ominous warnings.

"Hey, Reese!" Shane holds up a hand in greeting. "Glad you could make it."

I finger the snowflake necklace around my throat as Shane saunters over to Tim. Shane is making an effort because he knows Tim is important to me, and I appreciate that. The two of them start talking, and it looks friendly enough. I can't hear what they're saying—Shane is speaking quietly, and Tim is responding in an equally hushed tone. I strain to hear them over the sound of Chelsea and Kayla chatting a few feet away from me, but it's no use. They're talking too quietly.

But it doesn't matter what they're saying. They're not fighting, and that's all that's important.

I consider going over to join them, but before I can contemplate it further, the door to the kitchen swings open with a loud creak. Brandon bursts into the room, carrying two pizza boxes balanced in one hand and a bottle of vodka in the other.

"Ready to have some fun?" he calls out.

Shane jerks up his head at the sound of Brandon's voice. He backs away from Tim as if I've caught him doing something illicit, and he makes a beeline for the pizza and vodka. Whatever conversation the two of them were having is apparently over.

CHAPTER 10

PRESENT DAY

I finish suturing up the rest of Shane's laceration in silence. He doesn't ask me any other questions, and I'm grateful. I should never have told him anything about my life. That was a mistake. It just threw me off to see him again. It's like everything came rushing back. The good stuff over the course of our relationship and then the bad stuff at the very end.

"All set." I tie off the last suture and dab at his forehead to clean off the blood. "Good as new."

"Yeah."

"You need anything for pain?"

He makes a face. "No, thanks. If I ask for pain medication, I'm just going to get labeled as drug seeking."

He's right. Every time an inmate asks for pain medication, alarm bells go off in the back of my head. After all, the last NP who worked here got busted for selling narcotics. Still, Shane has a significant laceration on his head that I stitched up with no anesthesia. It wouldn't be terrible for him to ask for pain medication. But it's his choice.

"Anyway," I say, "I'll get Officer Hunt to—"

"Wait!" Shane's voice is hushed but urgent. "Wait, Brooke. Listen, I need to say something."

My eyes fly in the direction of the door. Hunt is waiting on the other side in case I need him. "Shane, I can't—"

"No. *No*. Please just listen to me, okay?"

I shake my head. "I can't. This isn't a good idea."

"I just need you to know"—his voice suddenly sounds hoarse—"I wasn't the one who tried to kill you, Brooke. I swear to you. I swear on my life."

I take a step back from the table. "I was there. I know it was you."

"You *don't* know that." He grits his teeth. "I didn't do anything. That asshole Reese knocked me out with a baseball bat, and then the next thing I knew, the police were shaking me awake and telling me I was under arrest."

"Shane," I hiss, "stop this *right now*."

"I would never have hurt you, Brooke." His eyes are wide and earnest, and he looks so much like the seventeen-year-old boy I fell in love with. "I've been wanting to say that to you for the last ten years. You have to believe me. I would never have done something like that. I couldn't. I *loved* you."

My right hand balls into a fist. How dare he? How dare he lie to my face that way? "Do you think I'm a complete idiot?" I say in a voice just low enough that Hunt won't hear.

"Brooke—"

Whatever Shane is about to say next is interrupted

by Hunt knocking on the door to the examining room. Without waiting for an answer, he pokes his head in. "You done yet?"

"Yes," I choke out. "We're done."

I help Shane sit back up on the table. Now he has to get off the table, which is a challenge with his ankles shackled. He's doing it carefully, trying not to fall. Hunt watches him, his lips twisting downward.

"Hurry up, you piece of shit," Hunt spits out at him.

I look at the guard in surprise. Hunt isn't exactly a picture of compassion with these prisoners, but he's polite enough. This is the first time I've heard him hurl profanity at one of them. And when Shane finally gets to his feet, Hunt jerks him forward much more roughly than he needs to.

Why does Hunt hate him so much? What did Shane do to elicit that kind of response?

The two of them leave the examining room. I watch Hunt take Shane down the hallway with the flickering fluorescent lights, back to his cell. When he gets half-way down the hall, Shane briefly turns his head to look back at me.

I touch my throat. I still wake up at night sometimes, covered in sweat, the memory of the necklace tightening around my windpipe still fresh in my mind. It was a long time ago, but I can still feel it happening like it was yesterday. I could feel the links of the gold necklace digging into my neck, I could smell Shane's sandalwood after-shave tickling my nose, and I could feel his hot breath on my neck.

But there's one thing I can't do. I can't see his face.

I never saw the face of the man who tried to kill me.

The power was out that night, and everything was pitch-black. But I knew Shane very well. I knew the feel of his body. The smell of him. I knew it was him.

It had to be.

Because if it wasn't him, I have made a terrible mistake.

CHAPTER 11

The entire drive home from Raker Penitentiary, I can't stop thinking about Shane. I had truly believed I would never see him ever again after his sentencing went through. I certainly never thought I'd be inches away from his face again.

After the visit, Hunt brought me Shane's chart. This time, I had permission to look through it without guilt. It was fairly slim, which made sense given that Shane is still young and in good health. Most of the notes were from injuries, likely sustained at the hands of other inmates.

The last note was written by my predecessor, Elise. Shane had come to her complaining of abdominal pain. She had prescribed him medication for acid reflux, but then at the bottom of the page, she wrote, "Manipulative, drug seeking." And she had underlined the word "manipulative."

I'm not sure if I would agree with that assessment. I even offered Shane pain medication, and he wouldn't take it. But seeing those words written in his chart made me uneasy.

Just as I'm pulling into my driveway, my phone buzzes in my purse. A text message came while I was driving. I sift through a surprising number of loose tissues in my purse—you can never have too many tissues when you have a young son—before I retrieve my phone.

Hey, it's Tim Reese. I got your number from the parent directory. Hope that's not too creepy.

Despite everything, I have to smile. Tim is a lot of things, but he's not creepy. But if he looked me up in the parent directory, he must have figured out that Josh is not a kindergartener. And inexplicably, he still wants to talk to me.

Only slightly creepy.

He writes back almost instantly:

So I was just thinking, coffee in the evening is just going to keep us up. How about getting a drink one night this week?

A drink. That's a bit more serious than coffee. That's a very date-y kind of get-together. Do I want that?

I have no idea. But I do know that if there's one guy I can trust to back off if I need him to, it's Tim. And I haven't socialized outside work in far too long. Maybe I should just let myself have a little fun for once. Don't I deserve it?

Let me check with the babysitter, and I'll get back to you.

Any negative feelings from work today and the shock of seeing Shane after so many years (and knowing I'll have to see him again in a week to take out the sutures) fade away as I contemplate a night out with Tim. It will be nice to hang out with him again. Growing up, Tim was always my favorite person in the whole world.

I feel bad that I shut him out for nearly eleven years. But it wasn't like I had a choice.

I get into the house, and this time, Josh doesn't come running when I call his name. I take it as a good sign though. If he were clingy, that would be worse. But he's got a few days of school under his belt now, and he seems more confident.

I reach the kitchen, where Margie is pulling another of her delicious concoctions out of the oven. It looks like some sort of lasagna. It's bubbling hot when she lays it down on the kitchen counter.

"Hey, Margie," I say. "That looks great. You don't have to cook every night though."

"Oh, I like it!" she says. "When my kids were growing up, I had a home-cooked meal for them every night. Home cooking prevents cancer, you know."

I'm not so sure about that, but I'm not going to say anything else to dissuade her from cooking for us. I am obscenely grateful that she does it.

"Listen," I say, "do you think you could watch Josh one night this week? I was going to go out for a drink with a friend. It shouldn't be long."

Margie's eyes light up. "A friend or a *man*?"

Oh God. I had a feeling when I hired this woman that she was going to be a bit of a yenta. "Just a friend."

"A male friend?"

"Yes…"

"So it's a date!" She claps her hands together. "That's wonderful, Brooke! A young single woman like you *should* be dating."

"It's not a date," I say through my teeth. "He's a friend. An old friend."

"Whatever you say."

I don't like the knowing look on Margie's round face. "It's not a date."

"Well, why not?" She blinks at me. "Is he ugly? Ugly men are good in bed, you know."

Oh *God*. "Margie…"

"I'm just saying," she says, "there's nothing wrong with going on a date. You don't have to feel bad about it."

Weirdly enough, she has hit the nail on the head. I already feel like I am spread thin, between work and motherhood. "It just doesn't feel like it's fair to Josh for me to be dating."

"Don't think that way," she says. "That boy could use a father."

I bristle at her comment—she touched a nerve. I have always tried to be enough for Josh. Mother and father. But I see this longing in his eyes when we're at the park and we spot a little boy playing with his dad.

"Is tomorrow okay?" I ask Margie.

"Absolutely," she says. "And stay out as late as you want. Josh and I will make chocolate chip cookies."

There's a part of me that sort of wants to blow off Tim and instead stay home to make chocolate chip cookies with Margie and Josh. But Margie is right. I deserve to have a night out to have fun. So as soon as Margie takes off, I shoot off a text message:

Tomorrow night okay?

Tim responds a second later:

You got it.

CHAPTER 12

ELEVEN YEARS EARLIER

"We're going to play Never Have I Ever."

Chelsea makes the declaration after we all have a couple of pizza slices in our bellies and Brandon has mixed us all cups of something called "screwdrivers." Apparently, they are a mix of vodka and orange juice, and they taste like paint remover.

We have gathered in the living room, seated in couples around the rickety coffee table. Shane and I are squeezed onto the tiny love seat. Everyone else is crowded onto the old sofa, which burped up a bunch of stray feathers when they sat down. Tim is by the armrest, and Kayla is squeezed in so close to him that their thighs are wedged together. Chelsea has her legs on Brandon's lap, and they're all lovey-dovey, even though Chelsea confided in me that she is sick of him cheating on her and she's going to break up with him after the next big game.

"What's Never Have I Ever?" I ask.

Chelsea clutches her chest in shock at my naivete. "Brooke, seriously?"

I shrug, trying to ignore the hot feeling in my cheeks. I'm not as experienced at drinking or partying as my friends or boyfriend are. This is only the second time I've had alcohol, and I've never been drunk before. To be fair, my parents barely let me out at the beginning of the year because they were so panicked after that girl Tracy Gifford was found dead.

"It's very simple," Chelsea explains. "So I say something I've never done, and anyone in the circle who *has* done that thing has to take a drink. For example, if I said, 'Never have I ever gotten a hundred on a math test,' then you two nerds"—she looks pointedly at me and Tim—"have to take a drink. Got it?"

Brandon runs one of his large hands over the curve of Chelsea's thigh. "It's not exactly rocket science."

"Sure," I say. "Sounds fine." Even though I am terrified this game is going to reveal my embarrassing lack of experience with just about everything. The best I can say is that I don't have any secrets.

Well, not many.

"Hey." Kayla is looking down at her phone. "I'm not getting any signal, Shane. What's going on?"

"Oh." Shane glances over his shoulder at the window, where the rain is pouring down in buckets. "Sorry, the signal out here is spotty. It dies completely anytime there's any kind of storm. But we have a landline if you need to make a call."

Kayla grumbles something under her breath and then slams her phone down on the coffee table. But she recovers quickly and smiles sweetly over at Tim. Now that she doesn't have her phone distracting her, she has refocused all her energy on him.

And that idea doesn't make me particularly happy.

Brandon rubs his hands together. "I'll go first. But it's going to be difficult to come up with something I've never done."

Tim's eyes meet mine for a split second, and he rolls them skyward. I have to suppress a giggle. Chelsea thinks Brandon is hot, and he is a big shot on the football team, but the truth is I can't stand him.

"I got it." Brandon lifts the paper cup containing his screwdriver. "Never have I ever…been dumped. What can I say—the ladies love me."

Chelsea and Kayla both drink to that. Tim and I keep our cups down. Shane is my first real boyfriend, so I've never had the opportunity to be dumped before. I look over at Shane, and he doesn't drink either. Interesting. This game is definitely going to be an opportunity to learn a little more about my boyfriend.

We go around the circle once, reciting our quasi confessions. Kayla has never been skinny-dipping, but to my horror, Chelsea has (with Brandon, apparently). Shane has never cheated on an exam, and nobody else will own up to that honor either. I admit that I have never used a fake ID, and Brandon drinks heartily to that. Shane doesn't, and I'm a bit relieved—maybe he isn't quite as wild as I thought he was.

"I've got one." Chelsea has a wicked grin on her bright-red lips, which have already stained the rim of her cup. "Never have I ever kissed my neighbor."

She's looking at me and Tim as she says it. Tim looks at me, and his eyebrows raise about a millimeter.

I shake my head, also by about a millimeter. Neither of us drinks.

Chelsea's face falls. "Liars," she says under her breath.

She's absolutely right. We're lying. Tim and I kissed once, but it was a long time ago. He was, in fact, my first kiss. But it wasn't a *real* kiss.

It happened the summer before high school started. Tim and I were hanging out in my bedroom, and I was bemoaning the fact that I was starting high school without ever having kissed a boy. Tim admitted he was in the same boat, and then he came up with the brilliant idea:

We should practice on each other!

I thought of him like a brother, but there was nothing objectionable about him. He was *cute*. So without much persuading, I agreed.

It was a good thing we decided to practice together because the first kiss was decidedly awkward. I didn't know what to do with my hands, I wasn't sure if I should keep my eyes open or closed, and I didn't know quite where my nose should go. And once our lips made contact, I was confused about what to do with my tongue. Should I put it in his mouth? That would be weird, wouldn't it? But would it be even weirder *not* to kiss with tongue? It was Tim who finally gently slipped me just the tiniest bit of tongue. And it was very nice, once I got used to it.

After twenty minutes, it felt like we were really getting the hang of this kissing thing. And of course that was the exact moment my mother chose to burst in on the two of us without knocking. It was also the last time we were allowed to be in my room alone together with the door closed, even though I kept explaining we were just *practicing*.

Tim and I never talk about it though. It's like it never happened. After all, it *was* just practicing.

Now that our little secret is still safe, it's Tim's turn. At one point, I saw Kayla's hand creep onto his leg, but I don't know what happened because it's not there anymore. Tim considers his confession, looking down into the orange liquid in his paper cup. Finally, he says, "Never have I ever beaten up a kid so bad he had to go to the hospital."

Brandon bursts out laughing. He raises his cup and takes a long swig of that awful screwdriver. Then he nudges Shane. "Take a drink, Nelson."

Shane squirms next to me. As I stare at him, he slowly lifts the paper cup and drinks from it.

"Shane?" I say.

Brandon takes another drink, even though he doesn't have to. "It wasn't a big deal. It was just that dweeby perv, Mark. And he deserved it."

Tim arches an eyebrow. "He *deserved* it?"

"We overheard him talking about Shane's mom," Brandon says. "Telling some of his weirdo friends that he thinks she's *hot*. He's been buying a few too many canned goods at that store where she works, if you know what I mean."

I glance at Shane, and there's a flash of anger in his eyes, but he doesn't say a word.

"The guy is such a weirdo," Brandon goes on. "You know he's always trying to peek in the girls' dressing room, right?"

Chelsea smacks him in the arm. "You guys are such assholes. Do you know that?"

I can't stop staring at Shane. The flash of anger has

faded, and now he's hanging his head. I knew he was kind of a wild kid in middle school, but I had hoped now that after joining the football team, he kept his nose clean. But maybe Tim is right. Maybe he *is* a bully.

"It was just a broken rib anyway," Brandon says. "He didn't even spend the night."

"Oh, is that all?" Tim retorts. "Just a broken rib?"

Brandon's eyes flash as a crack of lightning makes his face glow eerily. He throws his cup on the coffee table so harshly that the orange liquid splashes out. "You want to be next, Reese?"

"For Christ's sake, shut *up*, Brandon," Shane growls. He turns to look at me. "It was stupid. Really stupid. We had just lost a game the day before, and when I heard him say those things about my mom—I mean, it's my *mom*—anyway, I just...like I said, we were being stupid."

Tim's eyes meet mine. I can see the question written all over his face: *Are you buying this bullshit?* I have to look away.

"Brooke?" Shane says.

"Just..." I touch my snowflake necklace—my fingers always go there whenever I'm anxious. "Don't do it again."

After all, he's sorry. Everybody does stupid stuff in high school. I can't expect Shane to be perfect. I'm sure not.

"All right." Shane clears his throat loudly. "It's my turn again."

We all turn to look at him, our drinks ready.

"Never have I ever," he says, "been on a date with Tracy Gifford."

Shane is staring at Tim as a bolt of thunder shakes

the room. Tim raises his eyes, and a look passes between them that I can't quite identify. We all sit there, our hands frozen on our paper cups. Tracy Gifford is the girl who was found dead over the summer. Obviously, none of us have been on a date with her.

But then Tim raises his cup. And he takes a drink.

CHAPTER 13

PRESENT DAY

I can't believe after all these years, I'm going on a date with Tim Reese.

No, correction: it's not a date. We're just getting drinks. As friends. For all I know, Tim has a girlfriend. After all, he's good-looking and charming and has a decent job. Tim is a catch. It seems almost impossible that he would still be single.

But I get the feeling he is.

I had wanted to take separate cars, but Tim pointed out that we are leaving from pretty much the same block, so "for the sake of the environment, we should carpool." I couldn't argue with that logic. And I didn't argue when he offered to drive.

So that's why I'm wearing a pair of black skinny jeans and a flattering blouse while standing in front of my house, waiting for Tim to arrive. I never used to wear much makeup in high school, and I'm not going to wear much now. Just a bit of eyeliner and a slash of lipstick. I don't want to look like I'm trying too hard.

A white Lincoln Continental pulls up in front of the house, and before I have a chance to be surprised that this is the car Tim drives, I realize that there's a white-haired woman behind the steering wheel. When she emerges from the car, she pushes her oversize glasses up the bridge of her nose and smooths out her pink suit.

"Brooke?" She holds out her arms like I'm going to run into them for a hug. "Brooke! I can't believe it's you!"

I stare at her blankly. "Hello…?"

"It's Estelle!" She grins at me with bright-red lips. She wasn't nearly as subtle in applying makeup as I was. "Estelle Greenberg! We talked on the phone."

I cringe, wishing I could go back inside my house. Estelle Greenberg is Raker's premier real estate agent. In my parents' will, they earmarked money to pay for Estelle to sell their house and give me the proceeds. She called me up while I was back in the city, assuring me that she would take care of the sale of the house and I wouldn't even have to set foot in Raker if I didn't want to.

She was fairly shocked when I told her not only did I not want her to sell the house but that I would be *living* there.

"Oh, Brooke," she sighs. "I remember you when you were only *this* high!"

She holds up a hand at about mid-hip to indicate how big I was in her memory of me. I suppress the urge to roll my eyes.

"I have to tell you, Brooke," she says, "the real estate market is jumping right now. You can't even imagine what price I could get you for this house. Enough for you to buy your dream apartment back in the city. You could even live in Manhattan if you wanted."

A vein pulses in my temple. "I appreciate that, but I'm not interested."

"You know, the real estate bubble won't last forever. You should be smart about this."

"I'm fine," I say tightly. "Really."

"What do you want with that dusty old house anyway?"

Estelle fixes her brown eyes on me, waiting for my answer. It's not an entirely unfair question. It's not like my most recent memories of this town are good. But there was a time I *was* happy here. In some ways, I spent the happiest years of my life in this house. Back when I was young and carefree.

Or maybe part of me is still a rebellious teenager who wanted to come back here solely because my parents would never let me after I got pregnant.

"This is *my* goddamn house, Estelle," I say in a low voice. "And I'm allowed to do whatever I want with it without having to justify it to *you*."

Estelle's false eyelashes flutter as if she's shocked I spoke to her that way. I certainly would not have said something like that back when I was *this* high.

"You know," she says, "your parents would be very disappointed that you disobeyed their wishes."

Truthfully, I'm shocked my parents left me the house at all. After I started mailing their monthly checks back to them, uncashed, I figured I was out of the will. But there was no one else for them to leave their estate to. So I got it all by default.

I fold my arms across my chest. "Please don't bother me again, Estelle."

Her bright-red lips part, and for a moment, I'm certain she's going to argue with me. But instead, she turns on her heel and gets back into her Lincoln. Her car zooms away just as Tim's Prius slides into my driveway. I take a deep breath, trying to dispel the tension from our confrontation. It works—a little.

"Wow," Tim says when I climb into the passenger seat. "I haven't seen you dressed up in a long time."

I squirm as I slide the seat belt into place. "I'm not dressed up."

"Right. Me neither."

Although he does look a bit dressed up. He's wearing a light-blue dress shirt, and he's even put on a tie. Back when we were kids, I never saw him wear anything besides a T-shirt and jeans, but this suits him.

I don't invite him to come in, and he doesn't seem upset about it. I don't know what Josh will make of me bringing home some guy, especially if that guy is the assistant principal of his school. At the very least, it could start some uncomfortable rumors.

"Where are we going?" I ask him.

"It's a bar that opened up a few years ago—the Shamrock. It's pretty quiet, decent food. Or just beer, if that's all you want."

I nod, musing to myself that the last time I saw Tim, neither of us was old enough to drink legally. Now that milestone has come and gone.

"So how is Josh finding school?" Tim asks.

"Fine," I say. "He's making some friends."

"That's great. Kindergarten is such a hard transition, but I'm sure he'll do great."

I freeze. I had assumed that when Tim looked me up

in the school records, he figured out that Josh was in fifth grade. Apparently not. He still thinks my son is five years old. Which means he doesn't know that Josh is Shane's son.

And I really, really don't want to tell him. Not yet. Not when he's looking over at me during the red lights and smiling at me that way.

The Shamrock is only a five-minute drive away. Tim parks in the lot outside the bar, and he rushes around the side of the car to open the door for me, even though I have already got it open myself. This isn't a date, but he's being a gentleman, which is extremely sweet. Men aren't like that in New York City. You have to go upstate for good manners, apparently.

Inside the bar is about what I expected. Dark, a slight hint of smokiness hanging in the air, and a lot of sticky tables spread throughout the room. We grab a table in the back, and this time it comes as no surprise when Tim pulls out my chair for me.

"When did you get to be such a gentleman?" I tease him.

"I wasn't before?"

"Ha!" I snort. "I was lucky if you didn't pull my chair out from under me."

"Brooke!" He clutches his chest in mock horror. "I would never have done that. Unless you deserved it, of course."

"I'm just saying..." I look across the table at his twinkling blue eyes. "You don't have to act all formal with me. We've known each other since we were in diapers. We know each other pretty well."

He arches an eyebrow. "We used to. Now—not so much."

Before I can figure out what to say to that, a petite waitress in a tight T-shirt that shows off an impressive bust for her size comes over to take our order. She looks vaguely familiar, like many of the people in this town do—I think we may have gone to high school together. I let my hair fall in my face as I place my order, hoping I look different enough that she won't recognize me.

Before she leaves, she rests a hand with red fingernails on Tim's shoulder. "I'll be right back, Timmy."

"Thanks, Kelli," he says.

Kelli. It comes back to me in a flash—she was on the cheerleading squad like me and Chelsea but two years behind us. She looks almost the same as she did back in high school—same blond hair and heart-shaped face, although much larger boobs. Thankfully, she isn't looking at me and doesn't seem to recognize me.

Actually, she's only looking at Tim. She gives him an unmistakable look, and I'm surprised by the flash of jealousy. I haven't seen Tim in ages. I have no right to feel proprietary around him.

"I tried to find you, you know," he says after Kelli leaves with our drink orders.

I attempt not to react to that revelation. "Did you?"

"You are really hard to find though." He eyes me across the table. "No social media, huh?"

My parents did their damnedest to keep my name out of the news when it all went down, given I was a minor. And while I was in school, they also gave me a small stipend—a monthly check that along with my waitressing job just barely covered my expenses without leaving a penny left over—and one stipulation was I couldn't be on social media at all. No Facebook, no

Twitter, no Instagram. It was easy to agree to that because I didn't want to be on social media either. The last thing I wanted to do was catch up with my old classmates. *Hey, Brooke, remember when your boyfriend tried to murder you? Man, those were good times.*

"Sorry," I say. "I was being cautious."

"I know. But it's *me*, Brooke. I just wanted to know you were okay. You could have gotten in touch."

When I was nine months pregnant, about to give birth to the son of a convicted killer, I had no interest in talking to old friends. Even Tim. But I can't explain that to him. "I'm sorry," I say again. "I needed time to heal."

He's quiet for a moment, mulling over my answer. "Fair enough."

The waitress / former cheerleader, Kelli, returns with our drinks. She lays his glass down carefully in front of him and plunks my own more unceremoniously down on the table. She turns her attention back to Tim. "Are you getting any food today, Timmy?"

He looks up at her and smiles. "Not right now."

"I can't tempt you with any onion rings?"

Tim shakes his head no.

She winks at him. "Buffalo wings?"

"Nah."

"Curly fries?"

Oh my God, is this waitress going to offer him every item on the menu one by one? But thankfully, after he turns down the curly fries, she finally goes off to another table.

"We went to high school with her, didn't we?" I say.

Tim glances at Kelli, who is tapping her foot impatiently on the floor while she waits for two women to decide on their orders. "That's right. You've got a good memory."

"I think she was flirting with you."

"Actually..." He lowers his voice a notch. "We went out a couple of times."

My eyebrows shoot up. "Seriously?"

He shrugs. "It wasn't a big deal. Pretty casual."

"Did you kiss her?"

I laugh at the way his face turns slightly pink in the dim light of the bar. The freckles may have faded, but he is still fair, and his skin tone shows off his emotions way too easily.

"She and her boyfriend were on some kind of *break*," he explains. "We went out two times, then she went back to her boyfriend."

"She dumped you?"

"She didn't dump me. It was *two* dates." He glances behind him, where Kelli is taking some other customer's order. "And even if she didn't go back to her boyfriend, I don't think there was going to be a third date. We weren't a match."

"Oh, I get it. I didn't know you were so picky, Reese."

"I'm not picky!" He takes a drink from his beer and licks foam from his upper lip. "I'm just waiting for the right person. And Kelli was nice enough, but it wasn't her. Is that awful?"

"No, not awful."

He traces a pattern on the condensation of his glass. "So how about you? Were you married before?"

"No."

"Oh." He nods. "So Josh's dad..."

"Not in the picture," I blurt out. "At *all*."

And also serving a life sentence for murder. That too.

I'm used to getting a sympathetic look when I tell people I'm doing this all by myself, but that isn't the look Tim gives me. It's something different. I can't quite put my finger on it.

"That sounds hard," he finally comments.

"We're fine."

"I didn't say you weren't."

"Look..." I take a drink of my own alcoholic beverage for courage. "I just want to be clear that my life is kind of complicated right now, and I'm not looking for...you know, *anything*. Except friendship."

"Oh, good." He leans back in his seat, which squeaks under his weight. "Because that's exactly what I'm looking for too. Friendship."

"Good then."

"Perfect."

I study him across the table as he smiles back at me. Tim is a good guy—he always has been—and I believe that if I tell him all I want is friendship, he won't push anything further. He'll respect my wishes.

After all, ten years ago, he saved my life.

CHAPTER 14

It's sad that on a Saturday, I have nothing better to do than go grocery shopping. The shopping trip is literally the highlight of my weekend.

It was Josh who convinced me to go. First, he discovered we were out of Lucky Charms and wrote it in all capital letters on the shopping list that I keep on the fridge. He mentioned last night that we didn't have any. Then this morning, he looked especially forlorn as he poured himself a bowl of Cheerios instead of Lucky Charms, repeatedly mentioning that he wished there were some colorful marshmallows in his cereal. Then he wrote it on the shopping list a second time.

He also pointed out that I could go shopping without having to get a babysitter. Josh has been pushing for a little more freedom, and to be fair, he's old enough to stay by himself for an hour while I'm at the supermarket. So here I am, buying Lucky Charms and I guess eggs and cheese and bread and some other stuff we need.

While I am inspecting a head of lettuce in the produce aisle, I get the distinct feeling I'm being watched. I look over my shoulder and wince at the sight of a familiar face. It's Kelli—that girl who waited on us the other night at the Shamrock. The one who was on the cheerleading squad with me, back before my entire life went to hell.

Our eyes make contact. At this point, it would be worse to ignore her, so I wave hesitantly. "Hi."

The woman shoots daggers at me with her eyes. "I know you."

I freeze, not sure how to respond. Does she mean she knows me from when I was out with Tim? Or does she recognize me from all those years ago? I hope it's the former.

"You're the woman who was having drinks with Tim the other night," she says.

I let out a sigh of relief. "Uh, yeah."

Her lips curl in disgust. "So what are you—his *girlfriend*?"

"No," I say quickly. Not that I owe this woman any explanation, but I'd like to get out of this supermarket without her scratching my eyes out with those long red fingernails. "Tim and I are just old friends."

"Didn't look that way to me."

"It's true." I look over her shoulder, trying to catch the eye of a security guard. "If you want Tim, he's all yours. He told me you had a boyfriend though."

Her face fills with rage. "He was *talking about me* to you?"

Oh God. "No. Not at all. He just mentioned you went out, but now you had a boyfriend. That's it."

Kelli looks completely furious. I can see why Tim

wasn't eager to go out with her again if this is how she behaved. Of course, she seemed super nice around him. I'm sure if they started dating, she would have kept this side of her from him for as long as she could.

"You know," Kelli says, "Tim brings plenty of girls to the Shamrock. Don't think you're so special."

He does? I don't know why that revelation makes me sad. Maybe I *had* been hoping that the other night was more than just drinks with an old friend. "Like I said, it wasn't a date or anything."

Kelli narrows her eyes at me. Her lips turn down. "Do we know each other from somewhere else? You seem familiar."

I try to make my expression blank. "No, I don't think so. I just moved here."

Now would be a good time to make a gracious exit, before Kelli figures out who I am. But then her eyes widen into saucers, and I realize I'm too late.

"You're that girl!" She snaps her fingers. "You're… Bridget Something. You're the one who got Shane Nelson sent to prison."

Of course she'd get my name wrong but remember the name of the handsome star quarterback perfectly. For a moment, I consider denying the whole thing, but it's futile. She knows it's me. "That was a long time ago."

"That was total bullshit." Kelli practically spits out the words. "I *knew* Shane. He was a good guy. He would never have done those things."

I don't point out to her that the object of her flirtation, Tim Reese, was even more instrumental in getting Shane sent to prison than I was. But Tim's transgression was more forgivable than mine because he's hot.

Anyway, I'm not surprised she's defending Shane. This is nothing new—plenty of people in Raker, especially people who knew Shane well, were furious at me for testifying against him. Shane was a football star, and everyone loved him. I had been his girlfriend, and people felt I was betraying him. Even if I didn't have to leave for other reasons, I could never have stayed in Raker after what I did to him.

But I had to testify. I had to tell the truth about that night and get that monster locked away for good.

"You weren't there that night," I say quietly.

"I didn't need to be," she retorts. "You got it wrong. Shane was innocent."

"No," I say, "he wasn't. Believe me."

Before she can say anything else, I turn my shopping cart and speed walk to another aisle. After everything I've been through, the last thing I need is some scary waitress stalking me in addition to all my other problems. I go through the aisles as quickly as I can, gathering the items from the shopping list, mostly from memory.

It's only when I get into the car that I realize I forgot the Lucky Charms.

CHAPTER 15

ELEVEN YEARS EARLIER

"You went on a date with Tracy Gifford?"

Kayla's voice is so screechy that if it gets any higher, only dogs will be able to hear her. But I can't blame her because I'm feeling the same way. Tim went on a *date* with *Tracy Gifford*? How did that happen? In what universe did my neighbor go on a date with a dead girl?

"Two dates." Tim looks like he wants to disappear into the folds of the sofa. "That's it. It wasn't a big deal."

"Not a big deal!" Kayla bursts out. I notice her thigh is no longer touching his. "I'm sorry, but that's a *very* big deal."

Tim squirms. "It's really not."

Brandon's chiseled features are twisted in amusement. I always thought he looked like the handsome rich kid in every John Hughes movie. "I underestimated you, Reese. Nice going. Did you score with her?"

"No!" Tim's face is turning red. "I told you, it was just two dates."

"Exactly," Brandon says.

"Christ." Tim rakes a hand through his short hair, which is now sticking up a bit. "I'm telling you, it was nothing. *Nothing.* We met at the library, we got to talking, and we went out two times. Then she stopped returning my calls."

"Because she was dead?" Chelsea supplies.

Everyone else is firing questions at Tim, but I am completely speechless. I never could have imagined this in a million years. And how did *Shane* know about it? He must've known, because when he said it, he was looking right at Tim. I glance at Shane now, and he's watching everything unfold, a look of amusement in his eyes.

"Did the police question you?" Kayla asks.

"*No.*"

"Did they know you went out with her?" she presses him.

"I have no idea." He squirms on the sofa. "Whether or not they did, it wasn't a big deal. I mean, two dates, and it was, like, a month before she died."

"You mean," Chelsea says, "before she was *killed.*"

Tim shoots me a pained look, but I have to look away. I thought I knew him better than anyone else in the world, but I didn't know about this. I'm reeling from the shock. I can't wrap my head around it.

"You should go to the police," Kayla says. "Tell them what you know."

Tim grimaces. "I don't know anything. I have nothing to tell them."

With those words, he jumps off the sofa and stalks in the direction of the kitchen. He shoves the door open and disappears inside.

"Wow," Kayla breathes. "It just shows, you never know…"

I can't sit here another second while they speculate about what Tim might have done. I get up off the love seat and follow Tim to the kitchen. I can feel Shane's eyes on my back, but I don't turn around.

Inside the dark kitchen, Tim is leaning against the counter, his head bowed over the rusty sink. He looks like he's trying to get control of himself. I've seen him like this before. He had the same expression on his face when his dog of twelve years, Rusty, developed tumors all over his body and they had to put him down.

"Hey," I say.

Tim turns to look at me just as a crack of lightning illuminates his face. "Hey."

"You okay?"

The thunder that shakes the room is almost deafening. "I'm sorry I didn't tell you I went out with Tracy."

"Why didn't you?"

He rubs his hands over his face. "I was freaked out. We went out at the beginning of the summer, and then a month later, they found her dead. I thought I might have been the last guy she went out with. And I…I figured it wouldn't look good for me. Plus, it wasn't like I knew anything that would help."

It makes sense, but at the same time, it leaves me feeling a little uneasy. If he's completely innocent, why wouldn't he want to tell the police what he knows? Why would he hide it?

"I felt awful when I found out." He drops his eyes. "It didn't work out between me and Tracy, but she didn't deserve to die. She was a nice person. It tore me up."

"Yeah," I breathe. "I'm sure."

"I don't know how Shane knew about it." His face darkens. "I can't believe he's been sitting on that, waiting for the perfect moment to make me look bad."

I frown. "I don't think that was his intention."

"Oh, don't you?" Tim sneers. "Brooke, maybe I went on a couple of dates with some girl, but he really beat that kid up. For *no reason.* Put him in the freaking *hospital.* Is that really someone you want to be with?"

I flinch at his words. "He said he regretted it."

"Bullshit!" Tim's voice is loud enough that I'm worried the others will hear it through the door. "Shane Nelson is a bully, and he's a piece of shit. He only regrets that you found out about it because he wants to sleep with you."

My face burns. Tim hates Shane, but I can't believe he would say that to me. "That is so not true. And you have no right to say that."

We stare at each other for a moment. A muscle twitches under my eye. Tim breaks first.

"I'm sorry." He lets out a breath. "I'm sorry, Brooke. You're right. I shouldn't have said that."

"Damn straight."

"I'm just worried about you." The fear in his eyes is real. I know him well enough to know it. "I'm worried about you being with Shane. I don't think it's safe."

"Not safe?" I thought he was only worried that Shane was going to break my heart. "What are you talking about?"

"Listen to me, Brooke." He lowers his voice a notch. "Shane is—"

Before Tim can get out what he wants to say, the

door to the kitchen swings open. Shane is standing there, looking even more sexy than he usually does, with his dark hair slightly mussed and a lopsided smile on his face. "Hey, Brooke," he says. "You coming back out?"

It's hard not to notice he doesn't bother to ask Tim if he's coming out.

"Yes," I say. I look over at Tim. "You coming?"

Tim screws up his face. He looked like he had something important to tell me before Shane burst into the kitchen, but he can't very well do it now. And the truth is I don't want to hear it. Tim and Shane have some stupid little rivalry, but it's not my problem. Tim needs to get the hell over it.

"Fine," Tim finally says. "Let's go."

CHAPTER 16

PRESENT DAY

Today I'm supposed to remove the stitches from Shane Nelson's forehead.

I tossed and turned all night thinking about it. I dreamed of being back in that farmhouse. In my dream, the necklace was tightening around my throat, and the smell of sandalwood filled my nostrils. Then I heard a crack of thunder and some other noise in the background I couldn't make out, and then…

I was awake.

After the third time I woke up in a cold sweat, I gave up on sleep. I got up and made myself a cup of coffee. That was at four in the morning, and now I'm running on empty. Actually, it's a good thing. If I am exhausted, I'll be less panicked when Shane shows up.

At around two in the afternoon, Officer Hunt leads Shane down the long hallway to the waiting area outside the examining room. He takes a seat, his wrists and ankles shackled once again, waiting his turn after the two other men in front of him. Of course, after I spot Shane sitting out there, I can't think straight anymore. I have to keep asking the inmates to repeat what they just said five seconds earlier.

When it's Shane's turn to see me, Hunt grabs him by the arm and yanks him out of his seat. Shane needs a little help to stand, given his arms and legs are restrained, but Hunt is a lot rougher than he needs to be. And what's up with the shackles each time? I thought before it was because he had been in a fight, but now he's still cuffed.

Do they really think he's that dangerous? The only other guy I've seen in the last few days who was shackled like this had an angry sneer and hate symbols tattooed all over his face.

But what am I saying? *Of course* Shane is dangerous. I know that better than anyone.

But he doesn't look dangerous as he shuffles into my examining room and struggles to climb up on the table, a pained expression on his face. When he slips, he apologizes to me. "Sorry I'm so slow. It's just hard to do anything chained up like this."

You deserve it. The words are on my lips, but I don't say them. It would be unprofessional. Instead, I mutter, "Let's get this done."

He is struggling to find his balance on the exam table, and once again, I have to put out a hand to help him. He flashes me a grateful smile, and it looks so much like the old Shane, my cheeks burn, and I have to look away.

"Thanks, Brooke," he says. "I appreciate it."

"Uh-huh," I mumble.

"Okay. Let's get this over with."

I watch him attempt to scratch his nose with his

hands shackled together. Finally, I ask the question that's been running through my head since last week: "Why do they do this to you?"

Shane raises his eyebrows. "Do what?"

I nod down at the cuffs on his wrists. "Practically none of the other men get shackled this way. And I assume they're all just as bad as you here."

He cracks a lopsided smile. "Oh, I'm the *worst*."

I stare at him.

"That's what you think, isn't it?" His fingertips dig into the khaki of his prison jumpsuit. "That I'm a monster? That I deserve all this?"

His brown eyes hold mine, and this time, I refuse to look away. "Fine—don't answer the question. That's your right."

I expected some nasty retort from Shane, but instead, his shoulders sag. He nods his head toward the closed door separating us from the guard. "You want to know why I've always got shackles on? It's because he hates me."

"Who?"

"Hunt. He hates my guts."

"But why?"

He lifts a shoulder. "Who the hell knows? Maybe I remind him of somebody. Sometimes people just don't like each other. But it sucks if you're a prisoner and the guy who doesn't like you is one of the correctional officers. Makes your whole life a living hell. I mean, he has the power to make things really bad for me."

I hope he does. I consider saying those words, but what's the point? There was a time when I would have wanted to spit it in his face, but the years have taken some of the fight out of me. After all, Shane is in prison. He's serving his time for the terrible things he did. Everything that happened is in the past.

I wanted Shane to suffer after what he did, and I got my wish. He's stuck here, day in, day out, at the mercy of a bunch of guards who think he's the scum of the earth. Getting beaten up, and he can't even do anything about it or else it will be worse next time. Sleeping in a cell every night.

His life is hell.

"So how have you been?" Shane asks me as I peel open the suture removal kit.

"Fine." *Do not engage in conversation with this man.*

"Do you like working here?"

"Yes." It's the truth. Even though I'm still a little scared of the prisoners and I miss my heels, I find it to be rewarding work. And I want Shane to know that his presence here doesn't intimidate me. "The inmates are nice."

"Yeah. To *you*."

I get as close to Shane as I dare. It's not my first choice, but you have to get close and personal when you're removing stitches. "They're not nice to you?"

"Do you *see* the stitches on my head?"

I grab the first stitch with the forceps and snip it free. "I thought you walked into a fence."

"Yeah, well."

I snap the second stitch. "You know, my son got bullied a lot last year. It was really hard. The other kids even gave him a black eye."

Shane blinks up at me. "They gave him a black eye in *preschool*?"

For a second, I am lost for words. I don't know why I told him any of that. Five minutes ago, I swore to myself

I wasn't going to share any more personal information with this man. Especially not about my son.

Our son.

What would Shane say if he knew the truth? If he knew that a few weeks after that awful night, I started throwing up in the toilet. I had hoped it was a stomach bug, but when it didn't get better, I caved and bought a pregnancy test. And when I saw the two blue lines on the test strip, my entire world shattered into pieces.

I had to tell my parents. They leaned on me hard to get an abortion, but I wouldn't do it. But one thing we all agreed on was that Shane could never know. We carefully picked out the outfit I wore to Shane's trial so that nobody would see my growing baby bump. And after the trial was over, I left Raker and didn't return.

Until now.

Shane is looking at me curiously. I need to say something to fix this. So I smile and shrug. "Kids are tougher than they used to be."

"Guess so."

I snip the next few stitches in silence. When I lean over him to get out the last one, I notice his gaze lowering. I glance down to see where he's looking and…

Oh God.

My shirt is hanging open just enough to give him a fantastic view of my cleavage. And boy, is he taking advantage. I clear my throat loudly.

Shane rips his gaze away from my boobs. "Shit. I'm sorry."

He's not the first prisoner to look at me that way, although he is the first to apologize. "Don't ever let it happen again," I say sharply.

"It's just..." He scratches his neck, which is turning red. "There aren't a lot of, uh, you know, *women* here. And I don't ever..."

The last stitch comes free, and I straighten up. I realize what he is saying. He'll never be with another woman again. Ever. For the rest of his life.

"I'm really sorry," he says again. "That was incredibly rude, and...I should have controlled myself."

No, he should have controlled himself eleven years ago. If he had, he might not be here right now. I ignore his second apology as I run one of my gloved fingers over the laceration. "Looks pretty good. There will be a scar, but hopefully not too bad."

"I don't care, but thanks." He hesitates. "And I'm sorry about what I said last time. About that night..."

I put my hands on my hips. "So you admit what you did."

"No, I didn't kill anyone. But I understand you don't want to hear that you got it wrong."

He is so full of it. He's not apologizing for the sake of apologizing. He's apologizing because he wants to talk about it more. I remember the word Elise underlined in his chart:

Manipulative.

"I was *there*, Shane." I toss the tray with the stitches in the garbage, and I put the scissors and the forceps in the sharps container. "I know what happened."

"Obviously not. You said yourself you couldn't see anything."

I remove my gloves with a loud snap. "So if you didn't do it, who did?"

"You know who it was, Brooke."

I shake my head.

"It was Reese." His eyes are like saucers now that he has my attention. "It had to be. He's the only one who—"

This isn't the first time he has accused Tim. That was the crux of his defense all those years ago. But he couldn't convince a jury, and he sure won't convince me now. Does he think I'm stupid?

"Shane, stop it," I growl.

"No, please, Brooke. You have to believe that I—"

"Stop it!"

At the sound of my raised voice, Officer Hunt bursts into the room, ready for action. He towers over me, and his face is curled into a sneer. He has little semicircles of sweat under his armpits. "What's going on here? Is there a problem?"

Shane presses his lips closed. I shake my head. I don't want Hunt to know about the past Shane and I have together. "No, everything is fine."

Hunt narrows his eyes at Shane. "Are you done here?"

"Yes, all done," I say tightly. "Take him away."

Hunt nods briskly. "Great, let's go."

I see what's going to happen a mile away. Hunt grabs Shane by the arm to get him off the exam table, but because there is a step to get down and his legs are shackled, he can't keep his balance. He goes toppling off the table and clocks his head on the side of my desk with a sickening thump.

I leap into action, bending down next to Shane, who is now on the floor. He groans, his eyes cracked open, but he's woozy, and there's an egg rising just below his hairline.

This happened once on the football field during practice. I had been on the sidelines with my friend Chelsea when Shane got taken down by a brutal tackle. Just like now, there was a sickening crack as his body made contact with the ground. I raced across the field to make sure he was okay, my heart thudding in my chest. I was so scared he had been badly hurt, and I still remember the rush of relief as I slid my hand into his, and his eyes fluttered open as he squeezed my hand. It was the first time I realized I was falling for Shane Nelson.

"What the hell is wrong with you?" I snap at Hunt.

Hunt doesn't even look the slightest bit perturbed that he just gave one of the prisoners a concussion. "Relax. It was an accident."

I look at Shane's face—his eyelids flutter the way they did all those years ago when he got knocked out on the football field. "Shane, are you okay?"

"I'm okay," he mutters.

"Nelson is tough," Hunt speaks up. "He'll be fine."

Just when I think this situation can't get any more uncomfortable, I hear footsteps coming down the hallway. A second later, Dorothy peeks her head in. She is still wearing those half-moon glasses, and she peers at us over the rim, somewhat accusingly.

"What's all this commotion?" she demands to know.

Shane is struggling to sit up, but he's having a hard time of it, between the knock on the head and the shackles. I straighten up to look Dorothy in the eyes. "Officer Hunt caused Mr. Nelson here to fall, and as a result, he had a significant head strike. He definitely has a concussion. I'd like to admit him to one of the beds in the infirmary for observation tonight."

For the first time, Hunt looks like he cares about what just happened. "Dorothy, that is absolutely not true. I was just assisting the inmate to his feet, and he tripped. It was entirely unintentional."

Dorothy's shrewd blue eyes look Hunt up and down, then rake over the rest of the room, taking in the entire situation. I hold my breath—this woman is not known for advocating for the prisoners.

"Marcus," she says sharply, "why on earth is Nelson shackled for medical appointments? He's not a risk."

"I believe he is," Hunt says.

"Based on *what*?" she retorts.

He doesn't have an answer for that, which is a bit of a relief. Dorothy folds her thick arms across her chest and scowls at both of us, even though I haven't done anything wrong.

"Marcus, I want you to take those shackles off the inmate immediately," she snaps. "Brooke, admit him to the infirmary overnight. Can you both handle this, or do I need to babysit?"

Hunt and I exchange looks. Judging by his expression, he wants to knock me onto the floor right next to Shane. Lucky for me, I'm not a prisoner at Raker Penitentiary.

"We'll take care of it," he grunts.

"Good."

I help Shane sit up, and Hunt gets the key out to unlock the shackles on his wrists and ankles. Hunt hesitates for a split second before doing it, casting a glance back in my direction. I watch him fit the key into the lock, and my fingers fly to my neck. The last time I was alone with Shane, he tried to strangle me.

All of a sudden, I'm not so excited for his hands to be free.

But nothing happens. When the cuffs are off, all Shane does is rub his wrists, looking relieved to finally be free. He doesn't try to choke me. He doesn't even try to get off the floor right away. He looks like he's barely hanging on to consciousness.

"Can you walk?" I ask him.

He rubs his head. "I think so. I'm just dizzy."

Hunt helps me walk Shane down the hallway to the infirmary, and we get him settled in a bed. The bump on his head is swelling up, and he has to stop twice on the way to the infirmary because he's too dizzy to go on. It makes me think about the night Shane—or someone—tried to kill me. That night, Shane got a knock on the head the same as he did today—the EMTs on the scene found the lump on his skull to prove it. He claims he was knocked unconscious before anything even happened to me.

And for the first time in ten years, part of me wonders if he might have been telling the truth.

But he can't be telling the truth. Because if he is, the man who tried to strangle me all those years ago is still out there.

CHAPTER 17

ELEVEN YEARS EARLIER

After a few more rounds of Never Have I Ever, the six of us are sufficiently trashed. Tim's date with the murdered girl has been forgotten, and Kayla is all over him again. At first, he was gently pushing her away, but now he's letting it happen. As for Brandon and Chelsea, they are all but having sex on the couch.

"Hey." Shane punches his buddy on the shoulder. "Take it upstairs. Not on my sofa."

Brandon snickers. "Better in your mom's bedroom?"

Shane shrugs, but I'm just relieved the two of us won't be in Mrs. Nelson's bedroom. Even though her bed is nicer, I don't think I would enjoy it knowing that I was in Shane's mother's bed.

Shane turns to me, his eyelids slightly droopy. "Want to head upstairs?"

My stomach churns, which might be from the vodka in my belly, but not entirely. After all, I didn't even finish one entire screwdriver. (Brandon managed to put away six of them.) I suddenly wish I had a little more to drink, because maybe then I wouldn't be so damn nervous.

"Sure," I say.

Shane reaches out to take my hand. His palm is warm and dry and comforting. I let him lead me out of the living room to the flight of stairs to get to the second floor. The wood of the stairs warps slightly as my feet make contact—one of these days, I'll be climbing the stairs, and the whole damn thing will collapse. But not today, apparently.

As I climb the stairs, I get that sensation again like somebody's watching me. That creeping in the back of my neck. I turn my head, expecting to see Tim staring up at me. But instead, he's on the sofa making out with Kayla. Well, good for him.

When we get into Shane's bedroom and he closes the door behind us, my anxiety ramps up another notch. His bedroom is a typical teenage guy's bedroom. He's got a twin-size bed with a splintered wooden bed frame, and a striped black-and-white blanket is strewn across the mattress with no attempt to make it tidy. There's a pile of dirty clothing pushed into one corner of the room, which I suspect was his attempt to "clean" for me. A couple of posters of bands are tacked up on the peeling paint of his walls, and the top of his dresser is lined with a bunch of gold trophies that briefly glow when lightning fills the room.

Shane reaches out to turn on the light, but a second later, the bulb flickers and goes out. He swears under his breath. "Power must've gone out."

"Oh." I squeeze my sweaty palms together. I've been alone with Shane before in his bedroom, but it was always with his mother in the next room or about to come home any minute. We've never been alone quite this way before. "Should we…?"

"It's fine." I can just barely make out the rise and fall of Shane's broad shoulders. "Everyone is going to bed anyway. The power will probably come back in the morning."

"Yeah." I tug at the chain of my snowflake necklace. "That's true."

Shane reaches out for my hand again. He pulls me over to his bed, but he doesn't push me to lie down. I perch on the edge of the bed, and he sits beside me. He reaches out and gently runs his finger along the curve of my jaw.

"I lope you, Brooke," he says.

I shiver slightly, nervous but also incredibly turned on. "I lope you too."

A smile plays on his lips. "Good."

"I…uh…" I clear my throat. "I'm sorry, Shane. I'm just super nervous because…well, you know, I've never…"

"Yeah," he says. "Me neither."

I look at him in absolute astonishment. Is he really telling me that he…?

"You've never had sex before?" I blurt out.

"No." He frowns. "I haven't."

"But you…" I am utterly confused. Shane has dated other girls before. Maybe he hasn't been with anyone for very long, but he's gone out with a lot of girls who aren't exactly picky, if you know what I mean. And Shane is *hot*. His best friend Brandon—according to Chelsea—has slept with at least five or six girls in the time the two of them were *dating*.

"I don't know." His face is suddenly filled with uncertainty. "I didn't want some stupid one-night stand. I want to be with someone I actually like. Is that so much to ask for?"

"No." I squeeze his knee. I'm still nervous, but I feel a lot better after his confession. This is scary, but we're going to figure it out together. "No, it's not."

He squeezes my hand in his. "I love you, Brooke."

It takes me a moment to realize what he's said. He hasn't told me he "lopes" me like he usually does. He said he loves me. He *loves* me.

"I love you too," I breathe.

He leans in toward me. "And I'm going to show you how much."

And he does.

CHAPTER 18

PRESENT DAY

Before I leave for the day, I check on Shane in the infirmary.

The infirmary is relatively empty today. There were two patients there as of this morning, but they were both well enough to go back to their cells by the afternoon, so right now, Shane is the only occupant of one of the six beds. The other hospital beds lined up against the wall all sit empty.

There's a nurse who comes in the evening, but she hasn't shown up for her shift yet, so the only person around is a guard I vaguely recognize who sits outside the door, reading a thick paperback novel. The guard nods at me when I walk inside but then goes right back to his book. I look at the title—*Moby Dick*.

The lights are lowered in the infirmary, and since the sun has gone down, the room is dim. From the doorway, I can just barely make out Shane lying on the second bed from the end of the row. When I get closer, I can see all the features of his handsome face. In the dim light, he looks so damn much like the old Shane. The guy I fell in love with all those years ago.

His eyes are closed, and for a moment, a flutter of fear goes through my chest. I haven't checked on him for over two hours—what if he has a hematoma growing in his brain and lost consciousness while he's been lying here? He seemed neurologically stable when I left him, but a lot can happen in two hours. And since I was the last practitioner who saw him, it would all be on my shoulders. After all, it was my decision to watch him instead of sending him out for a scan of his head. If he died, it would be on me.

I take quick strides over to his bed. He doesn't stir when I'm standing over him. "Shane," I say.

Did his eyelids flutter? I can't tell. Oh God, please let him just be sleeping and not unconscious.

"Shane," I say again, and this time, I shake his shoulder.

My knees almost buckle with relief when his eyelids crack open. He's okay. "Oh," he says. "Hey, Brooke."

He's awake *and* he recognizes me. "Hey," I say. "I…I was afraid you were unconscious or something."

"No, just sleeping." He presses a button on the side of the bed that elevates him to a sitting position. "Were you worried about me?"

"No," I say too quickly. "I mean, yes, I was worried you might need a CAT scan."

But as I say the words, I realize it's not entirely true. Yes, I was worried that I had screwed up and made the wrong judgment call. I was worried about him in the way that I worry about all my patients. But that's not the only reason I was freaking out. He's right—I was worried *about him*.

And I don't entirely understand why.

For a long time, I felt only one emotion for this man. *Hatred*. I hated him for what he tried to do to me. I hated him for what he did to my friends. I hated him for knocking me up and leaving me to deal with the consequences all by myself. I hated him for not even having the guts to admit what he did and for making me get on the stand during a grueling trial to relive every moment.

But looking at him now, lying in this hospital bed, a bruise blooming on his forehead from the fall he took, his brown eyes staring up at me…

I…

I don't…

"I need to do a neuro exam." I clear my throat. "I need to make sure you're okay."

"Knock yourself out."

I run through the exam, making sure his pupils are equal, that he hasn't become weak on one side of his body, and I make him answer some basic questions to make sure his cognition is intact. It occurs to me that this is the first time I've interacted with him without any shackles on. If he wanted, he could reach out and wrap his fingers around my neck and squeeze as hard as he could—well, at least until the guard heard us and came running. But somehow, I'm not worried he's going to do that. Not even a little.

"Did I pass?" he asks me when I back away from him.

"You passed," I confirm.

"Great." He nods up at the clock on the wall. "I wanted to get out of here before dinner. It's taco night."

I can't help myself from cracking a smile. "Taco Tuesday?"

"You got it." He adjusts his position in the bed. "I don't want to miss taco night. I *lope* tacos."

My breath catches in my throat. *I lope tacos.* When was the last time Shane and I joked around about loping each other? That used to be our *thing*. I remember the last time I said the words to him: *I lope you*. Against my will, I feel a sudden rush of affection.

Yes, Shane Nelson did unspeakable things. But before he did those things, I had *loped* him.

No, I had *loved* him.

I look away before he can read the expression on my face. "Don't worry. I'll make sure they bring you a tray of food."

"Great. Thanks so much, Brooke. Really."

"Yeah."

He reaches behind his head for the pillow he's leaning against, which is almost flat as a pancake. He's trying to adjust it to make himself more comfortable on this hard hospital-bed mattress. I watch him struggle for a moment, then I lean in and fix the pillow for him.

My face moves close to Shane's as I adjust the pillow—closer than I was when I stitched up his head. I brace myself for the scent of sandalwood, but all I can smell is soap and shaving cream. The last time I was so incredibly close to him was over a decade ago. The night I lost my virginity to him. And he lost his to me.

When it was over, I felt so good. I had been so happy that this was the boy I gave myself to. I was so in love with him.

For a split second, our eyes lock together. And it

occurs to me that we're the only two people in this room. There's a guard, and if there were a problem, he would be here in an instant, but he wouldn't hear something quiet.

Like if Shane leaned in and kissed me.

I jerk my head back, shocked by the thoughts going through my head. What's *wrong* with me? Shane Nelson tried to kill me. He's a *monster.* He's spending his life in prison for murder. Even if I could ever forgive him for what he's done, I could never…

I cough loudly, and the sound echoes through the empty, dark infirmary. "I think we're done here."

"Great. Thanks so much."

"I'll make sure you get your dinner," I tell him in a squeaky voice that barely sounds like my own.

A smile plays on his lips. "My tacos."

"Right. Tacos."

"Thanks, Brooke." His eyes stay trained on mine. "I appreciate everything you've done for me."

"No problem."

I somehow manage to rip my gaze away from his. But as I walk out of the room, my sensible flats clacking against the linoleum floor, I can feel him watching me.

CHAPTER 19

I can't seem to stop shaking after my encounter with Shane in the infirmary.

I have spent over a decade now hating him. Glad that he was rotting away in prison because it was what he deserved. And even when I saw him last week and confirmed that he didn't have horns sprouting from his head or a devil's tail, I still thought of him as the man who tried to kill me.

Today was the first time since that night that I thought of him as the boy I used to love.

By the time I walk out to my car in the parking lot of the penitentiary, I want nothing more than to go home, eat one of Margie's delicious dinners, and crawl into bed. Ooh, and maybe take a hot bath. When Josh was little, taking a bath was impossible because I couldn't leave him alone for that long and there was no backup parent to watch him. But now that he's more independent, I've become addicted.

When I'm six feet away from my car, a large hand closes around my arm. I instantly go on high alert, whipping myself around to confront whoever grabbed me. But when I turn, I come face-to-face with Officer Marcus Hunt.

Outside the prison walls, he looks even more imposing. He towers over me, his lips curled into a perpetual sneer, and his biceps are about the same circumference as my thighs. He doesn't have any weapons on him at the moment, but he doesn't need them. He could crush me with one hand.

And we're the only two people in the parking lot.

"Brooke," he says, "I need to talk to you."

"I don't have anything to say to you," I hiss at him.

"Don't be like that."

My purse is flung over my shoulder. I've got a bottle of pepper spray in there, but I'm not sure I'll be able to get to it with him restraining me. "You need to let go of me."

"Brooke…"

"Let go of me or I'll scream!"

Hunt's eyes widen as he finally gets it in his head that he needs to let go of me. He releases my arm and holds his hands up in the air. "I'm sorry. I didn't mean to scare you. I just want to talk."

He didn't mean to *scare* me? Does he have a *clue* how scary he is? I can't imagine what it's like for Shane to deal with this guy every single day of his life.

"Please, Brooke." He takes a step back, his hands still in the air. "I just need to talk to you."

I don't want to talk to Hunt. I want to go home and have dinner and possibly a bubble bath. But I need to work with this guy—I can't be his enemy. And I'm admittedly curious about what he has to say.

"Fine," I say. "What is it?"

"Brooke." His forehead crinkles. "Look, I'm sorry about what happened with Nelson today. It wasn't like I meant to hurt him."

"Yeah, right."

"I didn't." He shakes his shaved head. "But you know what, even if I did, he deserves it. Do you have any idea what that guy did to land himself in here?"

I have some idea. "All these men have committed crimes…"

"This is different. Nelson is different. He's…he's really manipulative."

It's the same thing Elise wrote in his chart. And she underlined it. "I haven't seen him act that way."

"Right, because he's manipulating you. He's making you trust him, but you shouldn't."

I crane my neck to look up at Hunt's face. Whatever else I can say, I don't think he's making this up. He seems to really believe it. But the question is, do I believe it?

"I'm not going to let him manipulate me," I say.

"That's what Elise said. Now she's probably going to prison herself. Or at the least, she'll lose her license."

What is he saying? That Shane tricked Elise, and that's the reason she got in trouble? I find that hard to believe, especially after what she wrote in his chart. And Shane hasn't manipulated me. I even offered him pain medication last week, and he refused. "Don't worry about it."

"I *am* worried." He glances over my shoulder at my Toyota. "Look, I don't want to talk about this in the parking lot. Why don't we go get a drink together, and we can, you know, talk about this more?"

Oh. I get it now.

"No, thanks." I adjust the strap of my handbag on my shoulder. "I have to get home. The babysitter is waiting."

"Another night then?"

The concern on his face has vanished, and now he has a hopeful expression. So this is his game. He's torturing Shane to impress me and get a date. It's despicable, but I don't want to outright humiliate him. I do have to work with him, and I'm also counting on him to protect me if I'm ever in a dangerous situation.

"Maybe sometime next month," I say vaguely. "I'm just really busy now. And my sitter can't stay late."

"Oh, right, sure." Hunt rubs his shaved head. "Yeah, I have a busy month this month too. We'll have to do it next month. Or the month after. Whatever. No big deal."

"Yeah." I reach into my purse for my keys. "Anyway, I'm going to get going. I guess I'll see you tomorrow."

"Sure." He nods. "And, Brooke?"

"Yes?"

"Be careful."

CHAPTER 20

I can't sleep.

It's much quieter here than it was when I was living back in Queens. The block that we lived on had a lot of traffic at night, and at least once a week, I could be guaranteed to be woken up by a car horn or, worse, an alarm that wouldn't stop sounding off for the better part of an hour. But on this quiet block in our small town, the only thing you can hear at night is a few crickets chirping.

So I don't know why I've slept so terribly since I've moved out here.

Part of it might be how strange it is sleeping in my parents' bedroom. I was reluctant to take the master bedroom at first for this very reason. But it was the largest of the three upstairs bedrooms by far and the only one with a queen-size bed. So I tried to redecorate it to make it my own. I took down the seaside painting my parents always kept over their bed, swapped out the bedspread for my own royal-blue down comforter, and replaced nearly all the framed photographs on the dresser.

It doesn't help. It's still very much my parents' bedroom. It even still *smells* like them. The scent of my mother's perfume still lingers in the air, no matter how much I scrub the floors and the furniture.

I wish things hadn't gone the way they did over the last decade. It's not like I was ever close with my parents. My mother was strict, and my father was always traveling for work. And if the rumors were to be believed, he cheated on my mom a good amount. But still, I didn't expect the treatment they gave me when I decided to keep the baby growing inside me.

You're making a horrible mistake, Brooke, my mother would tell me practically every time we talked.

I wanted to stand up to them, but I was barely clinging to my sanity as it was. All I knew was that I wanted the baby. And I would do anything for my unborn child, including agreeing to live with a relative in the city, and I accepted their monthly checks to make ends meet and get an education. I didn't want to do it, but I also didn't want my son to suffer because of my own pride.

I even accepted that I wasn't allowed to return to Raker. Not even for a visit.

But when I finished nursing school, and I finally had a decent paycheck that would allow me to support myself without my parents' help, I stood up to them. I told them I wasn't going to take any more of their money. And I wanted the right to come back to Raker to visit them with Josh, or else we would have no relationship at all. I was tired of being their dirty little secret.

I really thought they would acquiesce. I was their

only child, and Josh was their only grandchild. I believed their love for us had to be larger than their shame at having a daughter who got knocked up in high school.

I was wrong.

A few months after I started returning their checks, my father drove out to Queens to surprise me as I was returning home from work. I've always thought of my father as being handsome compared with my friends' fathers—women used to turn to look at him on the street—but for the first time, I noticed how old he looked. He had bags under his eyes and a paunch straining the buttons on his shirt. His hair had always looked silver, but now it just looked dull gray.

Don't do this, Brooke, he pleaded with me. *Your mother and I love you. You know that.*

I snorted. *If you loved me, you wouldn't be ashamed of me.*

We're not ashamed of you. We just don't think it's a good idea for you to come to Raker.

But why?

The crease that was always between my father's eyebrows those days grew deeper. *Can't you just trust us for once, Brooke? We're doing this for your own good.*

I was utterly unsurprised that my father would not give me a logical reason why I couldn't ever visit my childhood home with my son. So I turned him away, and I continued returning their checks, uncashed. After a year, they got the idea, and the checks stopped arriving.

Now here I am, a few short months after their deaths, back in my hometown. Despite how terribly things went wrong, I had a happy childhood until that night. This is the kind of town where you want your child to grow up.

But I can't help feeling like this bedroom is haunted by their presence. Or really, the entire house.

I climb out of bed and walk over to the dresser across the room. When I arrived here after I got news of the car accident, I found this dresser littered with photographs of me and Josh. The photographs stopped after I cut them off five years ago, but there were dozens of pictures all over the house, spanning my life from when I was first born to that day I sent my father away because they couldn't accept my life choices. I took most of them down, but I left a couple. For example, a photograph on the dresser from when I was about Josh's age, posing with my parents for a Christmas card.

I pick up the photograph now, staring down at my smiling, unlined face. My parents each have one hand on my shoulder, and they are glowing with pride in our little family. I can't even remember them ever looking that way.

Despite everything, I believe my parents loved me. I can see it in their eyes in this photograph. But their stupid pride got in the way of our relationship. They chose to sever our ties completely rather than be humiliated by having me parade around in front of their friends with my fatherless son.

Except now when I look down at this photograph, I think back to that day my father came out to see me in Queens. He drove for at least five straight hours to get to me because it was that important to him. For the first time, I wonder if his motivation wasn't completely selfish.

Can't you just trust us for once, Brooke? We're doing this for your own good.

He almost seemed…

Afraid.

But that's silly. There was nothing to be afraid of. Shane was behind bars at that point, for the rest of his life. There was no way he could get to me. I was safe from that man.

And I still am.

CHAPTER 21

ELEVEN YEARS EARLIER

After you have had sex with your boyfriend for the first time, the absolute last thing you want to hear him say is "Shit." Well, maybe "I have herpes" would be slightly higher on the list, but this isn't good either.

"What?" I say. "What's wrong?"

Shane rolls off me, sweaty and flushed. I had been so scared before, but there was nothing to be afraid of. He was sweet and considerate, always making sure I was okay and that everything felt good…or at least not *bad*. I don't know if I would say it was mind-blowing, but it was pretty good for my first time. And now this is the part where he is supposed to be holding me and telling me how much he loves me and still respects me, but instead, he looks decidedly perturbed.

"What?" I press him.

"I think…" He frowns. "I think the condom came off."

"*What?*"

"I'm not sure," he says quickly. "But…well, it's off. And I didn't take it off. So I'm kind of wondering when it came off and…"

"Shit," I say.

My head is spinning. I'm seventeen years old. I can't be pregnant at seventeen years old. I have plans for the next ten years of my life, none of which involve a screaming child. I want to go to college. Graduate school. I want to travel the world. Oh my God, this is bad.

"Don't freak out, Brooke," Shane says. "It'll be okay."

I feel like I can hardly breathe. "How exactly will it be okay?"

"Look." He grabs my arm, which is trembling. "It was just one time. I'm not even sure if it came off. I'm sure it will be okay."

"You're kidding me. Girls get pregnant all the time from 'just one time.'"

"All right," he says with maddening calm. "Then we'll figure it out."

"*How?*"

"I don't know," he admits. "But whatever you decide to do, I'll support you."

My mouth falls open slightly. I look into his eyes, and I can tell he means it. Shane has plans for the future too. He's hoping for a football scholarship to college so he can have a better life than the one he grew up with. Those eight words are capable of destroying all his plans. *Whatever you decide to do, I'll support you.* But he said it anyway.

At that moment, I know I chose the right guy to lose my virginity to.

"I love you," I blurt out.

He runs his fingers along my cheek. "I love you too."

Even though I'm still freaking out about it, I force myself to calm down. Shane is right. It was just one time, and the chances are small that I got knocked up. And if I somehow did, he will support me. No matter what I decide.

Despite the thunder outside and my racing thoughts, I fall asleep in Shane's arms. And I don't wake up again until I hear the screams.

CHAPTER 22

PRESENT DAY

Josh is in heaven as he chomps on one of Margie's meatballs while the two of us share dinner at the kitchen table. "Mom," he says, "these are the best meatballs I've ever had."

"Oh yeah?"

"You know how Margie made them?" Without waiting for an answer, he answers his own question: "She put in meat but also eggs, bread crumbs, and also Parmesan cheese. She said Parmesan cheese was the secret ingredient."

"Yes, they're delicious."

Josh takes another bite of the meatball on his fork and chews thoughtfully. "How do you make your meatballs, Mom?"

Well, I open up the package of frozen meatballs, stick a few on a plate, and put them in the microwave for sixty seconds. If they're not done, I put them in for another thirty seconds. "Pretty much the same way, but without the cheese."

"Next time you make them," he says, "I'll help you. Margie told me exactly what to do."

It's nice Margie is so good with him, but it makes me sad that when my mother was alive, she never seemed to bond with Josh. She never would have made meatballs with him. She didn't even care that much when I cut her off.

The doorbell rings, and Josh leaps out of his seat with surprising energy for a kid who just ate about thirty meatballs. He loves answering the door though. It's one of his favorite things in the world, if you can believe that. I'm not sure why, because it's almost always just some guy delivering a package.

I hear the front door unlocking, followed by the sound of soft conversation. That's strange. Why is Josh talking to the delivery guy?

Unless it isn't a delivery guy.

I struggle to my feet, which isn't easy considering I have eaten about twenty-nine meatballs. (They were really good. Must have been the Parmesan cheese.) I shuffle over to the front door, and my mouth drops open when none other than Tim Reese is standing at the front door, talking to Josh. I freeze about ten feet away from the door, unable to move.

"Mom!" Josh calls out. "Look who's here! It's Mr. Reese. He's our assistant principal!"

I look over at Tim, who has a strained smile on his lips. "That's right. I…uh…I live just down the block, and my mom sent over these cookies from Florida, and I thought…"

He thought he would bring me some cookies. Except he got more than he bargained for.

"Cookies?" Josh asks hopefully. It will be a sad day when my son gets too old to be excited about cookies. Although to be honest, I *still* get a little excited about cookies. But at the moment, I'm having trouble dredging up any enthusiasm for them. "Can I have some, Mom?"

"Sure," I say tonelessly.

Tim looks down at the white box in his hand, as if he had forgotten he was even holding it. He shoves the box into Josh's arms without taking his eyes off me. "They're all yours," he says.

"Mom." Josh tugs on my arm. "How many am I allowed to have?"

"Um, one."

"One? That's *it*?"

"Okay, uh…two, I guess."

"But what if they're small?"

Oh my God, I would let him have the whole box if he would just leave the room right now. "You can have three if they're small."

"Yay!"

Josh takes off down the hall with the box of cookies, leaving me and Tim staring at each other in the hallway. Tim shakes his head. "That's your son? That's Josh?"

"Yes."

The confusion on his face almost makes me want to reach out and hug him. "You told me he was in kindergarten."

"I never told you that."

"But you…" He glances over my shoulder. "Can we talk outside for a minute?"

I'd *really* rather not, but I have a feeling I don't have a choice in the matter. This is a conversation we need to have, as much as I've been dreading it. And I don't want to talk about this within earshot of my son, and Tim knows it.

We step out onto my front porch, shutting the door behind me. I'm standing only a foot away from Tim, and I can almost make out the remnants of the freckles he used to have. I used to know his face so well, even better than my own.

We were inseparable when we were kids. And we thought it would always be like that—Tim especially. When we were six or seven, he used to talk about the future in a way that always included me. He'd say things like, *When we get married, we should get a big house with five bedrooms.* Sometimes I got the feeling he never stopped thinking that way—he just stopped saying it out loud.

"Brooke," he says quietly, "how old is Josh?"

I shut my eyes for a moment, hoping maybe when I open them, this will all be a really awkward dream. Then I open my eyes again.

Nope. Not a dream.

"He's ten," I say.

"*Ten*?" Tim's hand is shaking as he runs it through his hair. "He's ten years old?"

"Right."

"So does that mean Shane is…?"

He doesn't need to finish the question. We both know what he's thinking. I may as well tell him the truth. He deserves that.

"Yes," I say. "He is."

"Oh *God*." Tim looks like he's going to be sick. "I had no idea that you…"

"Well, now you know why I left town."

"Yeah, but..." He stares at the door to my house. "Does Josh know who his father is?"

"No. And I'd like to keep it that way."

"Does *Shane* know?"

I shake my head vigorously. "No. No way."

Tim looks again at the door of my house, his eyes growing wilder by the second. "Christ, he even *looks* like Shane."

"I know." I bite my lip. "He does look like him, but he's not anything like Shane. He's a really good kid."

"Oh *God*."

His reaction is about what I expected it to be. Tim never liked Shane, even before all the terrible things he did. I should have known he would react this way. But it's still hard to watch. Sometimes people do exactly what you think they're going to do, and they still manage to disappoint you.

"Look..." Tim takes a step back. "I think maybe I should go. This was...a bad idea."

He's not thinking anymore about how when we're married, we're going to build a giant two-story doghouse in the backyard. Which is fine. A doghouse that big wasn't practical anyway.

Tim is about to take off when Josh bursts out of the house. He looks slightly breathless, and his lips are covered in cookie crumbs. "Mom!" he says. "The kitchen sink is broken."

Oh great. This evening is just getting better and better. "Are you sure?"

Josh nods solemnly. "Yeah. When I turn the water on, it only comes out slow or really fast, and I got water all over me!"

I miss my old apartment in Queens. We had a landlord and a super, and if something was broken, all I had to do was call them. I suppose I have to figure out a way to fix the sink myself.

"Tim?" I better ask him before he makes a run for it. "You don't know a plumber I can call, do you?"

Tim looks over at the house, frowning slightly. "If you want, I can take a look."

"Do you know how to fix a sink?"

"Maybe. I've gotten pretty decent at fixing things around the house."

I'm not about to turn him down. Plumbers are expensive, and while my parents left me this house, they didn't leave me much money after taxes took their share. "Okay, thanks."

Tim follows me into the house. It's weird because he's been in this house hundreds if not thousands of times, but not for a long time, and not since the two of us have grown up. I never swapped out most of the furniture my parents had, but it's not the same furniture from when we were kids. It looks different but the same. Sort of like Tim himself.

"Do you have a tool kit?"

I think for a moment. "My dad kept one in the garage."

"I'll get it!" Josh says.

Tim and I stand there awkwardly while Josh runs to the garage to grab my father's toolbox. Fortunately, he doesn't take long. He comes back a minute later, lugging a black toolbox that looks like it weighs more than he does.

"All right," Tim says. "Let's do this." He looks down

at Josh, who is watching him with big eyes. "I don't know if I can handle this by myself. Do you think you could help me?"

"Yeah!"

He seems even more excited about fixing the sink than he was about cookies.

—

I spend the first five minutes watching Tim and Josh anxiously, but then I realize how boring it is to watch two people fix a sink, so I go to the living room to read. There's a lot of loud banging and intermittent running water, and at one point, I swear I hear both of them laughing.

About an hour later, Tim comes out of the kitchen, wiping his hands on his blue jeans. Josh follows a second later. "Mom, we fixed it! Mr. Reese fixed the sink!"

Tim's face breaks into a smile. "Actually, Josh here did most of the work. I was just sort of watching."

"And you helped me tighten that bolt."

"That's true. I did do that."

Josh beams at Tim. "Now you can fix the doorknob upstairs that keeps falling off. And I'll help."

Tim's smile falters. "Uh, well…"

I stand up from the couch. "Josh, Mr. Reese is too busy to fix everything in our house. And it's getting late."

Josh's face falls. He looks like someone told him his dog just died. "Oh."

"But I can come by tomorrow," Tim adds. "I mean, if it's okay with your mom."

"It's okay with me." My eyes meet Tim's. "If it's okay with you."

"It's okay with me."

Josh looks between the two of us, his face scrunched up. "So...are we fixing the doorknob?"

"Sure," Tim says. "Tomorrow, okay?"

I send Josh off to get ready for bed while I walk Tim to the door. I honestly didn't think I was going to see him again after the talk we had. But now it seems almost forgotten. Although I'm sure Tim hasn't forgotten.

We pause as Tim steps outside. "Thanks for doing that," I say.

"No problem." He looks at me for a moment, contemplating what to say next. "You were right, Brooke."

"I was? About what?"

"He *is* a good kid."

With those words, Tim turns around and starts on the path back to his own house.

CHAPTER 23

ELEVEN YEARS EARLIER

I jerk awake. My eyes fly open, and it takes me a second to remember where I am. I am at Shane's house, and he's lying in bed beside me, still breathing deeply. But I heard something. A scream. I'm sure of it.

I look down at my watch. It's three in the morning.

"Shane." I shake his bare shoulder until his eyes crack open. "I heard something."

"Huh?" He rubs his eyes with the back of his hand. "What's wrong?"

"There was a—"

And then we hear it again. A bloodcurdling scream, except this time I can clearly make out a word being screamed:

"Brooke!"

Shane sits up straight in bed, suddenly as wide awake as I feel. He throws his legs over the side of the bed and jumps into his pair of baggy blue jeans. He throws a T-shirt over his head while I'm struggling with my skinny jeans. He is still in his socks when he reaches for the bedroom door.

"Where are you going?" I ask anxiously.

His gaze darts down to the doorknob. "Somebody was screaming downstairs. I need to check it out."

"Not without me."

There is no way he is leaving me alone in this room. I button up my jeans and toss on my sweater.

"You should stay up here," Shane says. "It might not be safe."

"I want to come."

Shane opens his mouth to protest again, but the words are drowned out by another scream:

"Brooke!"

We get out of the room and run into Kayla and Tim at the top of the stairs. They both look like they've thrown on their clothes as hastily as we did. I wonder what they've been doing in there. Hopefully, mostly sleeping.

"You heard that?" Tim asks. Kayla is clinging to his arm.

Shane nods solemnly. We all look downstairs, and even from the second floor, we can see that the front door is wide open. Droplets of rain are dampening the carpet right inside the door.

"Chelsea," I murmur.

It had to have been Chelsea who screamed. Because it wasn't Kayla, and it wasn't me, so Chelsea is the only one left. But why would she call my name? Why wouldn't she call for Brandon if something was wrong? Unless…

If Brandon did anything to hurt her, I'm going to kill him.

Shane starts down the stairs first, taking them two at a time. Tim goes next, and I'm third. Kayla hangs behind, a distant fourth. I don't blame her. She's not great friends with any of us, and if there's trouble, she probably doesn't want to get involved.

Shane reaches the front door first. He hangs on to the doorframe, leaning out onto the small porch. Then he sees something that makes his eyes go wide, and he takes a step back.

And then I hear sobbing.

Tim gets out onto the porch second. He reacts much the same way Shane did. By this point, I am frantic to find out what's going on. I nearly trip over my feet getting to the front door. And then when I get outside…

Oh. Oh God…

Chelsea is on her knees next to Brandon, who is lying on the damp porch on his back, his chest a mess of dark-red blood. The same dark-red material is dripping out of his mouth, and his eyes are cracked open, staring at nothing. Chelsea is holding his hand, sobbing uncontrollably as the rain pours down on them.

"What happened?" I manage.

"Oh, Brooke!" Chelsea scrambles to her feet and throws her arms around me. She clings to me, even though she's getting blood and water all over my clothes. "I came downstairs because Brandon wasn't in bed. I saw the door was open so I looked outside and…"

"Is he dead?" Kayla squeaks. She looks like she's about to throw up.

Tim kneels beside the body. He places his fingers against Brandon's neck, searching for a pulse. He shakes his head. "He's gone."

Chelsea dissolves into louder sobs. She's still holding on to me, and I feel like I'm mostly keeping her upright. In another few seconds, the both of us are going to be on the floor.

"Get her into the house," Shane tells me. "We'll deal with what's out here."

Kayla and I help Chelsea back into the house and get her onto the sofa. She buries her face in her hands, unable to stop crying. I rub her back while Kayla reaches for her phone, which she had abandoned on a coffee table when she found out there was no service. She looks down at the screen.

"Still no service," she grunts. She looks up at the door and calls out, "Shane, you said there's a landline, right? Where is it? We have to call the police."

"It's next to the bookcase!" he calls back.

Quick as a flash, Kayla goes over to the bookcase. She picks up a cordless phone. She pushes a button on the phone and presses it against her ear. She frowns, pulls the phone away from her ear, and presses another button.

"Shane!" Her voice has taken on a hysterical edge. "The phone isn't working!"

A crack of thunder shakes the house, although it is softer than earlier in the evening.

"Shane!" Kayla screams.

After a few seconds, Shane comes into the house, slamming the screen door behind him. His face is slightly pink, and his hair and shirt are damp. He strides over to where Kayla is standing with the cordless phone and grabs it out of her hand. Kayla watches him, wringing her hands together.

"It's dead," he declares. "Storm must have damaged the phone lines."

Kayla's eyes fly around the room. "So there's no way to call the police?"

"No."

She shakes her head. "Then I'm getting out of here. Chelsea, where are the keys to your car?"

Shane presses his lips together. "Kayla, will you calm down for a minute?"

Lightning flashes, illuminating Kayla's small face, making her look almost demonic. "No, I will not calm down. Someone was just *murdered* in this house, and now the power and the phone are out. I'm getting the hell out of here *right now*. If you don't want to come, I'll send a police car when I get back to town."

Shane grimaces. "Kayla..."

Kayla gives him a look. "We need to leave, Shane. Why don't you want us to leave?"

Kayla makes a good point. We don't want to leave a crime scene, but we have to contact the police. And if the phone lines are down, we have to drive to the station. My parents are going to absolutely demolish me when they find out what I've been doing tonight, but I can't think about that. Someone is dead.

And there's a very real chance that somebody in this room is responsible.

Chelsea rises to her feet, her eyes still moist. "Kayla is right. We have to get out of here. I don't know who did this..." She raises her eyes to look at Shane and then at Tim, who is lingering in the doorway. "But we are obviously in some kind of danger. We need to get out of here."

I concur.

Chelsea and Kayla put on their completely inadequate

shoes and coats and march out of the house, ignoring the rain still falling heavily. I slide into my own sneakers, but they are no match for what feels like an icy river forming outside the front door. My sneakers fill with mud and freezing cold water. I can't wait to get home and away from this horror show.

But just before we can pile into Chelsea's Beetle and get back home, she stops short. I hear the sharp inhale of her breath a second before I realize what she's looking at.

All four of her tires have been slashed.

"What the hell?" she gasps.

We go around the side of her car to Shane's Chevy, and the situation is the same. Tires slashed to smithereens.

"What the hell?" Shane is furious now as he examines the damage to his tires. "Who would do this?"

Kayla steps backward, hugging her chest as she shakes her head. "Somebody doesn't want us to be able to get out of here."

"Kayla..." Tim reaches for her arm. "Look, we'll figure this out—"

"No!" Kayla jerks away from him, her eyes suddenly wild. "One of you killed him. One of you did this, and now you don't want the rest of us to get away."

"Kayla, that's ridiculous," Chelsea says.

"Is it?" Kayla blinks back tears.

"Yes!" Chelsea swipes a strand of her soaking-wet black hair with bleached tips from her face. "Tim and Shane are not murderers. They're *not*."

"Maybe it was *you*," Kayla shoots back.

"*Me?*"

"Sure, why not? After all, everybody knows Brandon

was cheating on you. Maybe the two of you had it out, and it didn't end well for him."

Chelsea's lips form a startled O. "You bitch..."

Kayla's wide eyes dart between the four of us, her breaths coming faster with each second. "I'm getting out of here—car or not."

"Kayla, don't—" Shane starts to say.

But it's too late. Kayla has turned around, and she's running in the other direction down the poorly paved path to the farmhouse, the rainwater reaching up above her ankles like she's wading through a shallow stream. Presumably, she'd thought she wouldn't be outdoors much during this sleepover, so she's wearing a pair of chunky heels with what had once been a stylish leather trench coat before the rain destroyed it. My coat and sneakers aren't much better, but I'm still tempted to follow her.

She makes it barely twenty feet. I don't know if her foot catches on something, but she takes a quick nose-dive into the muddy water on the ground. Tim swears loudly, then races out after her.

"Look at Prince Charming go," Chelsea mutters under her breath.

I shoot her a look. "What? You think he shouldn't help her?"

Chelsea doesn't answer. She just takes a ragged breath. Like Kayla, her makeup has run all over her face, making her appear almost maniacal. I'm glad I only wore lipstick tonight, which largely rubbed off when Shane and I were kissing.

Kayla looks like she's not going to let Tim help her at first, but she finally accepts his hand and allows him to pull her back to her feet. She casts a regretful glance at the road behind her, which is becoming more flooded with every passing second, and then follows Tim back to the farmhouse. It's hard to tell if her face is damp from tears or the rain.

Shane is hovering at the front door and gives Kayla a once-over as she steps back onto the porch. "You okay?"

She glares at him but doesn't say a word.

"Let's go inside," Tim says. "At least it'll be dry."

With that declaration, I can't help but notice how soaked he got while rescuing Kayla. We're all soaked, actually. We look like a bunch of drowned rats. Kayla got the worst of it though, when she slipped in the mud. Her dark hair is plastered to her skull, and her trench coat looks like it will need to be peeled off her skin. There are flecks of mud on her face, intermingled with her ruined makeup.

"You'd like that, wouldn't you?" Kayla hisses at him. "Trap me in the house with no way out."

"Hey." Tim raises his hands. "I'm just saying…we don't want to get sick out here."

"Sick!" She casts a horrified look at Brandon's body, still lying on the porch. "Someone is dead! And one of *you* did it! You had to have…"

"Kayla." Tim takes a careful step toward her. "You need to calm down."

"I'm not going to calm down!" She takes a step back, almost stumbling over her own heels. "I don't trust any of you. So until the power comes back on, leave me the hell alone."

With those words, Kayla runs back into the house. Her footsteps disappear up the stairs, and the sound of one of the bedroom doors slamming echoes through the house.

CHAPTER 24

PRESENT DAY

The next morning, before I start my clinic, I make a trip to the infirmary to check on Shane.

While I'm walking down another long hallway of flickering lights, a voice from behind me calls out my name. I pause and turn around in time to see Marcus Hunt sprinting down the hallway in my direction.

Great. What now?

I hope he doesn't start harassing me for dates. I can't deal with that on top of everything else. One thing I can say for sure though is that I'm going to start carrying my pepper spray in my hand instead of leaving it in my purse while I walk out to my car. One good spritz of that stuff, and he'll know to leave me alone.

"Brooke." He skids to a stop in front of me. "Hey."

"Hello." I avoid his eyes. "What do you need, Officer Hunt?"

He tugs at the collar of his stiff blue correctional officer uniform. "You can call me Marcus."

I don't respond to that. "What do you need?"

He grabs a few sheets of paper that he had stuffed into his pants pocket. He hands them to me—they're filled in with his spidery handwriting. The name on the top sheet of paper is Malcolm Carpenter.

"I know you were trying to get that mattress for Carpenter," he says. "We got one for somebody a couple of years ago, and I remembered these were the forms that needed to be filled out. I tried to fill in as much as I could for you."

I look down at the papers in my hands, stunned. I have been struggling to get that mattress for Mr. Carpenter with little success, and Dorothy has been actively trying to keep me from getting it. I even attempted to call Dr. Wittenburg, who is apparently my supervising physician, even though I have never met the man—and I wasn't able to connect with him either.

"Wow," I say. "Thanks so much."

"No problem." He winks at me. "Hey, we're on the same team, right?"

"Right." I wait for him to follow up by asking me for drinks again, but he doesn't. "Anyway, I better stop in the infirmary. I'll release Nelson if he looks okay."

At the mention of Shane's name, Hunt's eyes darken. He swivels his head in the direction of the infirmary door, his gaze seething. He hates Shane, and it's not clear why. According to Dorothy, Shane hasn't done anything particularly terrible during his time at the prison.

"I'm sorry you have a problem with Shane Nelson," I say. "But he's been perfectly fine with me."

Well, except for trying to kill me that one time.

"I'll just bet he was nice with you," Hunt grumbles.

"And if I have any concerns about my safety, you'll be the first to know." I meet his eyes. "I promise."

He considers this. "Just be very careful."

"I will."

He shakes his head like he doesn't think I'm actually going to be careful, and he's right. Whatever harm Shane tried to bring to me all those years ago, I don't think he's going to try anything now, surrounded by guards capable of shooting him if they need to. And the truth is, when I look at him now, it's hard to imagine he was ever capable of it. Even when we were in the courtroom, when the memory of the air in my windpipe being cut off was still fresh in my head, it was hard to look at Shane and imagine him trying to kill me. He just seemed like Shane—the boy I fell in love with on the football field.

I still can't wrap my head around what made him do all those terrible things. Split personality? A moment of insanity? But it doesn't matter. Either way, he's paying the price.

The infirmary at the Raker Penitentiary is a small unit with six beds where we can administer basic medical treatments. We can do IV antibiotics, give fluids, and monitor patients who are too sick to be in the general population but not sick enough to be in the hospital. I've been stopping there first thing in the morning to do my rounds, then I make another stop before I leave.

Shane is the only prisoner who is currently occupying a bed in the infirmary. He is lying flat on one of the mattresses, his eyes shut, the bruise on his forehead much darker than it was yesterday. Even though Dorothy said yesterday that he didn't need to be in shackles, he's got one leg chained to the bed rail.

There's a fresh-faced young nurse's aide named Charlene who is sitting at the infirmary desk. I walk over to her and nod toward the beds. "Nelson do okay overnight?"

"Yes, no problems."

I can't help but ask, "Why is he shackled to the bed rail?"

Charlene shrugs. "Hunt came in here before he went home yesterday and put the cuffs on him. I don't know why. He's mostly just been sleeping. He only woke up for breakfast. I gave him some Tylenol for a headache, and he was really nice. Very polite."

"Good," I say.

"He's cute too, isn't he?" She giggles, then her face turns red. "I need to get out more, huh?"

"Yeah."

She looks at the third bed, where Shane looks like he is still asleep. "I wonder what he did to end up here."

Charlene is young enough that she wouldn't remember the excitement around Shane's trial, even if she is from the Raker area. But I'm not going to be the one to clue her in. "I…I don't know."

"I used to look them up on Google," she goes on. "A lot of these guys have done something bad enough that it was in the news. But it was always such a bummer to find out. I'd rather not know."

"Yeah," I say. "I know what you mean."

I leave Charlene to her paperwork and walk over to the bed where Shane is still asleep. I watch him for a moment, blowing air softly between his slightly parted lips. I had been hoping that my hovering over his bed would wake him up, but it hasn't. So I reach out and touch his shoulder.

Shane's eyelids flutter, and he reaches out and rubs them with the balls of his hands. When he takes them away, he blinks up at me. His eyes widen, and he sucks in a breath. "Brooke…"

"Shane?" I say.

He blinks again. "Oh, sorry, I…it was just weird waking up and you're there. It was kind of like, you know, déjà vu a little."

"Yes, I get it." I grimace. "How are you feeling?"

He yawns as he uses the button to lift the head of the bed. "Kind of like my head got slammed into a desk." He offers me a weak smile. "I'm okay. Just a headache."

"How bad on a scale of one to ten?"

"I don't know. Four maybe. Five?"

"Nausea? Dizziness? Confusion?"

"No, I'm okay." He struggles to adjust his position in bed, thwarted slightly by the cuff holding his right ankle in place. "Just the headache. That's it."

I look down at the shackle on his ankle. "I can tell Officer Hunt to take that off."

"Nah." He waves a hand. "Honestly, I'm used to these things by now. It's not a big deal. And if you push the issue, he's just going to hate me more."

"Fine. If you say so."

I perform a neuro exam, verifying that there's nothing concerning that would require me to send Shane out for a scan of his head. He looks fine though, like he said. Just the bruise on his head. Although I notice the way he winces when I shine my penlight in his eyes. He has a worse headache than he's letting on.

"Do you want anything stronger for that headache?"

He massages his fingers into his temple. "No, it's fine. I had a Tylenol. I can manage."

I have no idea why Elise wrote "drug-seeking" in his chart. The guy is clearly in pain, and he doesn't even want to ask for anything. "You look pretty uncomfortable. I can give you a Fioricet, if you want?"

He nods gratefully. "Okay, sure, I'll have some of that."

"No problem."

"Also..." His brown eyes peer up at me. "I promise I won't bring up that thing we were talking about yesterday ever again."

My jaw tightens. "Good."

"I know what you think of me," he says, "and I know whatever I say to you, you won't take it seriously."

"Shane..."

"But there's just one thing I have to tell you." His words come out quickly, like he's afraid I'm going to leave before he finishes, which is a real possibility. "I'd never forgive myself if I didn't say it."

"Please don't do this, Shane."

"You need to stay away from Reese." His slightly bloodshot eyes are huge staring up at me. "Just do that for me. Okay?"

"Shane..."

"I don't care if you think I'm a...a killer," he chokes out. "Just...you've got to stay away from Tim Reese. He's dangerous. *Please*, Brooke."

I look into his eyes, and there's real fear there. A chill goes down my spine. I don't know how he could think Tim is dangerous. Tim is so obviously not dangerous. I could never believe that about him. Shane has to be faking it.

He has to be.

"Fine," I say.

"Really?"

"*Yes.*"

He leans back against the bed, his facial features relaxing. "Thank you, Brooke."

It won't be the first time I've lied to him.

CHAPTER 25

ELEVEN YEARS EARLIER

Chelsea is kneeling over Brandon's body, sobbing quietly. She reaches out a hand and runs it over his slack jaw. The rest of us stand on the porch, the boys shifting uncomfortably. Shane must be gutted over this too—Brandon was his best friend—but he hasn't said much of anything since we discovered the body. Not that I'd expect a teenage guy to start bawling the way Chelsea is.

Chelsea raises her tear-streaked face to look at us. "What are we going to do with the body?"

Shane and Tim exchange looks. "We're going to leave him here," Shane says.

"You're just going to leave him?" Chelsea bursts out as she rises to her feet. "Out in the cold?"

I don't say what the rest of us are thinking, which is that Brandon isn't going to be bothered by the cold. Not anymore.

"I've got some extra blankets in the linen closet," Shane offers, "if you want one."

Chelsea hesitates for a second, then nods. Shane goes back into the house while the three of us wait on the porch. Tim is standing just a couple of inches away from me—so close that I can almost feel the heat of his body. He reaches out his hand and makes contact with mine, giving it a comforting squeeze for a split second before the door bangs open again and Shane returns with the blanket.

The wool blanket is sky blue and looks like it would be itchy, except Brandon isn't going to mind very much. Chelsea gently lays the blanket over his lower body, pausing as if not sure if she should put it over his head or not. Finally, she covers his face too, turning her boyfriend into nothing more than a darkening lump on the front porch.

She presses her fingertips to her lips, then holds them out to him. "I love you, baby."

Did she though? Did she really? Only yesterday, we were talking on the phone and she said, *I hate that cheating asshole.*

She looks back at the rest of us as if expecting us to chime in. I hardly knew Brandon, and what I knew of him, I didn't much like. But I don't want to leave Chelsea hanging, so I murmur, "We'll miss you, Brandon."

"Miss you," Tim chimes in after a beat, even though he disliked Brandon as much as I did.

Chelsea looks at Shane, whose eyes have gone glassy. "We're going to find who did this to you, man," Shane says. "And we're going to make him pay."

—

Now that we've said our goodbyes to Brandon, Chelsea consents to going back into the house to figure out our options for our next move. Unfortunately, those options are limited. The phone lines are dead, either from the storm or from something more ominous. The tires are slashed on both of our two vehicles. And the storm outside is still raging as bad as it ever was.

"Kayla didn't have much luck walking back to the main road." Chelsea stands in the middle of the living room, wringing water out of her long hair. "But I bet one of you guys could make it. It's not that far, is it? Like, a mile?"

"A mile and a half." Shane makes a face. "And you saw how slippery the road is, so it's a difficult hike. But what worries me more is that with the amount of wind, there could be some power lines that came down. One wrong step and you could get electrocuted."

Great. So our choices are to stay here with a murderer lurking around or risk getting drowned or electrocuted.

"I think we should stay put until the storm dies down," Shane says. "At the very least, we might get our phone service back. And the roads will dry out."

I look at Tim with my eyebrows raised. He lets out a long sigh. "I agree. It's not safe out there right now."

Both of the boys seem firmly in favor of staying put. I look over at Chelsea, who is completely waterlogged. Her mascara has dissolved into streaks running down her cheeks, even though she always gets waterproof. I guess waterproof mascara isn't a match for the storm.

"Brooke," she says, "can I talk to you?" She eyes the boys. "*Alone.*"

She doesn't wait for an answer. She seizes me by the

arm and pulls me out of the room, leaving Shane and Tim staring after us. She doesn't stop until we're at the back door, which she wrenches open and then pulls me outside, slamming the door closed behind her.

"Chelsea, it's cold out!" I hug my arms to my chest. "Can we go back inside?"

"No." Chelsea glances at the back door almost accusingly. "I'm really freaked out, Brooke. Somebody did this to Brandon. They…he was stabbed. Someone stabbed him to death! He's dead!"

"I know."

She swipes at her eyes with the back of her hand. "We're not safe here. You know that, don't you? We need to get out of here."

"You saw what happened to Kayla when she tried to make a run for it."

Her eyes look wild with the leaking mascara. "Kayla was the worst cheerleader on the squad—she could barely make it through a practice session. You and me—I bet we could make it. And if not us, the boys could for sure."

"But you heard what Shane said about the power lines."

"Or maybe he doesn't want us to leave. Did you think of that?"

Yes, I did think of that. But it still makes sense. I'm not excited to wander out in the mess outside, especially without proper footwear. Isn't that how people get frostbite?

"Shane's not a murderer," I say firmly. "It was probably some drifter wandering through the area. There's no way it could have been one of us."

Chelsea is gulping as she tries to take in air. She looks like she's seconds away from having a panic attack.

"Chels?" I scrunch my eyebrows together. "Chelsea, you have to breathe. Take some deep breaths, okay?"

"I'm okay." She closes her eyes, concentrating on her breath. "I'll be okay."

I'm not sure what to do. Don't they say you're supposed to put your head between your legs in this situation? But Chelsea seems like she's got it under control. She's hanging on to me, taking deep breaths until her shoulders relax. I wait outside with her, even though it's pretty cold out here. Although now that the power is out, it's pretty cold inside too. But at least the wind wouldn't be flicking droplets of water at us.

"You okay now?" I ask her when she finally opens her eyes.

Chelsea nods.

"We need to go back inside." I don't phrase it as a question. If she doesn't come with me, I'm going anyway. "We can't stay out here."

She looks at me for a moment, then she nods. I turn the doorknob to the back door and push it open, feeling obscenely grateful for the dry air in the kitchen. It's dark in the kitchen, and we both jump when we hear the door to the room crack open.

"Brooke?" It's Tim's voice. I'm relieved. While I know Shane isn't a murderer, there's nobody I trust more than Tim Reese. "That you?"

I nod but then realize he probably can't see me. The room is all shadows. "Yes, we're back. Where's Shane?"

"He went outside to see if he could get a cell phone signal."

Chelsea tugs on my arm. "I need to sit down, Brooke."

Chelsea feels really shaky again, so I help her across the kitchen and into the living room. Tim helps support her, and we get her up on the sofa. She ends up lying down, her hand strewn across her face. Whatever comes of this, Chelsea will never be the same. Finding her boyfriend murdered has done a number on her.

"Hey." Tim taps me on the shoulder. "Can I talk to you for a second in the kitchen?"

I squint at Chelsea in the darkness. She looks okay for now. "Fine. But I don't want to leave her for too long."

Tim leads me into the kitchen. As we disappear behind the door, the thought flits through my head that none of us should be alone right now. We should stick together. Yet we're leaving Chelsea alone in the living room, and Shane is wandering around outside.

What if something has happened to Shane? What if he's lying on the ground dead like Brandon?

"So I took another look under the blanket." Tim winces as he says the words. "It looks like Brandon was stabbed to death."

"He…he was?"

Tim's face is so close to mine, I can make out all his features in the dark. But I can't see the freckles that are usually slightly visible when I'm close to him. "But there wasn't a knife next to him. I couldn't find one anyway."

"Oh."

Tim jerks his head at the kitchen counter. "I got worried that whoever it was would come back, so I went to get a knife from the kitchen. And guess what? All the knives are gone."

I stare at him. "What?"

"Right? Pretty weird. There's a knife block on the counter, but it's empty."

I shiver and hug myself. "So what does that mean?"

"I'd say it means that whoever did this planned it in advance and got rid of all the other weapons in the house."

"Tim." I feel like I'm choking. "What are you saying?"

"I think you know exactly what I'm saying, Brooke."

CHAPTER 26

PRESENT DAY

It's a month into the school year, and Tim Reese has become a frequent visitor to our house.

After he fixed the sink and the doorknob, he and Josh embarked on a seemingly endless list of projects to tackle in the house. After all, the house is kind of old, so there was a lot that needed fixing. And after they got done fixing everything, they got the idea to build a bookcase for Josh's room. This weekend, they're going to be painting it. (Neon green, apparently.)

Although I was anxious about moving here, my reservations have all melted away. Working at the prison has its ups and downs (I haven't seen Shane once in the last month, but he is still very much *there*), but I have never seen Josh happier than he's been out here. He loves school, and more importantly, he's bonded with Tim in a way that has really surprised me.

When I get home tonight, I smell the delicious aroma of garlic and butter. I'm pretty sure those are Margie's two favorite ingredients in the whole world. And there is no nicer smell to come home to.

I find Margie in the kitchen, arranging a tray of garlic butter shrimp. I want to just inhale them, they look so good.

"I made extra," Margie tells me, "since I assume that nice Tim will come for dinner."

I start to protest, but then I realize Tim has come over for dinner at least half a dozen times in the last two weeks. And he's had us over to his house three times.

"Yes, he said he was probably coming," I mumble.

Margie laughs. "You don't have to be embarrassed about having a boyfriend, Brooke."

"He's not my boyfriend." Margie gives me a look, and I shake my head. "He's *not*. We're just friends."

It's the truth. Tim has hung out here a lot in the last month, but nothing has happened between the two of us. He hasn't tried to kiss me. When we watched a movie a few days ago, he didn't yawn and attempt to put his arm around my shoulder. We are friends—like always. His realization that Shane and I have a kid together has vanquished any feelings he had for me.

"I should warn you then," Margie says, "Josh is asking some very interesting questions about him."

Oh no. What does *that* mean?

After Margie has taken off for the night, I go into the living room, where Josh is playing with his Nintendo. He is entirely focused on the game, his tongue sticking out slightly as he concentrates. His expression is strangely familiar, and it takes me a second to realize with a jolt that Shane used to make that same exact face when he was concentrating on something.

"Hey, Josh." I sit down next to him on the couch. "How was school today?"

He doesn't take his eyes off the game. "Okay. Is Tim coming for dinner?" At school, Josh has to call him Mr. Reese, which makes him giggle, but at home, he's just Tim.

"Josh…" I slide a few inches closer to him. "Margie told me you were asking some questions about Tim."

Josh pauses his game and throws the controller to the side. I don't know what he's thinking. He probably thinks Tim is my boyfriend, just like Margie does. I'm going to have to set him straight. I'm not sure if the truth will disappoint him or if he'll be relieved.

"Well," he says, "I was wondering…"

"Yes?"

He takes a deep breath. "Is Tim my dad?"

I feel like I just got punched in the gut. I had no idea whatsoever that he had been thinking that. "Josh…"

"Because you knew him from before you moved away," Josh points out. "And you were really close. And also, he's really nice."

He's looking up at me with a hopeful expression on his face. I wish more than anything in the world I could tell him that Tim is his father. I wish Tim *were* his father. Or that his father were a decent human being who there was some chance in hell I could possibly end up with… or at least allow my son to spend a few minutes in his company.

"I'm sorry, sweetie," I say. "Tim isn't your dad."

Josh looks crushed. He looks so sad that a tiny part of me wishes I had just lied about it and dealt with the consequences later. But of course, I couldn't do that. I had to tell him the truth.

I start to put my arm around him, but the doorbell rings, echoing through the house. When Josh hears it, he grabs his Nintendo controller and restarts his game. "I just want to finish this level before dinner," he says.

"Josh," I say, "I want to talk to you more about this… I know you're disappointed."

"No, I'm not." His eyes are back on the TV screen. "I don't want to talk about it."

Fine. There's no chance of competing with Nintendo, so I may as well answer the door. Of course, it's almost certainly Tim, having arrived for dinner. I should just give him a key. Not in a relationship kind of way but in the kind of way that you give your neighbor a spare key. Like for if I get locked out or something. I mean, the only other person who has the key is Margie, and she lives all the way in the next town.

Tim is standing at the front door, wearing the same khaki pants and dress shirt that he wore to work but minus a tie. He holds out his arms, because every time he comes over, we hug at the door. That's what friends do, right? We hug. It's not like we greet each other by making out.

"Hey, Brooke," he says. "Smells great in here."

"Thanks," I say, even though it's not like I was the one who cooked the shrimp.

It does smell good in the entire house though. I could smell it down the hallway. And it's only when I'm in Tim's arms that I notice another smell. Something extremely familiar, but not nearly as pleasant as garlic and butter.

It's *sandalwood*.

I jerk away from Tim, my nose crinkled in disgust. "Oh my God, what are you wearing?"

Tim's eyes fly open, and he grasps at the collar of his shirt. "What? This is just a cotton dress shirt."

"No! I mean, that smell!"

"Smell?" He runs a hand along his clean-shaven jaw. "I did shave before I came over, and I put on some aftershave. But—"

The smell of sandalwood has embedded itself in my nostrils. Every time I inhale, I feel the chains of that necklace tightening around my throat. I take a step away from him. "Please go wash it off. Now."

"But—"

"Now. *Please.*"

Tim obediently trots off to the bathroom. I hear running water, and he's in there for quite a few minutes, which I think is a good sign that he is making a serious effort to get all the aftershave off. When he comes out of the bathroom, his skin looks slightly pink.

"Okay," he says. "I think it's off."

I take an experimental breath. I don't smell it anymore. Thank God. "Thank you."

"Sure." He has a deep groove between his eyebrows. "No problem."

Well, now he thinks I'm out of my mind. I need to explain this to him. Unlike other guys, he'll get it. "When Shane tried to…you know…he was wearing sandalwood aftershave. The smell of it makes me sick now."

"Oh!" Tim rubs his jaw. "Jesus, Brooke, I'm so sorry. I had no idea. I got that aftershave as a present, but I'm going to throw it away."

"You don't have to do that."

"Obviously I do." He flashes a lopsided smile. "It's okay. I hate aftershave anyway."

I return his smile. "Then why were you wearing it?"

"I don't know. I was probably trying to impress Josh."

We stand there in the hallway, staring at each other for a moment, and there's a sudden jolt of electricity between us. I study his face, wondering if he feels it too. Even when I think Tim is firmly in the friend zone, I wonder if there's a possibility I'm wrong.

As long as he never wears that sandalwood aftershave ever again.

CHAPTER 27

After dinner is over and Josh has brought his plate to the sink, he turns to Tim: "Can we toss around the ball in the backyard?"

I'm relieved that Josh still seems to like Tim, even though he isn't his father. But as much as I want them to bond, I need to intervene. "Did you do your homework?"

Josh averts his eyes. "No..."

"Well, that's your answer then."

Josh groans, but Tim confirms my verdict—I love having another adult on my side. "Get your homework done," Tim says, "and tomorrow we can go to the park with your bat. We can get in some *real* practice without breaking any windows."

Josh nods eagerly and hurries up the stairs to his room. Tim has taken him to the park a few times, in between their home-improvement projects. I feel kind of guilty that my family is eating up his entire social life. I mean, he *is* a single guy. It's not like we are in a relationship. He shouldn't be stuck with us every single weekend, fixing stuff around my house and taking my kid to the park.

"You don't have to do that," I tell him after Josh's door slams shut. Even though if he says he's not going to take Josh to the park tomorrow, I might cry. I've gone to the park to let Josh practice batting, and I am epically bad at it. I couldn't catch the ball if my life depended on it, so I spend most of the afternoon either ducking to keep the ball from hitting me in the head or chasing down the ball while Josh stands there.

"It's fun for me too." He lifts a shoulder. "You know, he's a *really* strong hitter. He can hit that ball farther than I can."

"He had the most home runs on his Little League team last year," I say proudly.

"I believe it. He's a natural athlete."

Even though it's a compliment, Tim's comment sits heavy in my stomach. Because Shane was a natural athlete as well. Star quarterback and all that. If Josh ever asks to join the football team, I'm going to try my best to talk him out of it.

Tim gathers the remaining dishes from the table and brings them over to the sink. He turns on the hot water and grabs the bottle of dishwashing soap.

"I can handle it," I insist. "There are only a few dishes."

"I want to help." He tugs the pan from the stove right out of my hands and dips it in the sud-filled sink. "Come on. What kind of jerk would I be if I came here, got a free dinner, and then took off?"

"To be fair, you did, like, six figures worth of repair work in this house."

Steam comes out of the sink as Tim scrubs at the pan. "No way. It was *at most* high five figures."

I smack him playfully in the arm. Or I start to, but then my hand lingers on his biceps. He must…you know, work out. Tim looks over at me, his eyebrows practically at his hairline. For a moment, we just stand there, our eyes locked together. Then he reaches over and shuts off the water in the sink. He dries off his hands on a dish towel.

Then he grabs me and kisses me.

I let him do it. Okay, I more than let him. More like I grab him by the collar and pull him closer to me like I haven't kissed a guy in the last decade, which is scarily close to accurate. For a good sixty seconds, we stand in the kitchen, making out like the world is about to end. That's how long it takes me to remember that my son is right upstairs and then push Tim gently away.

His face is flushed, and he's looking at me like if I said the word, we would go straight up to my bedroom. "Jesus, Brooke," he says.

I have to take a second to catch my breath. "I thought you were only looking for friendship."

"Yeah, well, that was bullshit, and you knew it."

"No, I didn't."

He gives me a look. "Come on. You know I've been in love with you since I was four years old."

My heart skips in my chest. Yes, I knew on some level that Tim felt that way about me. Even though he dated other girls, he never looked at them the way he looked at me. But I never felt that way about him. Not until recently.

"I just…" I glance up the stairs, hoping Josh's door is

closed. "We have a good thing going here. Josh adores you. And you're my best friend. I feel like…I'm scared of messing that up, you know?"

"I agree—we have a good thing going." He reaches out and takes my hand in his, and again, I let him. "But I think we could have a *better* thing going."

He's right, of course. As wonderful as it has been having him hanging around the last month, it would be better if he were here more. If our friendship were more. Tim and I—we could have it all.

"My life is just so busy between my job and Josh," I point out. "Maybe you'd be better off with somebody simpler. You could still go out with that waitress from the Shamrock. Kelli, right?" Kelli was a little out there but she definitely liked him a lot, and she sure as hell didn't have a ten-year-old son with her incarcerated ex-boyfriend.

"Brooke, listen to me." Tim squeezes my hand as he looks me right in the eyes. "I haven't seen you in ten years. In that time, I've dated a fair number of girls. But it never worked out—it couldn't. And it was all because I couldn't stop thinking about you. Anyone else I dated, it wouldn't be fair to them." His Adam's apple bobs. "I'll never feel about anyone else the way I feel about you."

I might cry. It's the nicest thing anyone has ever said to me. Tim is so sweet and sexy, and he's great to my kid. I should be throwing myself into his arms and just thank my lucky stars.

But for some reason, I can't turn off Shane Nelson's voice inside my head.

Stay away from Tim Reese. He's dangerous.

Please, Brooke.

It's ridiculous, of course. I knew it when he was saying it, and I know it now. But I can't shake the feeling that this has worked out just a little too well. That Tim is just a little too perfect. Especially for someone like me.

"Brooke?" Tim is frowning. "Look, I don't want to pressure you. If you don't want this, we can pretend it never happened. If you just want to be friends, that's fine. I mean, it's not *fine*. It would completely suck. But—"

"Shut up," I say. I'm not sure if I'm saying it to Tim or to Shane's voice in my head. But it doesn't matter. "You're right."

A smile creeps back across his face. "I am? About what?"

"Not being together *would* completely suck."

I grab him by his shirt and pull his lips onto mine. He kisses me back just as eagerly. And all the while, I ignore the tiniest hint of sandalwood clinging to the collar of his shirt.

CHAPTER 28

ELEVEN YEARS EARLIER

Tim hates Shane. He thinks I should break up with him. But what he's accusing Shane of is a step beyond that. He's accusing my boyfriend of murder.

"Tim," I whisper, "are you saying you think Shane…?"

Tim's eyes flash as the room briefly glows from a bolt of lightning. "It's his house. If anyone were going to plan it…"

"Why would he do that though?"

"Why would he beat up some innocent kid? Because he's a terrible person. That's what I've been telling you, Brooke."

My legs feel rubbery beneath me. Shane isn't a terrible person. Tim doesn't know him the way I do. If he had been in the bedroom and seen how sweet and caring and *loving* Shane was, he wouldn't be saying that. Shane would never hurt anybody. "Why would he kill Brandon? Brandon is his best friend."

"Best friend?" He shakes his head. "I don't think either of those assholes has the capacity for that kind of loyalty. They're friends, but they hate each other."

"I don't believe that."

"Believe what you want to believe."

"Tell me something." I narrow my eyes at him. "When you and Shane were huddled in the living room earlier, what were you talking about?"

He's quiet for a moment. "What?"

"When we first came in, the two of you were talking. What did you say to him?"

Even in the dark kitchen, I can see his jaw twitch. "I just told him he better treat you right."

"I see."

"Listen to me." His fingers close around my wrist. "This isn't a joke. Shane is dangerous. And while you've been gone, I've been searching the house for something I could use as a weapon."

That's when I noticed the object in Tim's other hand that he's been holding onto since Chelsea and I got back into the house. I squint into the darkness.

It's a baseball bat.

"It's longer than a knife," he says. "If he tries to come at me, I'm clocking him right in the head."

"Fine." If Tim gives Shane a concussion, it won't be the worst thing that happens here tonight.

He gives me a long look. "Let's make sure we stay together, okay? I won't let anything happen to you."

I believe him.

When we return to the living room, Chelsea is still lying on the sofa, but on the plus side, her chest doesn't appear to be covered with blood and stab wounds. Shane is also in the living room, shaking water out of his clothing and his hair. I can see him just barely well enough to recognize he got drenched out there.

"Any luck finding a signal?" I ask.

"Sorry, no." He stomps his sneakers against the ground, trying to get some of the water and mud off them. "I think we're stuck here until morning."

Chelsea struggles into a sitting position on the couch. "I hope Kayla is okay upstairs."

I tug on the snowflake on my necklace. "Maybe we should check on her?"

"Why?" Shane says. "She didn't seem to want us anywhere near her."

"I know, but she was freaked out," Chelsea says. "She's probably calmed down by now. It's better if none of us are alone, isn't it?"

There's a long silence as we contemplate Chelsea's suggestion. Kayla seemed hysterical earlier, and I'm not eager to see her again right now, when I'm already a little hysterical myself. But on the other hand, I'm also worried about her. When someone is that upset, they can do stupid things.

"We'll just knock on the door," Tim says. "If she tells us to go away, we leave."

Nobody wants to stay behind in the living room, so we all go together up the steps to the bedrooms. The stairwell is dark, and I cling to the banister to keep from falling. Even though it's hard to see, I can feel Tim's presence right next to me, hovering over me with that baseball bat clutched in his right hand.

Kayla had gone back into the bedroom where she and Tim had been sound asleep when Chelsea's scream woke us all up. At least that's what I would deduce based on the fact that it's the only door that is closed. Chelsea goes first, picking her way carefully down the hallway until she reaches the closed door. After a hesitation, she raps her fist against it.

No answer.

"Kayla?" Chelsea calls out. "Are you okay?"

Again, no answer.

Chelsea clears her throat. "We won't try to come in. We just want you to tell us you're all right." She pauses. "Kayla?"

In the slit of light coming in through the upstairs windows, I can see Tim looking at me. My eyes meet his, and he shakes his head. I can hear the bat shifting in his hand.

Chelsea turns to us. "She's not answering. What should we do?"

"The door doesn't have a lock," Shane says.

"I..." Chelsea's voice trembles. "I can't do this."

Before there can be any more debate, Shane pushes past her. There's a creaking noise as the knob twists open, and a second later, the door to the room swings open.

Even though it's dark in the room, it's lighter than it was in the hallway, so our eyes are already adjusted. Which means I'm able to make out details I wouldn't be able to otherwise. Like the bookcase in the corner. Or the bed in the center of the room.

Or Kayla lying on the bed, her chest covered in fresh blood, her eyes staring up at the ceiling.

CHAPTER 29

PRESENT DAY

Mr. Fanning has a broken finger.

I don't know how he got the broken finger. I asked him before I sent him over to radiology for an X-ray, but he was squirrelly about the details. The X-ray showed a fracture of the middle phalanx of his little finger, and I called the radiology department at the local hospital that provides official reports of our X-rays to confirm that the fracture didn't go through a joint and wasn't displaced. It looks like a simple fracture—one that can be treated easily with buddy taping.

After I get off the phone with radiology, I emerge from the examining room to find Mr. Fanning sitting in one of the plastic chairs in the hallway, joking around with Officer Hunt. Hunt is outright hostile to most of the inmates, so I'm surprised to see him on good terms with Fanning.

"Mr. Fanning," I say, "come on inside."

Mr. Fanning grunts slightly as he gets out of the chair. He is in his early fifties with a large gut that stretches his khaki jumpsuit. He has that central obesity that makes me think he's within five years of a major heart attack. Hopefully, by the time he starts getting those crushing chest pains, I'll have moved on to a better job.

I assume Hunt doesn't think Fanning is a safety concern because he closes the door 90 percent of the way. Fanning climbs up on the examining table, cradling his right hand. It's not a bad fracture, but it sucks for him that it happened on his dominant hand.

"So is it broken?" The bags under Fanning's eyes seem to deepen. "It is, isn't it?"

"It is," I confirm. "But it's a minor fracture. We can treat it here."

Fanning looks doubtfully at his right hand. His pinky finger has turned almost purple, and his ring finger doesn't look great either, but at least that one isn't broken. He's lucky he wasn't wearing any rings, because we'd probably have to cut them off.

"It will heal fine," I reassure him. "I promise. We just need to immobilize it."

"Okay, Brooke," he says. "If you say so."

I'm glad he goes along with this plan. It's not exactly easy for a prisoner to get a second opinion, especially since I don't seem to have a doctor backing me up. The inmates have rights, and if he lawyered up, we would be in trouble. But most of the men either don't know they can do this or don't care enough. In any case, I try to give them the best medical treatment I can.

I grab some paper tape from a drawer so I can bind his fourth and fifth digits together. Fanning watches me, a look of growing concern on his face. "That's all you're going to do?"

I wrap the tape around his fingers. "This is the standard treatment. It was a simple fracture—we just need to immobilize it."

"And it will heal?"

"Absolutely."

Fanning grimaces with pain as I stretch out his fingers to wrap the tape evenly. "Goddamn Nelson."

I jerk my head up. "What?"

"Nothing," Fanning says, his eyes suddenly wide with panic. "Never mind."

"Mr. Fanning." I wrap one more layer of tape over his fingers. "Can you please tell me how this happened?"

"I already told you." He averts his gaze. "A door closed on my hand. I swear."

Of course, he could be telling the truth. Maybe a door did close on his hand, and that's how he broke his finger. But then the question would be was somebody holding his hand in the door when it closed? If they were, that person meant business. They meant to smash two of the fingers of his dominant hand to smithereens.

And why did he say the name *Nelson*?

Then again, it's not like Nelson isn't a common name. No, I don't remember there being any other Nelsons when I was looking through the file cabinet. But it could be somebody's *first* name. Couldn't it?

I ensure that the tape has secured his fingers so he can't bend them, and then Mr. Fanning is good to go. He holds up his hand, still looking skeptical that a roll of tape can heal his fracture, but he accepts it.

"Come back in a week," I tell him. "We'll see how it's healing."

He nods. "Thanks, Brooke. I appreciate it."

"Just don't slam your hand in any other doors, got it?"

He winces. "Yeah. I'll try. Believe me."

Fanning slides down off the table, and I let Hunt back into the room to escort him to his cell. I watch the two of them disappear down the hallway, and I still can't help but wonder how he got that fracture.

Goddamn Nelson.

He couldn't have been talking about Shane. Maybe Shane was dangerous on the outside, but not here. If anything, Shane has been a target here in prison. He certainly isn't going around breaking other people's fingers.

But the truth is I don't entirely know what he is capable of.

CHAPTER 30

Tim has come by this weekend to build a birdhouse with Josh.

At least that is what Josh has told me about a thousand times over the last hour. Seriously, I thought kids get *less* annoying as they get older. But it's sweet that he's so excited. I thought Josh might cool to Tim after finding out that he wasn't secretly his father, but that hasn't been the case at all. If anything, they've gotten closer in the last couple of weeks.

So have Tim and I.

At about eleven o'clock on Saturday morning, Tim rings the doorbell. We did exchange keys *for safety reasons* since he's my neighbor, but he usually rings the bell. I appreciate that. We have to keep some boundaries here. I mean, we know each other so well, it would be easy enough for him to just move right in. But we are intentionally taking it slow.

When I open the door, Tim is standing there holding

a few wooden boards in his right arm and a thick hard-cover book in the other. He looks over my shoulder. "Josh is upstairs?"

"Yes."

He nods and leans in to kiss me. We have been making an effort not to let Josh know we are more than just friends. We'll have to tell him eventually, but the thought makes me anxious. I've never had a relationship important enough to let my son know about it. This is a big deal.

Thankfully, Tim gets it. He's fine about waiting.

He pulls away from me as soon as we hear Josh's eager footsteps on the stairs. A second later, Josh bursts into the room. "We're going to make a birdhouse!"

"You got it!" Tim dumps the wooden boards on the ground, then holds up the book in his other hand. "But first, I have a surprise for you."

I get a good look at the book that Tim is holding. When I see the cover, my stomach sinks.

It's our high school yearbook.

Why on earth would Tim bring that over here? I don't even know what happened to my copy—I don't think I even saw it, since I relocated before the end of the school year and was homeschooled for the remainder of the year. But our high school yearbook is the last thing I want to look at. And it's the last thing I want Josh to see.

Oh my God, what if he sees a photograph of Shane and notices the resemblance?

"This is our high school yearbook," Tim says to Josh. "Want to see how dorky your mom and I looked when we were kids?"

My panic level shoots up. "Tim…"

"Don't worry," he murmurs in my ear. "He's not in it."

Oh. Well, I guess it makes sense that they would leave the student responsible for multiple murders out of the yearbook. That part is a relief at least.

Josh is weirdly eager to look through the yearbook. We sit at the kitchen table while he flips right to the portrait photo of me, which had been taken about one month before my life changed forever. It's not a bad picture. I didn't have an embarrassingly cringy hairdo, and the white shirt my mother had me wear for picture day looked crisp and professional. There's a softness to my face that I don't see anymore when I look in the mirror. Not since that night.

"Look! It's Tim!" Josh cries. He holds the yearbook up near Tim's face. "You look so different! You were so skinny!"

"Yeah, yeah."

I manage a smile. "You were cute back then."

"Oh yeah?" Tim squeezes my knee under the table. "I didn't realize you thought so."

He *was* cute. But he wasn't *hot* in the same way Shane was back then. Between the two of them, it was obvious which one the girls went wild over.

Josh continues to flip backward through the pages, studying the pictures with surprising intensity. When he gets to the *N*s, I hold my breath. But Tim is right. They left Shane out of the yearbook.

I look over Josh's shoulder at all the old faces. Flipping pages backward, he passes Kayla Olivera followed by Brandon Jensen, and my chest tightens at the words "In Memoriam" under his name. That should never have happened.

"Wait," I say. "Stop."

Josh freezes on the page with the *H* names. I slide the book away from him and look down at the page on the right. I stare at the photograph in the bottom right-hand corner. The name underneath is written in bold capital letters.

Marcus Hunt.

Oh my God, it's Officer Hunt.

I would never have recognized him if I didn't know it was him. He had hair back then—fine and golden, like on a baby chick. I recognize him vaguely, remembering him as being a tall and gangly boy with thick glasses.

Why didn't Hunt tell me we went to high school together?

I tap the photograph with my index finger. "Tim, do you remember this guy?"

"Yeah. Mark Hunt. I remember him."

I shake my head. "I'm having a little trouble placing him."

"He was kind of a weird kid." Tim drops his voice a notch. "Some football players you might have known beat him up bad enough to put him in the hospital once."

And suddenly, it all makes sense. Why Hunt hates Shane so much. Why he's made it his mission to torture him.

That asshole lied to me. And I'm going to make sure he knows that I know what he's doing.

CHAPTER 31

ELEVEN YEARS EARLIER

Kayla is dead.

It's obvious—I know it right away. I know it before Tim goes to feel for her pulse with a shaking hand, the bat gripped in his other hand. I know it before Chelsea collapses onto the ground, kneeling with her face inches from the floor. I feel like doing the same thing.

Keep it together. You've got to keep it together, Brooke.

Tim backs away from Kayla's body. He looks even more shaken than he did when we found Brandon. After all, he was kissing this girl only hours earlier. That's got to be a shock.

And this is different. When Brandon was found dead outside the farmhouse, it seemed possible that some random psycho had been wandering by, and maybe Brandon got in a fight with him because that's what Brandon does. But this is different. Kayla was *inside the house*. Which means whoever did this to her was inside the house.

And they're probably still here.

"You!" Shane's pointing a finger at Tim. "You did this."

"Me?" Tim clutches his chest. "Are you out of your mind?"

"You were alone here while the girls were out back and I was out looking for a signal." Shane's voice is hoarse. "You're the *only one* who had a chance to do this. It was you."

He makes an excellent point. Tim is the only one who had the opportunity. But it couldn't have been him. Not Tim. Never. I'd sooner believe that I killed Kayla myself.

"Why would I do this?" Tim shoots back.

"I don't know. Because you're crazy?" Shane says. "Maybe she rejected you, and you got angry."

"This is ridiculous!" Tim's eyes bulge. "You were alone outside for all that time. Maybe you're the one who did this! You went in through the window and stabbed her while we were all downstairs."

"Come on. This is the second floor. Who am I—Spider-Man?"

Another excellent point.

Tim takes a step toward Shane, raising the bat in the air. "I don't know how the hell you did it. Maybe you had a ladder—I don't know. But it wasn't me, and it wasn't Chelsea or Brooke. So it had to have been you."

"Watch it, Reese." There's a menacing edge to Shane's voice. "You better not be thinking about swinging that thing at me."

"I will if you give me a reason to."

My heart is jack-hammering in my chest. I look back at Chelsea, who has scrambled back to her feet. We exchange looks in the darkness. I don't know what's about to happen, but it's something bad. I try to figure out what I could say to make this right, but it's gone too far.

"Brooke." Tim's voice breaks into my thoughts. "You believe me, don't you? I wouldn't hurt anyone. Shane… he must have done this."

Shane swivels his head in my direction. "Brooke, you can't seriously think I would kill somebody. Tim was the one in the house!"

I open my mouth, even though I'm not sure what I'm going to say. But before I say the wrong thing, a hand grips my arm. It's Chelsea.

"You can both go to hell!" she spits at them. "Come on, Brooke."

I allow Chelsea to drag me out of the room while Shane and Tim stare at us. She pulls me over to Shane's bedroom and slams the door shut behind us. She leans her weight against it for a moment, breathing hard.

"I don't know who killed her." She's blinking back tears. "But it was definitely one of them. We've got to stay in here until somebody comes for us. Help me barricade the door."

I stare at the door, not sure what my next move should be. She's right. We are the only people here, which means Tim or Shane must have killed Kayla. Which means the only way we're safe is if we stay away from them.

But that also means one of them *isn't* the killer. And we have effectively left that person alone with a murderer.

"Chelsea," I say.

"Brooke!" Her voice is strangled. "Do you want to live through the night or not?"

I want to live through the night. Of course I do. But

so did Kayla, and she also barricaded herself in a room. And now she's dead.

Still, I go along with the plan to humor Chelsea. Shane's bookcase is too heavy to move, so we build a wall of books in front of the door. In reality, I'm not convinced the boys couldn't get through it easily, but it's better than nothing.

A hand raps against the door. "Brooke? Chelsea?"

It's Shane's voice.

"Go away!" Chelsea screams. "We're not coming out until morning!"

I'm not sure about the validity of this plan. Both of our phones are downstairs, so if one of the boys is looking to kill us, they'll still be able to do it in the morning as soon as we emerge from the bedroom.

"Come on. This is ridiculous!" Shane yells through the door. "Just come out. We're safer if we stay together."

"We're not coming out, Shane." Chelsea folds her arms across her chest. "You're wasting your breath."

Although there's a part of me that thinks he's right. We might be safer if the four of us stay together. After all, the killer can't get all of us. Their only hope is to take us down one by one.

"Brooke?" It's Tim's voice this time. "Are you okay?"

I touch my fingers to the door. "Yes, I'm okay."

He's quiet for a moment. "I think you should stay in there. Both of you."

There's something about the way he says it—a tremor in his voice—that makes me back away from the door, my hands shaking. Tim is right. We need to stay in this room for the rest of the night.

It's our only chance.

CHAPTER 32

PRESENT DAY

Marcus Hunt greets me at work in the morning with a cup of coffee.

It's become a routine for us. Before Hunt brings me my first patient, he comes by the examining room with a hot cup of coffee for me. It's nothing special. It's just a coffee from the pot in the guard break room. But it's nice of him, and a hot cup of coffee is always appreciated first thing in the morning.

My mother would say that boys don't do anything nice for you if they're not expecting something in return. Of course, she's not around anymore to lecture me, but she may have a point in this case. I had been working out a way to mention offhand that I have a boyfriend.

But today, I'm too pissed off to be polite and spare his feelings.

"Here's your cream and sugar." Hunt holds out my coffee in his left hand and a couple of packets of cream and sugar in the right. "I know you like to add your own."

I clear my throat. "Can I talk to you for a moment? *Alone.*"

Hunt's eyes light up. "Sure, Brooke."

Great. He thinks I'm going to make out with him.

We get inside the exam room, and I shut the door behind us. A voice in the back of my head tells me it might not be the best idea to be alone with this guy, especially when I'm about to confront him, but I can't have this conversation with him in the hallway. Unfortunately, this is definitely encouraging the idea that I am hot for him.

"Marcus," I say in a low voice, "why didn't you tell me you were in my class in high school?"

He freezes, his mouth open but no words coming out.

"Don't say you weren't," I say. "I was looking through the yearbook and saw your picture. You were in my class. You must have known who I was when you first met me." He starts to say something when I add, "Don't lie."

"Fine." His shoulders droop. "Yes, I knew you right away. I mean, it's pretty hard to forget the girl who almost got murdered by her boyfriend during senior year."

"You also never mentioned that Shane and his buddies beat you up." I fold my arms across my chest. "That they put you in the *hospital*. And you've been harboring a grudge against him for years, and now you're making him pay for what he did to you."

"That," he says, "is an exaggeration."

"Is it? Tell me he did anything here in prison to warrant the way you've been treating him."

A dark expression passes over Hunt's face. "He doesn't *have* to do anything here. I already know what kind of person he is. He's the kind of guy who would kick me in the ribs while laughing about it." His hand balls into a fist. "You know what he's like too, Brooke. I don't know why you're defending him."

He makes an excellent point. I should hate Shane. I should be happy to see him locked up here, his hands and ankles shackled together. I should want to see him suffer after what he put me through.

But ever since I saw him lying in that infirmary bed, all the angry feelings I held toward him seem to have evaporated. Maybe it's because he's my son's father. Or maybe there's another reason.

When I testified against Shane, I felt so certain he was the one tightening that necklace chain around my neck, trying to kill me. But the more I think about it, the less certain I feel. There was something that happened that night I am missing. One little detail that has escaped me.

I'm sure of it.

Hunt leans in close to me—too close. "I could make him really pay for what he tried to do to you. Nobody on the outside gives a shit about him. I'll do whatever you tell me to do. I could throw him in isolation for weeks—or months. I could have him beaten up so badly, he won't be able to *walk* anymore. Just you say the word." He winks at me. "Nelson thinks I've been torturing him, but he has no idea."

My chest tightens. "I don't want you to do that."

"What part?"

"*None* of it." I swallow a hard lump in my throat. "I...I want you to lay off Shane."

"Excuse me?"

"You need to stop." I raise my voice, trying to seem more confident than I feel. "You need to treat him like a human being. *Now*."

He cocks his head to the side. "I don't think you're in any position to be making demands. You're the one who took a job where one of your patients is a man who tried to murder you. What do you think Dorothy would say if she knew about that?"

Wow, yet another excellent point. This guy is on a roll.

"In fact," he says, "if you want to keep this job, maybe you should think about making some time to grab that drink with me after work."

I lift my chin. "Actually, I have a boyfriend."

"You mean Tim Reese?" Hunt laughs at the shocked look on my face. "Come on. The guy's at your house every night. You don't have to be Sherlock Holmes."

I can't believe my ears. I'm suddenly incredibly sorry that I started this conversation. And even sorrier that we're alone in this room together. "You're spying on me?"

He shrugs. "I drove by your house a few times. I recognized Tim from high school. A boring but safe choice. Also…" He bares his slightly yellowed teeth at me. "I find it kind of interesting that you have a kid in fifth grade. You're kind of young to have a son that old, aren't you? Who were you dating ten years ago anyway?"

Oh no. No, no, no…

"I bet Nelson would be *really* interested to hear about that," he muses. "I'd sort of like to see the look on his face, you know?"

"Please don't tell him," I gasp. "Please."

Hunt flashes me a smile that makes me want to punch

him in the nose. "Don't worry, Brooke," he says. "Your secrets are safe with me. But you better be a little nicer to me. For starters, from now on, *you* can bring coffee to *me* every morning."

"Fine," I snap.

He gives me a long look, and I brace myself for more demands. But they don't come. He just shakes his head at me.

"What a waste, Brooke," he mutters. "All for that scumbag."

With those words, he jerks open the door to the examining room and storms out.

CHAPTER 33

My daily goal is to get Correctional Officer Steven Benton to smile.

Officer Benton is my first stop every day when I enter the penitentiary. I can't say that I still don't get a little jolt of fear when I walk past the prison yard with the guard towers lining the fence. I've never seen any of the guards up there with their rifles, but I know they are there. Ready to shoot if they need to.

But once I'm inside, it's the same old routine. I pass the waiting area, and Jan at the front desk knows my face by now, so she immediately hits the buzzer to open the metal bars and waves me inside—I barely even jump anymore at the sound. And my next stop is the security check-in with Officer Benton.

"Good morning!" I chirp as I lay my purse down on the table in front of him to go through the metal detector. "How are you?"

Benton grunts. "Fine. You?"

"Oh, the usual." I step through the metal detector, holding my breath like I always do. It doesn't make sense, but I do it automatically. "I had a visit with Mr. Barrett yesterday—you know, the guy who was an English teacher on the outside? He's such a flirt."

He looks up with mild interest. "Oh yeah?"

I nod. "He told me he wanted to marry me when he gets out of here."

"Did he?"

"Yes, but unfortunately, you can't end a sentence with a proposition."

It's such a cheesy joke. It's true on some level—Mr. Barrett *was* an English teacher, and he does flirt with me shamelessly. But the corny dad joke was entirely for Benton's benefit—and it pays off when his lips twitch just a bit. An *almost* smile. I'll count it as a win, and I have a little extra skip in my step as I walk down the hallway to the examining room / office.

Until I find Dorothy waiting for me outside the room, her beefy arms folded across her chest.

Great. What now?

"Brooke," she says sharply, "I need to talk to you."

"What about?" I glance at my watch. "I've got patients to see shortly."

"I'd rather not talk out here. Let's go to my office."

She cocks her finger at me, and I follow her wordlessly to her office. We could have talked in the examining room, where I would've had some leverage. Instead, Dorothy gets to sit at her desk, while I sit at the small chair in front of her desk, feeling very much like a child being disciplined by the principal. I rack my brain to think of what I might have done to upset her. Really, it could be anything. It doesn't take much to set Dorothy off. I've been doing my best to stay out of her way.

Dorothy settles into her ergonomic leather chair, her eyes boring into me. "We got a delivery this morning. A pressure-relief mattress."

Despite everything, I feel a jolt of happiness. It's been weeks since I filled out the forms Officer Hunt gave me, and after a few frustrating phone calls, I had started to lose hope. "Mr. Carpenter's mattress came?"

"Brooke." Her lips set into a straight line. "I already told you we don't have the resources to provide every patient with a special customized soft mattress. You're going to bankrupt the prison."

"Mr. Carpenter isn't every patient. He's a paraplegic, and he has a nonhealing pressure wound on his sacrum. This is a medical treatment."

"A comfy mattress is *not* a medical treatment."

When I first started at the prison, I had thought Dorothy looked familiar to me. It suddenly hits me who she reminds me of—my *mother.* As I stare across Dorothy's desk at her square face with her tan chin tilted slightly up in the air, I can't help but remember how my mother used to boss me around. She always believed she knew better than me, and she couldn't stand it if I ever disagreed with her—it was her way or the highway.

You can't possibly be thinking of keeping that monster's baby, Brooke. I won't allow it.

But I kept my baby. I didn't let her push me around that time. And I won't let Dorothy push me around anymore. I'm sick of being a victim.

"It's a pressure-relief mattress." I stare at her, unblinking. "Without this mattress, he is for sure going to end up in the hospital and maybe need surgery to get this repaired."

Dorothy snorts. "Please don't be so dramatic. How long has it been since you graduated from school? Five minutes? When you've been a nurse as long as I have, you know what patients need and what they just *want*."

I can hardly believe my ears. My right hand balls into a fist, and I have to shove it between my knees. Honestly, I'm shocked one of the men hasn't taken a swing at Dorothy by now. Maybe they have. If it has happened, I'd love to have seen it.

"Listen, Dorothy," I say. "I may not be as experienced as you, but I know enough to know that Mr. Carpenter has a serious pressure ulcer, and it's just going to get worse if we don't treat it properly. I ordered him the bed, and if you keep him from getting it, I'm going to call the local newspaper and let them know how the inmates at the prison are being deprived of appropriate medical care."

Dorothy's mouth falls open. "Are you *threatening* me?"

"Absolutely not," I say. "I'm simply advocating for my patients to get adequate care. If you're not on the same page as me, then perhaps you can explain why to the local media."

"Brooke…"

"Also," I add, "you need to keep lidocaine in stock in the pharmacy. I'm not sewing up anyone else with no anesthetic. It's inhumane. Next time there's no lidocaine, I'm sending the inmate to the emergency room, and you can eat the cost of transportation."

Now it's Dorothy who looks like she wants to hit *me*. I can see her jaw working as she debates whether it's worth it to fight me on this or not. She doesn't like the idea of a twenty-something-year-old nurse practitioner pushing her around. But she's got to realize that I'm right. She could never justify her behavior to the newspaper or, worse, in a courtroom if things went south for Malcolm Carpenter.

"The mattress is already here," she finally says. "I suppose it's all right for him to keep it. *This* time."

She's trying to save face. She doesn't want to admit that I have won this argument, and I'll let her have that much. But I'm going to advocate for my patients. They are human beings, and they deserve to be treated that way, despite what Dorothy might think.

CHAPTER 34

Today is my birthday.

Compared with last year, I have a lot more to celebrate. Last year, I was living in a one-bedroom apartment where my son slept on a cot in the living room, and the landlord had just hiked up the rent by two hundred bucks a month. I hadn't been on a date in two years. Josh was coming home in tears every day because of the bullies at school. I had a babysitter who didn't show up half the time and kept making me late to my urgent care shifts. And even though my parents were alive, we hadn't spoken for years.

This year, Josh is happy in school. We've got a big house to live in, and we each have our own room. And of course, there's Tim, who I've only been dating for a month, but I'm starting to think I'm really falling for him.

I spend an extra long time getting ready tonight. Tim is taking me out to dinner, just the two of us. I had been planning to include Josh, but when I mentioned it to Margie, she looked horrified. *You need to have an adult night out*, she insisted. She'll be coming to watch Josh so Tim can take me to a nice restaurant.

When I look in the full-length mirror in my bedroom, I'm pleased with what I see. I'm wearing a little black dress that makes my boobs look big, paired with black kitten heels, and my dark hair is loose and silky around my shoulders. And when I come downstairs and Josh sees me, his eyes turn into saucers.

"Mom," he says, "you look pretty."

He means it as a compliment, but the fact that he sounds so shocked when he says it makes me wonder how he thinks I look the rest of the time.

"Thank you," I say.

He puts down his Nintendo and looks at me expectantly. "Are we going out to dinner?"

I settle down next to Josh on the sofa, tugging on the hem of my dress. "Actually, Margie is coming. Just Tim and I are going out tonight."

"Oh." He looks confused. "So is Tim your boyfriend?"

I knew that question was coming eventually. Tim and I have been careful about how we act around each other when Josh is around so he won't realize we're a couple. Tim spent the night a couple of times, and he set the alarm on his phone for six in the morning so he could vacate the house before Josh woke up. But it was inevitable that Josh would figure it out. And I owe him the truth.

"Yes, he is," I say. "Are you okay with that?"

Josh hesitates, thinking it over. "Yeah, that's okay. Tim is cool."

"I'm glad you think so."

"Also, he's the assistant principal of the school, so I could get away with stuff if he's your boyfriend."

I burst out laughing. Josh is like the best-behaved student ever, and I doubt there's anything he would do in school worse than, I don't know, reading a book under the table during movie time.

Unlike his father.

The doorbell rings, and I run to answer it. There was a fifty-fifty chance it might be Margie, but I'm glad to see Tim standing at the door. He's wearing a dark-gray jacket over a blue dress shirt and a tie. He looks achingly handsome, and all I can do is stare at him. I barely even notice he's looking at me the same way until he lets out a low whistle.

"Damn," he says. "You're going to give me a heart attack, Brooke."

He leans in to kiss me, but before he can, we hear Josh's footsteps racing toward us. He pulls away just as Josh bounds into the foyer. Josh points a finger at Tim.

"You're my mom's boyfriend," he announces.

Tim looks at me with his eyebrows raised, and I nod. "He asked," I explain. Then I add, "He thinks you're cool."

"Wow, Josh, I'm honored." He places a palm on his chest. "That might be the first time anyone has called me cool in my entire life."

Josh giggles. Tim reaches over and takes my hand in his. I don't know if we want to be super affectionate in front of Josh, but I think holding hands is okay.

"So," Tim says, "I've got your birthday present in my pocket. Do you want it now or later?"

I wink at him. "Immediate gratification, please."

"Some things never change."

Josh doesn't seem interested in a present that isn't for him, so he goes back to playing Nintendo while Tim and I head out to the kitchen table. I sit down next to him, and he reaches into his jacket pocket to pull out a blue rectangular box that is clearly jewelry.

"I hope you didn't spend too much," I blurt out. Maybe I shouldn't have said that, but Tim can't be raking it in at the elementary school. I don't want him to spend tons of money on me.

"You're worth it." He lays his hand on top of mine as he looks into my eyes. "But no, I didn't spend a fortune. It's something special. I think you'll really like it."

"I know I will."

Tim used to be so thoughtful about getting presents. I'm sure whatever he got me is going to be wonderful. I gently pry the lid off the box—a gold necklace is nestled inside, resting on a little square of cotton. I pick up the necklace, holding it up until I can see the charm hanging off the gold chain.

It's a snowflake.

I drop the necklace like it's made of acid. I think I'm going to be sick. It's the same kind of snowflake necklace that I used to wear years ago. The same kind of snowflake necklace that Shane tried to strangle me with a decade earlier.

I jump up from the table so quickly that the chair wobbles on its legs. I feel a tightening in my throat. That necklace. It looks so much like the one I used to wear.

Tim jumps out of his own seat. "Brooke? What's wrong?"

"Why would you get me that?" I shriek.

"I…I don't understand." He wrinkles his forehead. "It's the same kind of necklace that I got you for your tenth birthday. I haven't seen you wear it, so I figured you lost it. I saw this one at the town flea market last month, so I—"

"Shane tried to strangle me with that necklace!"

Tim looks baffled. "He did? I thought he tried to do it with his…with his hands."

My breaths are coming fast. Too fast. "No, he used my necklace. *That* necklace!"

"I'm so sorry, Brooke. I didn't realize—"

He reaches out to put his arm around me, but I jerk away. Instead, I sprint in the direction of the bathroom, and before he can reach me, I slam the door shut. And lock it. I need a moment to collect myself.

When I'm alone in the bathroom, I stare at myself in the vanity mirror. I put on makeup for our date tonight, but you wouldn't know it from looking at me now. My face is about the same color as a sheet of paper, and the purple circles under my eyes are as visible as ever.

How could Tim forget about that necklace? I testified during Shane's trial about how he tried to strangle me with it. Tim was sitting right in the audience. I remember because whenever I was nervous during my testimony, I would look at him and feel less alone. After all, he was there that night too.

How could he possibly forget that the snowflake necklace almost killed me?

Stay away from Tim Reese. He's dangerous.

Okay, I need to calm down. Tim heard my testimony, but it's not like he's been having nightmares involving a snowflake necklace for the last decade. It's understandable he might have forgotten that little detail. It certainly makes more sense than the alternative of him intentionally buying me that necklace to freak me out.

"Brooke?" Tim knocks gently on the bathroom door. "Are you okay?"

I take a deep breath, then blow it out slowly. I can't spend the rest of the evening in this bathroom. I need to come out.

I open the door. Tim is standing in front of me, and he looks stricken—almost as bad as I feel.

"I'm so sorry, Brooke," he says. "I'm such an idiot. I completely forgot."

"It's okay," I say, even though it's not really.

"I'll get you a different present," he vows. "Something way better."

He holds out his arms, and I reluctantly allow him to put them around me. After a few seconds, I melt against his chest.

"I hope I didn't ruin the night," he murmurs.

"You didn't."

I can't let this bother me. He was just trying to be sentimental and get me a gift he thought I would love. He had no idea I would react that way. I need to put it out of my head and enjoy the evening.

CHAPTER 35

ELEVEN YEARS EARLIER

We don't start breathing easier until Tim and Shane's footsteps disappear down the stairs. Two sets of footsteps, it sounds like. Which means they're both still alive.

"We need to find a weapon." Chelsea rifles blindly through Shane's desk drawer. I can't help but think about the bat Tim has been wielding as his weapon. "Because eventually, we're going to have to leave this room."

I plop down on the bed where Shane deflowered me earlier in the evening. Was that only a few hours ago? It feels like another lifetime. When I touch my fingers to my lips, I can still taste him. I can still smell the sandalwood of his aftershave.

I should help Chelsea look for a weapon. She's right—we shouldn't just sit here, twiddling our thumbs. But I can't help it. My thoughts won't stop racing.

"Do you really think one of them could be a killer?" I blurt out.

Chelsea pauses in her search. She straightens up. "Oh, Brooke."

She settles down beside me on the bed and throws her arm around my shoulders. And for the first time this evening, I burst into tears. It all just hits me at once. Brandon is dead. Kayla is dead. And one of the two boys I care about most in the world is responsible.

And I don't even know which one.

"They couldn't have done it," I sniffle. "Neither of them. It's not possible." I lift my eyes. "Right?"

She squeezes my shoulders, pulling me close to her damp, blood-stained shirt. "Listen, I know Shane is your boyfriend, and you and Tim go way back, but look at what happened. There is nobody else here. It had to have been one of them."

I rub my runny nose. "Who…who do you think it is?"

She pauses. "I don't know."

"Yes, you do. You just don't want to say."

Chelsea lets out a long sigh. "Fine. It was Tim."

I lift my eyes in surprise. That wasn't what I thought she was going to say. "Tim? But…"

"It makes the most sense, Brooke." She tucks a strand of wet hair behind her ear. "Shane's right—Tim's the only one who had the opportunity to go up there and do it. And he was the one who was cuddling up with Kayla all night. Shane barely knew her."

"But…"

But it can't be Tim. Not my first best friend. My first kiss. The guy I've known all my life, who would do anything for me. I touch the snowflake necklace, remembering how pleased he looked when I opened the box.

"And he dated Tracy Gifford," she reminds me.

"What's up with that? He had a bunch of dates with a girl who turned up murdered, and he figures he doesn't need to mention that to anyone? That is hella suspicious, Brooke."

"I know, but..."

"Plus, he's *frustrated*," Chelsea adds. "Because you're dating Shane, and of course he wants you for himself."

I swivel my head to stare at her. "What are you talking about?"

She lets out a dramatic sigh that lasts several seconds. "Come *on*, Brooke. You must realize that Tim is madly in love with you."

I snort. "No, he's not. We're *friends*."

"Right. You think of him as a friend, and he's in love with you." She cocks her head to the side. "I thought for sure you knew. You really don't see it?"

I reach for the charm on my necklace again, my fingers shaking slightly. Is Chelsea right? I always thought Tim and I were on the same page about our relationship. I mean, yes, he used to talk about us getting married back when we were little. But we were *children*.

And yes, we kissed that time. But it was just once, even though it lasted twenty minutes. And we were *practicing*. It wasn't like it meant anything...

Oh God.

She's right.

Tim is in love with me.

CHAPTER 36

PRESENT DAY

"Okay," Tim says, "I'm going to need you to rate this birthday compared with all other birthdays you've had in your life."

Tim and I are in the car driving back from the restaurant. After my panic attack over the snowflake necklace, we ended up having a wonderful time. It was nice just the two of us. We could be as affectionate as we wanted without worrying about freaking out Josh. And Tim is *very* affectionate. Especially after a glass of wine.

"Rate it on a scale of one to ten?" I ask. It's hard to break my habit from nursing school of rating everything on the visual analog pain scale.

"No." He grins at me as we come to a stop at a red light. "I mean how does it rank compared to your other birthdays? Like, are we talking top five…?"

"Top ten," I say.

"Top ten!" He looks affronted. "I *told* you that you

should have gotten the lobster. That would've definitely taken it into the top five."

I laugh. "Stop it. The chicken was great."

"I just feel like..." He rests his right hand gently on my knee as he starts driving again. "I mean, you don't remember your first, like, five birthdays. So really, top ten isn't *that* good."

"It's pretty good."

"Well, maybe I can do something else for you tonight that could take it into the top five."

"Maybe you could."

Although the real reason tonight can't make the top five has nothing to do with dinner, which was delicious, or with what he will do in the bedroom, which I'm sure will be amazing as usual. The second he presented me with that snowflake necklace, the night was ruined. As much as I tried not to think about it, I couldn't put it entirely out of my head.

"Also," he adds, "I have some good news."

"What's that?"

"I got a great lead on a new job for you." He squeezes my knee. "I have a friend who works at a primary care practice, like, fifteen minutes away from here, and he said they're looking for a nurse practitioner. They're desperate, actually. They want to meet you ASAP."

"Oh," I say.

"Isn't that great? It sounds perfect for you. And then you wouldn't have to work at that prison anymore."

"Yes, but..." I tug at the hem of my black dress. "I have a one-year contract at the prison, so..."

"Oh, come on. They won't hold you to that. Just give them, like, a month's notice."

"I don't know."

Tim turns to look at me at another red light. The whites of his eyes glow slightly in the moonlight. "You do want to leave that job, right? You don't want to keep working at a *men's penitentiary*, do you?"

I squirm in my seat. "It's not as bad as you think. Most of them are just so happy to be getting medical care."

"And not to mention," Tim continues like I hadn't even spoken, "the fact that Shane Nelson is a prisoner there. I don't know how you could even work there knowing he's around. What if you had to treat him?"

We talked briefly about the fact that I was working at the same prison where Shane is incarcerated. Tim was flabbergasted, but when I explained it was the only job I could find, he eventually calmed down. But I had to swear to him that I never treated Shane.

That is to say, I lied.

"If I had to treat him," I say, "I could do it."

"Seriously? Because you took one look at a necklace that reminded you of that night, and you almost had a panic attack. And Christ, what if he found out about Josh?"

I frown. Tim is worried about me working at a maximum-security prison, but it's not as bad as he thinks. And maybe Shane isn't as bad as he thinks either.

"What if…" I clear my throat. "What if I got it wrong? What if Shane wasn't the one who tried to strangle me that night?"

Tim's hand abruptly leaves my knee. "*What?*"

I hug my chest. "I'm just saying, it was so dark in the living room. I couldn't see a thing. I never even saw his face."

Tim slams down on the brakes, inches away from

rear-ending the car in front of us. "You have *got* to be kidding me, Brooke."

"I just think—"

He swerves the car to pull over to the side of the road. I can make out a vein throbbing in his temple. "Maybe it was too dark for you to see him, but *I* saw him. He came at me with a goddamn knife and buried it in my gut. All I could do was hit him with that bat, but the bastard didn't go down. He looked right into my eyes, Brooke, and he told me you were next. Trust me—it was him."

The police found Tim unconscious and bleeding on the floor of the farmhouse with a stab wound in his belly. In the last month, I've had the opportunity to see the scar left behind from that night. It's a one-inch line of raised skin just above his belly button. I always thought it would be bigger.

"It was just very dark that night," I murmur. "That's all I'm saying."

Tim turns away from me. He looks down at the steering wheel, his eyes glassy. After a second, he puts the car back in drive. We travel the rest of the distance to my house in silence.

"I'm sorry," he says as he pulls up in front of my house. "I shouldn't have…look, I get why you might have mixed feelings about Shane, given—"

"Right," I say before he can complete that thought.

"But you need to know that he is an evil human being. He's *sick*. And if you ever see him at the prison, you need to turn around and run the other way."

I lower my eyes. "I can take care of myself, Tim."

He doesn't have anything to say to that. I unbuckle

my seat belt, but he is still quiet. I don't offer to let him come inside, and he doesn't ask. I think this birthday has officially fallen out of the top ten.

When I get back into the house, it's quiet except for the sound of water running in the kitchen. Margie is probably cleaning. She may be old, but she never sits still. Honestly, I wish I had her energy.

I walk into the kitchen in time to see Margie scrubbing at a pan and humming to herself. "Hi, Brooke!" she chirps. "Josh is asleep. Did you have a nice time?"

"Uh-huh."

"Oh, I'm so glad!" She sighs. "To tell you the truth, I miss dating. I love my Harvey, but I sort of miss that excitement. And Tim is *so* handsome."

"Yeah…"

"He has great eyebrows," she adds.

"Does he?"

"Oh yes. You can tell a lot about a man from his eyebrows. Nice eyebrows mean he's wise."

"Interesting."

"Also," she adds, "he has a nice butt."

Oh my God. Although she's right—Tim does have a nice butt—I'm sort of embarrassed that Margie noticed. "Uh, thanks?"

"And that's such a beautiful necklace he got you! But you should put it in your jewelry box where it will be safe."

My stomach drops. I had abandoned the necklace on the kitchen table and then forgotten all about it. Well, I didn't forget about it so much as I hoped it would vanish into thin air while I was out with Tim—or at least that he would know enough to throw it in the garbage bin, where it deserved to be.

But he didn't. He left it there for me.

Margie grabs her coat and takes off for the night. It's only after she's gone that I dare to approach the blue rectangular box left behind on the kitchen table. It looks like either Tim or Margie put it back in the box, so all I need to do is toss it in the garbage.

But instead, I find myself opening the box.

I hold up the necklace, letting the snowflake charm swing back and forth. It looks exactly the same as the one I used to wear—the one Tim bought me for my tenth birthday. It's a gold chain with a gold snowflake with white diamonds set into the six spokes of the snowflake.

I look closer at the necklace and notice something else that makes my heart stop.

The second spoke on the snowflake is missing a diamond from the edge. Exactly like the one I used to wear.

This necklace is identical to the one I wore in high school. And it has the exact same defect in the exact same place as that necklace did.

Is it possible that it's the same necklace?

I never found out what became of that necklace. After it broke, I never saw it again. I had assumed the police kept it as evidence, but maybe they didn't. Maybe somebody else had it this whole time.

Tim claimed he got it at the town flea market. A *flea market*? What flea market is he talking about? I have lived in this town since I was a baby, and I never once heard about any sort of flea market.

Was he lying?

Stay away from Tim Reese. He's dangerous.

Is it possible that Shane was telling the truth about that night? Is it possible he wasn't the one who tried to strangle me with that necklace? I never got a look at his face. The only person who testified with absolute certainty that they saw Shane with a knife was Tim. Even though my testimony was damning, Tim was the one who put the final nail in his coffin.

What if Tim was lying about everything?

No, I can't think this way. Tim is my boyfriend. I've known him my whole life. He's a good guy. He wouldn't lie, and he sure as hell wouldn't kill anyone. I know it better than I know my own name.

But then how did he get that necklace?

CHAPTER 37

Tim and I have made up since the night of my birthday.

He came by the next evening with a bunch of roses and a pair of beautiful earrings. We never discussed the necklace again, but I did do one thing he asked. A few days ago, I scheduled an interview with that primary care practice. He was right—working at a maximum-security prison isn't exactly my dream job, and at the very least, the primary care practice is much closer.

If I quit my job at the prison, I'll never have to see Shane ever again. It will be a relief.

Mostly.

Tim and I are engaged in what has become our nightly routine of washing the dishes together after dinner. We've been together for about two months now, and since we told Josh about our relationship, Tim has been spending three or four nights a week here. Of course, he lives right down the block, so he hasn't relocated too much of his stuff here, since it's easy enough for him to go back and forth to get whatever he needs.

"Are we becoming like an old married couple?" I ask him as I slide the last of the dishes onto the dish rack.

Tim chuckles. "Do you remember when we were kids, and we always used to talk about what life would be like when we got married?"

It was mostly Tim who used to talk that way, but I do remember it. "Yes, of course."

"I just assumed we would end up together, you know? Like there was nobody else in the world that I could possibly marry."

"I know." I allow him to pull me close to him. "When did you stop thinking that way?"

"Never."

I laugh, but Tim isn't smiling. He's looking into my eyes with a serious expression on his face.

"Brooke," he says, "I just want you to know that…I love you. I have always loved you, and I'm pretty sure I'm always going to love you."

Even though it's the first time he's said that, his declaration of love doesn't come as a surprise. I could tell he was itching to say it to me. And even though I felt it too, I was scared to hear him say it.

Because the last man who told me he loved me tried to kill me.

But there is no way I can leave him hanging. It's obvious how badly he wants me to say it back. I'm sure he would pretend it's all right if I didn't, but inside, it would kill him.

"I love you too," I say.

He kisses me, and I want it to be this wonderful

moment when we tell each other we love each other for the first time, but I can't stop thinking about the last time I said those words. *I love you, Shane.*

Then a few hours later, he was tightening that necklace around my throat.

Our kiss is interrupted by the sound of Josh yelling at the TV screen. I had told him to go up and do his homework, but apparently, he decided to play more Nintendo. "Oh my God," I say. "That kid is in serious trouble."

I go out to the living room just in time to see something exploding on the television screen. I poke Josh hard in the shoulder. "Up to your room now, buddy."

"But, Mom—"

"Josh, *now*."

"I'm right in the middle of this level!"

"Listen to your mom," Tim says sternly.

I love the way Tim is with Josh. He respectfully defers to me on everything, but he always backs me up if I need him to. And Josh really loves him. The two of them are pretty adorable when they're doing something together—Nintendo, baseball, home repair.

Josh grumbles, but he shuts off his game and throws the controller down on the sofa. With the Nintendo off, the television turns to cable, which is showing the evening news. Josh stomps up the steps one by one, then the door to his room slams loudly.

"Am I that mean?" I ask Tim.

"No way," he says. "I used to teach fifth grade when I started, and sometimes these kids need a push in the right direction. But he's a good kid. He wants to do well in school, and he'll be grateful that you made sure he did his work."

"Maybe."

My eyes go straight to the television screen, which is showing a local news story. It's about a missing woman. Kelli Underwood, who disappeared two days ago. She was discovered to be missing when she didn't show up for her waitressing job.

Waitressing job?

I look closer at the television. There's a photograph of the missing woman plastered on the screen. And right away, I recognize her.

It's that waitress from the Shamrock. The one I knew from high school. The one I ran into at the grocery store, who yelled at me for testifying against Shane and told me to stay away from Tim.

Tim is also staring at the television screen. His eyes widen when they show the photograph of Kelli. His fingers grip the edge of the sofa, his knuckles turning white.

"Isn't that the waitress from the Shamrock?" I say as casually as possible.

"Um." He rips his eyes away from the television screen. "Is it? Maybe. I haven't been there in a long time. Not since we went together."

"You're not sure? Didn't you say you went out with her?"

"No," he says. "I mean, barely. We got a drink together when she was done with her shift. That's it. It was nothing."

"I see."

I'm almost certain he told me they went out on two dates. And Kelli certainly seemed to remember it when she confronted me at the supermarket. But he doesn't want to admit it.

Maybe because this isn't the first girl he's gone out with who suddenly vanished.

"Listen, Brooke..." He runs a slightly shaky hand through his hair. "I think I might head back to my place. I'm kind of beat, and we've got an early meeting tomorrow morning. So I'm just going to sleep at my own place."

I had assumed after we exchanged *I love you*s for the first time, we would make passionate love soon after. But instead, Tim can't seem to get out of here fast enough. And then when he's walking down the steps of my front porch, he trips and almost falls on his face.

But I can't say I'm not entirely disappointed he's gone, because now I get to google Kelli Underwood.

The details are extremely easy to find. Kelli (with an *i* at the end) is a twenty-seven-year-old waitress who was also taking art history classes at the local college. She lived alone in a small basement apartment, and they discovered she was missing when she didn't show up for her shift at the Shamrock two nights ago. One story mentions she has a boyfriend, but it doesn't say whether he's a suspect.

Two days ago...was Tim here that night? I can't remember.

Fortunately, Kelli was extremely active on social media. Unlike me, she has plastered photographs of herself all over the internet. I look back on her various social media feeds, searching for anything that jumps out at me. Finally, I spot a post from the beginning of the summer:

Fact: Assistant principals are GOOD KISSERS!!!!!

Unless there's some other assistant principal Kelli went out with, I'm going to assume she is referring to Tim. Which means he went out with her during the summer, and it was enough of a date that they kissed at the end. Or during. And apparently, she liked it.

But that's the only mention I can find about Tim. He has minimal social media presence himself, and she hasn't tagged him or anything. Aside from that one kiss, I can't prove anything else happened between them.

But he definitely went out with her. He was lying when he played it down.

Still, I can't entirely blame him. I'm sure he's not eager to talk about a waitress he went out with before we were together. And after what happened with that Tracy Gifford girl, he would rather not associate himself with another missing girl.

It doesn't mean he's responsible. Hell, Kelli probably just took off somewhere without telling anyone. She's probably fine.

I'm sure of it.

CHAPTER 38

ELEVEN YEARS EARLIER

Chelsea has been rifling around in Shane's desk drawers for the last twenty minutes, but her search for a weapon is not going well.

"There's nothing!" she declares. "He doesn't even have a pair of scissors!"

I don't know what to say. Even if Shane had a sharp pair of scissors in his drawer, I don't know how I would feel about using them. I don't think I'm capable of stabbing somebody.

"What about a pen?" she asks me. "There are a lot of those."

I draw my knees to my chest, hugging them close to my body. "What are we supposed to do with a pen?"

"I don't know. Poke him in the eye?"

I shake my head. "I don't think I could poke somebody in the eye with a pen. Could you?"

She straightens up and turns to look at me. It's so dark in the room that it's hard to make out her expression. I only catch glimpses of her when there's a flash of lightning. "I could if I had to. If it were Tim or me."

She's talking about it now like the whole thing is decided. Tim is the one who killed Brandon and Kayla. But I still can't wrap my head around it. I know Tim too well. He couldn't do something like that. Okay, maybe I wasn't aware of his crush on me, but that's different.

"I don't think Tim killed them," I say. "I don't believe it."

Chelsea plants her hands on her hips. "You have a serious blind spot when it comes to Tim. He isn't as great a guy as you think he is."

"Yes, he is."

"Trust me—he isn't."

It sounds like she has something specific in mind, but I'm sure whatever it is, it's stupid. "Look, he's not a killer."

She lets out an exasperated sound. "Don't you get it, Brooke? It had to be him. He's the only one who had the opportunity. He was alone in the living room, and he could've gone up and killed her. Nobody else had the chance to do it."

I chew on my lower lip. My lips have gotten very chapped in the last couple of weeks, as the weather has turned. Licking them and biting them makes it worse, but I can't help it.

"Actually," I say, "one other person had a chance."

"Who? Shane was outside. And nobody else is here. Who else had a chance?"

"You." I try to pick out her features in the dark room, but all I can see are her dark eyes with leaked mascara. "You were alone in the living room when Tim and I were in the kitchen."

Her jaw falls open. "*Excuse* me?"

"Well," I say thoughtfully, "it *does* make sense. More sense than Tim or Shane randomly killing Brandon and Kayla. I mean, Brandon was cheating on you. A *lot*. And then Kayla was accusing you of killing him. It stands to reason—"

"Oh, this is good!" Chelsea sounds like she's trying to be sarcastic, but there's a slightly hysterical edge to her voice. "First my boyfriend is murdered and I have to find his dead body. And now you think I killed him and apparently busted down Kayla's door and did her in as well?"

"No, I'm not saying that," I say carefully. "I'm just pointing out that you had an opportunity and a motive."

She stands there for a moment, her silhouette completely still. "If I am the one who killed them, why am I bothering to look for a weapon? If I did it, that means I've got a knife stashed away somewhere, doesn't it?"

"I…I guess so."

"Damn straight." She shakes her head. "I mean, you are seriously out of your mind if you think that I'm capable of killing two people."

My stomach churns as a thought hits me. Tim was looking for the knife while Chelsea and I were in the house. He didn't find it, but that was information he told to me alone. So how could she know the killer has a knife stashed away? Unless…

"I think we should go downstairs." I scramble to my feet. "I want to make sure the guys are okay. And…I think it's better if we're all together."

"Are you out of your mind? For all we know, Tim has already stabbed Shane to death, and he's waiting for us at the bottom of the stairs!"

"No," I say firmly. "He's not."

I've got to get out of this room. Now that Chelsea knows I'm onto her, I'm not safe here. I don't want to end up like Brandon and Kayla—I can't. I go over to the door and turn the knob, but the wall of books we built in front of it keeps it from opening.

"Hey, hey, hey!" Chelsea slips in front of me and puts her hand on the door, holding it closed. "Seriously, what are you doing? It's not safe down there."

"I want to go." I kick some of the books away. "Let me go."

"Brooke, you're being ridiculous! You don't seriously think I killed Brandon and Kayla, do you?"

"I don't know." I push a few more books out of my path. "I just need to get out of here. I have to use the bathroom."

I try to reach for the doorknob again, but Chelsea is blocking it with her body. I raise my eyes to look at her round face, her black hair with the pale tips that I helped her bleach in the bathroom at her house, and her brown eyes that suddenly look like pools of blackness in the dim light of Shane's bedroom.

"Chelsea," I say firmly, "step aside. *Now*."

Her gaze zeroes in on my face. "No. You're not leaving."

Chelsea had been searching the room for a weapon, but she didn't need to search. She had a knife on her all along. The same knife she used to kill Brandon and Kayla. The same knife she'll use to kill me.

Except when I look down at her hands, they are empty. Where is the knife? Did she stash it somewhere?

"Chelsea..."

"You need to stay here, Brooke. You *can't* leave."

If I can get past her and escape this room, Tim and Shane will help me. And I've got an advantage over the other two she's killed—I know what she's capable of. And I know from cheerleading practice what her weaknesses are.

I draw back my sneaker and kick her as hard as I can square in the shin, right where she always gets splints when we run. Chelsea crumples to the floor, moaning as she clutches her leg. "You bitch!" she cries.

I grab the doorknob again, and this time, I'm able to get the door open a few inches. I say a little thanks for all the hours I spent keeping my weight down to fit into my cheerleading uniform, and I squeeze my body through the tiny gap between the door and the doorframe.

"Brooke!" she shrieks.

I don't turn around to watch Chelsea attempting to scramble back to her feet. There's not much time, but I only need a few seconds' head start. I sprint into the hallway, which is pitch-black, and I feel around for the banister of the stairwell. I've got to get downstairs.

"Tim!" I call out. "Shane!"

No answer.

It's not a good sign. I had assumed the two of them would be downstairs in the living room, keeping an eye on each other, but the living room is dead silent. Nobody is down there.

I suddenly wonder if I have made a terrible mistake leaving the bedroom.

I pick my way down the stairs as quickly as I dare. I hear noises coming from Shane's bedroom. "Brooke!" Chelsea calls out again, but her voice is muffled like she's still in the bedroom. It's strange—I hit her hard, but not *that* hard. She ought to be back on her feet by now and running down the stairs after me.

"Tim!" I call again, bordering on screaming now. "Shane!"

When I get to the foot of the stairs, I let out a yelp as I trip and go sprawling. Something was lying in my path, blocking me. Something soft.

Oh my God. It's a body.

I squint down, trying to see who it is, but the living room is too dark. I lift my hands off the floor, and there's something sticky and wet coating my palms.

Blood.

Oh my God. Chelsea was right. Someone else was killed while Chelsea and I were hiding up in the bedroom. Chelsea was never trying to hurt me—she only wanted me to stay in the room so I wouldn't end up like the others. I let out a choked sob, knowing I need to get back up and run, but my body feels frozen.

And then the weight of a body crushes me, keeping me from getting back on my feet. And fingers grab the chain around my neck, pulling it tight.

CHAPTER 39

PRESENT DAY

When I come out of the examining room to see who my next patient is, the only person waiting is Shane Nelson.

Once again, Officer Hunt has shackled both his wrists and his ankles. And it's obvious what Shane's reason is for being here: somebody beat the crap out of him. His lower lip is split open, he's got a deep bruise blossoming on his left cheekbone, and when Hunt helps him to his feet, he flinches with pain.

"I thought we weren't doing the shackles anymore with him," I say to Hunt.

The guard shoots me a look. Our relationship has been decidedly frosty since I confronted him about our shared past, but I'm feeling braver since I had an interview yesterday at the primary care practice, and it went well. If he wants to get me fired, that's fine with me.

"He was fighting," Hunt snaps at me. "The shackles are required."

Considering I don't see any abrasions on Shane's knuckles, it seemed less like he was fighting and more like he was getting beat up. But I don't push the issue. I do, however, close the door once Shane is in the exam room.

"Jesus," I comment.

"It's not as bad as it looks," he says. "Really."

I give his face a once-over. The bruise from when he hit my desk is completely gone, and he still has a light-pink scar from the laceration I sewed up the first time he was in here. He has that cut on his lip and some bruises on his face, but nothing that looks like it needs stitches. But I notice every time he shifts his weight, he winces.

"What hurts?" I ask him.

"I have a broken rib."

I raise my eyebrows. "How do you know that?"

"Because it feels exactly like it did last time I had a broken rib."

I wonder how many broken ribs he's had since he's been in here. "I'll order a chest X-ray," I tell him.

"Great."

Despite everything, I feel a rush of sympathy for Shane. In the short time I've worked here, I've seen him come in here with significant injuries at the hands of other inmates on two separate occasions. Even if he is "evil" like Tim claims he is, it seems wrong that the prison is allowing this to happen.

"Are you sure you don't want to report the men who did this to you?"

"Very sure." He snorts. "You think I want this to happen to me every day?"

"You know," I say, "sometimes you need to stand up

to bullies. Last year, when my son was in fourth grade, he was getting pushed around every day. But now—"

I stop short because Shane is staring at me like I just punched him in the gut. I rewind what I just said in my head, trying to figure out why he looks that way. Then I realize.

"You have a son in fifth grade?" he asks in a hoarse voice. "You said he was in *kindergarten*."

I open my mouth, but no words come out. Just a little squeak.

"Brooke." He squeezes his knees with his hands. Hunt must've made the cuffs extremely tight because I can see the metal biting into his wrists. "How old is your son?"

I could lie. There's no way he would figure out the truth. But then again, I'm sure he can see the truth written all over my face. "He's ten."

"Is he…?"

"Yes." I nod slowly. "He's yours."

Whatever those men did to Shane that landed him in here, what I have just done to him is far worse. He looks like he's having a lot of trouble catching his breath, which is a bit disturbing if he really does have a rib fracture, but I don't think that's why.

"Why didn't you tell me?" he manages.

I shake my head, but I don't answer. I don't think he expects me to. The answer is obvious.

"Brooke, can I…?" He hesitates, and I'm afraid he's going to ask me to bring Josh to visit. I won't do that. There's no way he can convince me. But instead, he says, "Can I see a picture of him? Please?"

I shouldn't. I really shouldn't. But the way he's

looking at me is breaking my heart. And really, what harm could it do?

So I dig out my phone. I bring up a recent photo of Josh, and I hold out the screen so he can look at it. He stares down at the photo, his lips parted.

"My God," he breathes. "He looks like me."

"Yes."

"Can I see one more? Please, Brooke?"

I really, really shouldn't, but I can't seem to say no. Shane will never meet his son, but I can at least give him this. So I show him a few recent pictures. One of Josh playing baseball. One from a birthday party. I show him some old ones too. Josh on his first day of kindergarten, proudly posing with his Teenage Mutant Ninja Turtle backpack. Shane eats it all up. In all my years of being a mother, I don't think I have ever met anyone this mesmerized by pictures of my son. Even my parents never seemed that interested.

We could have easily looked at these photographs for the next several hours, but then Hunt knocks loudly on the door. "You wrapping things up?"

I shove my phone back into my pants pocket. Shane's face falls. "Sorry," I say.

"It's okay," he says. "Thank you. For showing me those pictures. I know you didn't have to do that."

"You're welcome."

His brown eyes are so sad, it almost breaks my heart. "I'm glad you never brought him here. I wouldn't want him to see me like this. I wouldn't want him to know that his dad is…"

"Yeah."

Shane stares at the wall. There's something in his

expression I can't quite read. "You know," he says, "sometimes I almost get used to how much it sucks being stuck here, especially for something I didn't even do. I accept the fact that I'm going to have to ask permission to use the bathroom for the rest of my life, I'll never get to hold a real job, I'll never get to drive a car again, I'll never get to be with…with a woman again. That every meal I'll eat for the rest of my life is going to taste like slop. That once a month, a bunch of guys will jump me in my cell and beat the shit out of me for no reason except maybe I looked at one of them wrong." He takes a shaky breath. "But then I find out about one more goddamn thing being in here has taken away from me, and it's just…it's…"

He presses his lips together hard, even though it must hurt like hell with that cut he has on his lower lip. It takes me a second to realize that he's trying not to cry.

"Shane," I say, "why don't we get that chest X-ray?"

"It's fine," he mutters. "Don't bother."

"You just told me you have a broken rib. We at least need to make sure you don't have a pneumothorax. That could kill you."

"I doubt it. I'm not that lucky."

"Shane…"

"I'm allowed to refuse, Brooke," he says sharply. He drops his voice. "At least give me that."

Our eyes lock. For a moment, he's the boy who I used to watch playing football when I was a cheerleader. He was so great at it. And he looked so hot in his football uniform. But most of all, I loved how excited he used to be when he would spot me on the field and wave to me.

I would never have believed that boy was capable of trying to kill me.

The truth is I still don't believe it. There was something else that happened that night—something important I'm missing. Something tugging at the periphery of my memory. I feel like if I could think hard enough, I would figure it out. But the harder I try to remember, the more it eludes me.

Shane breaks eye contact first. "I'd like to go back to my cell now."

"Are you sure you don't want—"

"*Yes.*"

I do as he says—I ask Hunt to bring him back to his cell without getting the tests he needs. He's depressed—that much is obvious. Suicidal? I don't know. We have a psychiatrist who allegedly comes once a month, but I've yet to see him once during the months I've been here. I consider calling Shane back to ask him more about it, but I don't want to torture him.

I'm not sure I'm going to see Shane again while I'm working here. He'll probably do his damnedest to avoid any medical visits, and if the primary care practice offers me a job, I'm out of here. It's been too hard seeing him. It has been nothing like I thought it would be.

I'm glad this is almost over.

CHAPTER 40

ELEVEN YEARS EARLIER

I'm going to die.

My beloved snowflake necklace—the one I have worn every day for the last seven years—is cutting off my oxygen supply. Strong fingers are pulling it tight, closing off my windpipe as I gasp for air.

"Please…" I try to form the words, but I have no air.

He's going to kill me. Tim is going to kill me with the necklace he bought me for my tenth birthday. The irony of it.

Except then I catch up with a whiff of something. Something in the air. A familiar scent close to me, coming from the guy holding me down.

Sandalwood.

Shane's aftershave.

It's not Tim after all. Tim is the one lying dead on the floor. Shane is the one holding me down, trying to choke me to death. Shane is the one who had the opportunity to plan this. To get rid of all the knives and weapons in his house except for the knife used to stab Brandon and Kayla—and now Tim—to death.

But he's chosen a different end for me.

"Shane," I try to choke out.

But it's no use. My head starts to swim as I cling to consciousness. I struggle against him, but he's too strong, and he's got the edge lying on top of me.

Where is Chelsea? I don't understand. She was trying to get out of the room. She should be out by now—she should be able to help me. But she's not here. Maybe she decided to hide out when she heard me scream. I couldn't entirely blame her.

Lightning flashes, and I catch a glimpse of the blood in a pool beneath me. It feels hopeless. Shane already killed three people tonight. And one of them was a football player even bigger than he is. My consciousness is slipping away. I'm going to die. This is going to happen.

A crash of thunder shakes the foundation of the house. It's the loudest one yet, and vaguely, I'm aware of another sound in the background. And one other thing.

The snapping of a link in my necklace.

All at once, the air comes rushing into my lungs. I can breathe again. A rush of adrenaline hits me, and I sense Shane has been thrown off balance by my necklace breaking loose. If there's ever been a chance, this is it. I swing my elbow back as hard as I can.

When he grunts with agony, I know I have hit the money spot. The pressure on my body eases up, and I manage to roll out from under him. I'm sure in a minute, he'll have recovered, so I've got to run. I can't look back.

I make it to the front door and yank it open so hard that the hinges scream. I burst out into the night, barely aware of how cold it is and the fact that I don't have a jacket on. The rain is coming down hard, and there's practically a river in front of Shane's house, but I can't think about that. I have to run. Maybe there is a fallen power line out there waiting to electrocute me, but I have to take that chance.

I run out onto the flooded road, grateful that my hours of cheerleading practice have kept me fit and nimble. Of course, Shane is pretty damn fit too. He's a quarterback. And his legs are a lot longer than mine. All I've got going for me is a head start and the fact that nobody has elbowed me hard in the testicles.

"Brooke!"

I hear my name called out from somewhere behind me. Or maybe I'm just imagining it. Maybe it's the wind. But I have to believe he's close behind me. He can't let me leave. If I live, I'll tell everyone what he's done.

"*Brooke!*"

Tears are streaming down my cheeks. My feet are numb from the ice-cold water, but I've got to keep going. This is my only chance. I've got to live.

"Broo—"

And then I see it. A set of headlights in the distance. It looks like a pickup truck. Under ordinary circumstances, it's the kind of vehicle I would keep my distance from late at night because you never know what kind of axe murderer is driving, but right now, it's my only chance.

I run toward the truck, waving my hands in the air. "Stop!" I scream. "Help me!"

Thank God, the truck stops, and the night doesn't end with me being hit and killed by a pickup truck. I hazard a look behind me, but there's nobody there. I'm not sure Shane was ever following me in the first place, but if he was, he's gone now.

I run up to the side of the vehicle. The driver is a big guy with a full beard. He's bigger than Shane. He looks tough, but his eyes go wide, and all the color drains from his face when he looks at me, standing there dripping wet, blood all over my shirt.

"Please help me," I say.

And then I collapse.

It's over.

CHAPTER 41

PRESENT DAY

When the police arrived at the Nelson farmhouse, they found five bodies. Brandon Jensen on the porch—dead. Kayla Olivera in an upstairs bedroom—dead. Chelsea Cho in Shane's bedroom—stabbed to death between the time I ran out of the room and the arrival of the police. Tim on the floor of the living room—bleeding and unconscious but still alive. Shane on the floor of the living room—knocked out cold. Three dead, three survivors.

I was the one who told the police that Shane had tried to strangle me with my necklace. When Tim regained consciousness, he confirmed Shane had come at him with a knife and taken him down. But Tim forced himself to get off the floor and had hit Shane on the head with a baseball bat and knocked him out to keep him from following me out the door—just before collapsing himself. Shane's fingerprints were found all over the knife.

Shane was the only one who told a different story. He claimed that he never stabbed Tim—and it was *his* knife, so of course his fingerprints were on it. He claimed Tim had knocked him out, and he couldn't remember anything that happened afterward. He alleged that Tim must have stabbed himself to make it look like he was the innocent party. But of course, I was the tiebreaker who backed up Tim's story. When I told the police about what Shane had done to me, he was the one arrested.

Even though I never saw his face through the whole thing.

And now Shane is spending his life in prison. Tim, on the other hand, is my boyfriend. Someone who I'm beginning to think I might have a future with, for the first time since I became a single mother at eighteen years old. He's a great guy. The best, really.

Shane was the one who tried to strangle me that night. He had to have been.

Tonight, Tim and I are celebrating. I got the job at the primary care practice, and the salary and benefits are amazing, not to mention it's much closer and much less scary than the prison. The interview went really well, and they even apologized for not responding to my first request for an interview when I was sending my résumé all over town—apparently, some disgruntled patient had called and warned them about me. I felt terrible that a patient disliked me enough to do that, but I tried to put it out of my head. At least I have the job now.

So I handed in my notice at Raker Penitentiary, and even though Dorothy made a bit of a fuss about it, when I pointed out the fact that I hadn't once met the physician who was supposed to be supervising me, she quickly changed her tune and wished me luck at my new position.

I won't have to deal with Dorothy or Marcus Hunt ever again. I won't have to see Shane ever again. Thank God.

Margie comes over to babysit for Josh so that Tim and I can have a night alone. Tim got it in his head that he wanted to cook dinner for me, so right now, I'm heading down the block to his house. I'd love to spend the night there, but it's not fair to ask that of Margie, so the two of us will go back to my house at the end of the night.

As I press my finger against the doorbell, a random thought floats into my head: I wonder if Kelli Underwood ever came over here. I'm certain Tim told me the two of them had a couple of dates, so it's not impossible he might have invited her over. She might have stood in this very spot, ringing the doorbell.

She's still missing. It's been a week now. I've been checking the news daily for updates, and the tone of the stories is sounding less and less optimistic. By now, if she were able to, she would have contacted somebody. The longer somebody is missing, the less chance there is of them turning up alive and well.

I tried to bring it up last night with Tim, and he changed the subject. I suppose I don't blame him. He seems uncomfortable talking about his exes—as do I.

Tim opens the door to the house, wearing a T-shirt and jeans. His whole face lights up when he sees me at the door, the way it always does. You would think now that we've been dating for over two months, he wouldn't always look so excited to see me. But he does. It feels like fate that we ended up together after all these years.

"Brooke!" he says. "Get in here. It's cold!"

He's right—the temperature has dropped in the last week, and my thin jacket doesn't seem nearly warm enough. Raker gets a lot colder than Queens.

Once I'm inside the house, Tim helps me out of my coat and then wraps his arms around me to warm me up. I rest my head on his shoulder, feeling a rush of happiness. I never thought I'd have a relationship this good ever again. With every passing day, I'm more and more certain that Tim is The One. And he's made it no secret that he feels the same way about me.

"Hey," he says, "how did Josh's math test go?"

Last night, Josh and Tim spent an hour studying the addition of fractions with different denominators for his test today. I had tried to explain it to Josh the week before, but somehow it didn't get through. Luckily, Tim is a professional elementary school teacher who taught this very subject.

"He got a hundred," I say.

"All right!" Tim does a fist pump. "That's great."

"I'm glad one of us is good at teaching math to ten-year-olds."

"Don't feel bad. You're cute at least."

I laugh and smack Tim on the shoulder. "You know what you've done, don't you? You're going to have to do this from now on every time Josh has an exam. You are now the designated teacher."

He smiles at me. "I don't mind that."

As I head to the living room, I smell something tantalizing coming from the kitchen. It's not as good as Margie's kitchen aromas, but it smells pretty damn good. I inhale deeply as I settle down onto his sofa. "What are you cooking for me?"

Tim sits beside me on the sofa. "Guess."

I take another sniff. "I smell tomato sauce."

"Ding ding ding."

I remember the one other night I came over, Tim cooked spaghetti and meatballs. "Spaghetti and meatballs?"

He makes a face at me. "Should I be offended that the fact that you smell tomato sauce makes you assume I must have made spaghetti and meatballs? I *am* capable of making other things, you know."

"Well, what is it then?"

"It's spaghetti and meatballs," he says, a touch defensively. "But it *could've* been something else. It could've been lasagna. Chicken parmigiana. Just saying..."

I lean in to kiss him. "I love spaghetti and meatballs."

He kisses me back, pulling my body close to his. Is this the way he kissed Kelli Underwood? She certainly seemed to think he was a good kisser.

No, stop it. Why am I thinking about that?

"I love you, Brooke," he murmurs in my ear.

Since the first night he said it to me, we have opened up the floodgates. He loves telling me he loves me. And I can't say I don't love being loved. "I love you too."

He pulls away and glances back at the kitchen. "Do you smell something burning?"

"No."

He frowns. "I better go check on the food. I'll be right back."

As Tim dashes into the kitchen to tend to the spaghetti and meatballs, I lean back against the sofa cushion. I notice something bunched up against my thigh, causing an uncomfortable pressure, and I reach back to see what it is. Between the sofa cushions, my fingers locate a balled-up cloth.

I tug on the cloth until it comes free. That's when I realize it wasn't a cloth at all. It's a green silk scarf, which had blended into the fabric of his green sofa.

Whose silk scarf is this? It sure as hell doesn't belong to Tim. I bring the fabric close to my nose, inhaling the scent of a woman's perfume. The smell is vaguely familiar.

"The sauce is fine," Tim declares as he returns to the living room. "I'd say the food should be ready in about ten minutes. I hope you're hungry, because I made way, way too much."

I can't even manage to force a smile. My fingers are wrapped around the silk scarf in my hand. "Tim, whose scarf is this?"

He barely glances at it. "I don't know. Yours?"

"It's *not* mine."

He looks more carefully at the green fabric in my hand, his eyes narrowing. "It doesn't look familiar to me. Maybe it's my mother's?"

Of course, that makes sense. This is, after all, Tim's parents' house. It shouldn't be suspicious to find a piece of women's clothing stuck in the furniture. Maybe the perfume I was smelling seemed familiar because it was the same one that Mrs. Reese used to wear all those years ago.

Yes, that must be what it is. After all, it's not like Tim is bringing other women here. He wouldn't cheat on me.

Tim tugs the scarf out of my hand and tosses it onto the coffee table. Then he slides onto the couch next to me, so close that his thigh is pressed against mine. "Listen," he says, "there's something I want to talk to you about."

"Oh?"

"Yeah." He reaches out and squeezes my hand. "I just…I'm wild about you, Brooke. I always have been. And I know we haven't been together that long, but I hate being away from you for even one night. So I was thinking…maybe…"

Is he asking me if we should move in together? If that's the question, I don't know what to say. I'm wild about him too. But I have Josh to think about. I can't uproot his life by having another person move in with us just to have it all fall apart. I can't give my son a father and then take it away from him.

And there's another reason why I'm not sure I'm ready to take things to the next level with Tim. I can't shake the feeling that he's hiding something from me. Why has he been so evasive every time I have tried to ask him about Kelli? He already told me he went out with her. Why won't he admit it?

And who does this scarf really belong to?

Tim must notice the look on my face because he releases my hand and backs away on the sofa. "You know what? Let's talk about this later."

My shoulders relax. "Good idea."

"Hey." He squeezes my knee. "Why don't you grab a bottle from the wine cellar? I think we could use a drink."

It's sort of adorable that Tim calls their basement a wine cellar, but he's already run off to the kitchen to take care of whatever is burning, so I don't have a chance to tease him about it. It's not a wine cellar—at all. It's a basement with, like, a dozen bottles of wine and a wood rack that his dad built. But I suppose if he wants to call it a wine cellar, I won't begrudge him that.

While Tim is in the kitchen, I turn the knob to the basement door. Like my house, his house is old, and the door sticks, so I have to wrench it open. And of course, the basement is pitch-black. I feel around for the drawstring to turn on the lightbulb. After grasping around blindly for about thirty seconds, my fingers make contact. A single bulb flickers on, dimly illuminating the basement.

The basement of Tim's house feels colder than it is outside—almost frigid—and the air is slightly moist. As soon as I enter, I identify an unpleasant musty odor that wasn't here the last time I retrieved a bottle of wine from the basement—he's probably growing mold down here. I make my way down the lopsided wooden stairs, holding on to the icy metal banister so I don't go flying. It's dark enough down here that I am nervous about the placement of my feet on the ground.

When I get to the bottom, the wine rack is waiting for me. He seems to have added a few extra bottles since the last time I was down here. Not that Tim is any sort of wine connoisseur, but he just gets a kick out of having a wine cellar.

After pulling out a few bottles to check the labels, I select a bottle of merlot. Does merlot go well with spaghetti and meatballs? I have no idea. But it will taste good and give us both a nice little buzz.

Just as I'm about to go back upstairs, I notice a gray tarp rolled up on the floor of the basement in the corner of the room. I hadn't noticed that tarp the last time I was down here looking at the wine collection. What is Tim doing with a giant tarp?

I creep over to the rolled-up material—the strange smell is stronger over here. Even in the dim light of the basement, I can tell something is sticking out of the end. I bend down and realize what it is—it's a shoe. No, not just a shoe; it's a high-heeled red pump.

And it's still on a woman's foot.

I stare at the foot sticking out of the tarp, unable to comprehend what I'm seeing. I look closer and can make out another shoe peeking out of the tarp as well. Does Tim have a mannequin wrapped in a tarp in his basement?

Don't kid yourself, Brooke. You know exactly what you're looking at. Her scarf is lying on the coffee table upstairs.

I've got to get out of this basement.

I drop the merlot on the ground, and the bottle shatters into dozens of pieces. I run for the stairway, taking the steps two at a time, not bothering to be careful this time. I place my hand on the knob and…

It doesn't turn.

Oh God. It's locked.

CHAPTER 42

Tim sent me down here to get wine. He wanted me to see that dead body wrapped in the tarp. And now he has trapped me down here.

"Tim!" I bang on the door to the basement. "Tim!"

Everything makes sense in a horrible sort of way. He's been toying with me all this time. That sandalwood aftershave—he must have known how I felt about it. What if he was the one who splashed it on that night at the farmhouse so I would think he was Shane? And then, of course, that damn snowflake necklace. He's the one who gave it to me. He knew that was the necklace used to choke me that night—because he was the one who did it. He kept it all these years, and he gave it to me just to freak me out.

Why did I trust him? I should have listened to Shane. He *warned* me. He told me that I couldn't trust Tim Reese. He begged me not to have anything to do with him. But I didn't believe him. There were so many signs, and I ignored every single one of them because I blindly trusted Tim—the boy I knew since we were babies.

Tim is sick. I never realized it until this moment.

"Tim! Let me out of here!"

He can't keep me down here, can he? He would never get away with it. Margie knows I'm here, and so does Josh. If I didn't come home, they would know. They would call the police and tell them where I am.

Unless he plans to do something to them too…

I've got to get out of here. I can't let him do to me what he did to Kelli. But how? I brought my phone with me, but it's in my purse, which I left on his living room sofa.

The knob shakes slightly. I hear Tim grunt, and I take a step back as the door pops open. He is standing in front of me, his eyes looking almost hollow in the light of the hallway.

"Sorry about that," he says. "Door must have stuck."

I stare at him. Is he really pretending like I didn't just see what I saw down there?

He raises his eyebrows. "What wine did you pick out?"

I glance over my shoulder at the bottle of merlot that is lying shattered on the floor of the basement. "Actually, I'm not feeling so great. I…I think I'll head out."

"Seriously?" His jaw tightens. "I just spent the last hour cooking dinner. You're really going to leave?"

"I…" I press my fingertips against my temple. "I have a migraine."

"You get migraines? You never mentioned that to me."

"Well, I do."

"Because this is the first time you have had a migraine the entire time we've been together."

My temple throbs. In another second or two, I really will have a migraine. "So I'm not allowed to have a goddamn migraine? Is that what you're saying?"

He jerks his head back. "That's not what I'm saying. I'm just saying…don't go. Let's talk for a minute."

"I'd rather not."

"Is this about what I said earlier? I'm sorry I said anything. I didn't mean to pressure you."

"I want to *leave*, Tim."

I don't wait for an answer. I push past him to the front door, snatching my purse off the sofa. My phone is in there and so is my pepper spray—I'll use it if I have to, although I hope I don't. Tim races to catch up with me. His legs are much longer than mine, and he grabs my arm before I even make it to the living room. His fingers encircle my forearm, digging into my skin.

"Brooke," he says. There's a look in his eyes that I barely recognize. This is not the Tim I know—it's another side of him I've never seen before.

"Let me go," I hiss at him.

"Brooke, what—"

At that second, the doorbell rings. Tim looks at the door, then back at me. He releases my arm, and I back away from him, my body trembling. At the same moment I do, he notices the flashing red-and-blue lights through the window by the doorway. "What the…?"

It's the police. What are they doing here? It's like I called them psychically.

I hang back as Tim marches over to the door. He twists the locks and throws the door open. He seems taken aback by the appearance of a uniformed officer on his front porch. Relief washes over me. The officer is tall and muscular and looks like he could take Tim in a fight.

"Thank God you're here!" I gasp before the cop can open his mouth. "He wasn't letting me leave, and...and there's a dead body in the basement."

Tim's jaw drops. "A *dead body*? Brooke, how could you—"

The police officer seems just as shocked as Tim. I'm still not sure how he ended up here or what he wants with Tim, but he takes a step into the house, his hand on his holster. "Are you Timothy Reese?"

"Yes." Tim's eyes are bulging out. "But...but this is ridiculous! Brooke, what are you thinking?"

"You have a body in the basement," I spit at him. "I saw it! Is it Kelli?"

"Kelli! Are you out of your mind?" He looks between me and the cop. "Officer, this is completely absurd. There's nothing in my basement."

"And her scarf is on the coffee table," I tell the officer.

Tim gapes at me. "What are you talking about? That's my *mother's* scarf."

The officer speaks into what looks like a walkie-talkie mounted on his chest. A second later, a second officer appears at the door. "Mr. Reese," the first officer says, "we came here because of an anonymous tip that a missing woman named Kelli Underwood was seen entering your home the night of her disappearance."

I think I'm going to throw up. All this time, I believed Tim was a good guy. How could I have been so wrong? I wish I could take back the last ten years.

"This is ridiculous," Tim says. "I didn't even know Kelli Underwood."

"How can you say that?" I cry. "You went out with her! You kissed her!"

The color drains out of Tim's face. He flashes the officers a helpless look. "Okay, I went out with her *once*. Months ago. I haven't even seen her in at least two months."

"He's lying!" Tears gather in my eyes. "She's down in the basement, wrapped in a tarp. I saw her!"

"This is ridiculous!" Tim cries. "I promise you, Officer, there is *no* dead body in my basement. All I've got there is a wine cellar—I swear."

The first officer locks eyes with Tim. "You mind if we take a look in your basement?"

There's a look of growing panic on Tim's face as he looks between me and the policeman. "Listen…" His voice trembles. "Just wait. *Wait*. You don't need to—"

I don't know the law, but I'm guessing that the officer has probable cause at this point. He brushes past Tim, who looks like he's going to have a stroke. Tim starts to follow him, shouting protests, but the other officer, who is older with gray hair, drops a firm hand on his shoulder.

"You stay right here, son," the cop says to Tim.

"There's nothing down there." Tim's eyebrows are scrunched together. "It's just my wine cellar."

The tears are dripping down my face now. I can't stop them. The cop notices me crying and flashes me a sympathetic look. "Are you okay, miss? Did he hurt you?"

"I didn't hurt her!" Tim bursts out. His face is bright red. "Brooke is my girlfriend. I would never—"

A voice floats up from the basement. "We got a dead body down here! Looks like Underwood!"

Quick as a flash, the older officer whips a pair of handcuffs off his belt. Tim looks like he's about to be sick now. "Timothy Reese, you are under arrest for the murder of Kelli Underwood."

"Please." Tim's face is turning pink as the cop snaps the cuffs on his wrists. "I don't know what's in my basement, but I didn't put her there. I swear to you..."

But the cop isn't listening. He reads Tim his rights as he hustles him toward the front door. I watch the entire thing, and it's so surreal, I feel like if I pinch myself hard, I might wake up in my bed in a cold sweat. Tim killed Kelli Underwood and stashed her body in his basement, likely intending to get rid of it at some point. He probably also killed that girl Tracy Gifford all those years ago. And I'm almost certain that he was the one who strangled me that night.

I got it all wrong. I made a terrible mistake and trusted the wrong person. Because of that mistake, a murderer went free, and now a girl is dead.

I have to do whatever I can to make this right.

CHAPTER 43

The police keep me at Tim's house for over an hour, questioning me over and over again. I tell them about how I found the body in the basement, that Tim wouldn't let me leave, and I mentioned my suspicions about that night at the farmhouse over a decade earlier. They want me to come down to the station with them, but I explain to them I've got to get home to my son, and I'm not going anywhere with them unless they want to arrest me. They reluctantly let me leave.

When I get back to my house, Margie and Josh are in the kitchen. They're sitting at the kitchen table, painting decorations on sugar cookies shaped like Christmas trees. The scene is so sweet, I almost burst into tears.

"Hi, Mom!" Josh excitedly holds up one of the finished products. The tree has been painted with green icing with red trimming. "Look at what we're making!"

He takes a bite out of the cookie. I'm afraid to ask how many of those he's eaten. Margie is great with him, but she's not good at enforcing *moderation*. On any other night, it would've upset me. But tonight, I can't make myself care about my son eating too many cookies.

"Where's Tim?" Josh asks.

There's a hard lump in my throat. "Um…"

Margie's wrinkled forehead crinkles deeper. "Is everything okay, Brooke? I…I heard the sirens…"

"It's fine." My voice sounds unnaturally high. "Margie, thank you so much for coming tonight. We'll see you on Monday, okay?"

Margie looks at me curiously as she tucks a strand of gray hair behind her ear, but she obediently collects her coat and her purse. I walk her to the door, and before she leaves, she gives me one last look. "Are you sure everything is okay?"

I nod, barely trusting myself to speak. "Uh-huh."

With Margie gone, I return to the kitchen, where Josh is polishing off the rest of the tree-shaped sugar cookie. He frowns when he sees me. "Where's Tim?" he asks again.

"Tim…" Oh God, how am I supposed to talk to my son about what just happened? The reason I never told him about his father was to spare him this. "He isn't coming over tonight."

"What?" Josh juts out his lower lip. "But he said that we could play Nintendo together if I got a hundred on my test, and I did!"

"Something came up."

"But that's not fair! I got a perfect score! He said he would play with me. He promised."

"I know, but…" I slide into a seat next to Josh. "He wanted to come, but something happened. He did something bad, and the police found out and had to take him away."

Josh stares at me. "What did he do?"

It's the most obvious question he possibly could have asked, and I am utterly unprepared for it. "He committed a crime."

"Did he steal something?"

"No."

"Then what did he do?"

"He…he hurt somebody."

Josh scrunches his face up. "Tim wouldn't hurt anybody on purpose."

He has no idea.

"He did, honey," I say. "And…he's probably going to go to jail. For a long time."

"You mean he's not coming back here?"

I shake my head slowly. Tim will never set foot in this house again. Not over my dead body. It makes me sick the way I allowed him into our lives.

Josh leans back in his chair. His face turns pink, and I don't realize he's crying until he swipes at his eyes with the back of his hand. It's so hard to watch him cry quietly. I miss those loud, dramatic tears from when he was little. This is so much more heartbreaking.

"Josh," I say, "please don't cry."

"*You're* crying."

I touch my eyes and realize he's right. My entire face is wet with tears. Josh climbs into my lap like he used to when he was a toddler, and I hold him close to me while we both mourn the loss of yet another person from our lives.

CHAPTER 44

TWO MONTHS LATER

The sight of the barbed wire fence around the maximum-security prison still makes me edgy.

I quit my job at Raker Penitentiary about two months ago. I've been here several times since then, but only as a visitor. In the parking lot, you can see the sharp spikes at the top of the fence and the guard towers flanking the outdoor yard.

I won't be here long though. I'm barely going to get out of the car. And after today, I'll never come back here again.

A lot has happened in the last two months. Aside from my new job, which I love, Tim is currently incarcerated, awaiting trial for multiple murders. While he was dating me, he was also stalking Kelli. I had no idea, of course. From my end, he seemed like the perfect boyfriend. Although several people from the elementary school claimed that they knew there was something a little off about him.

I recanted my testimony about the night at the

farmhouse. Even though I knew I could get in a lot of trouble for it, I had to do it. I had to tell the police that I realized I got it wrong. Shane hadn't been the one who tried to strangle me that night. It was Tim. He was the one twisted enough to try to kill me with the very necklace he bought me.

And then he saved it for an entire decade. Waiting for the right moment to use it against me.

Fortunately, I didn't get into a lot of trouble after I recanted the testimony. It was an honest mistake on my part—it was, after all, an extremely traumatic night. And this paved the way for Shane to get a new lawyer and have the verdict of his trial overturned.

Today, after eleven years, Shane Nelson is being released from prison.

And I am picking him up.

The doors to the prison open, and Shane comes out, wearing an old black coat, a pair of blue jeans, and sneakers that likely used to be white but are now a shade of gray. He's got a duffel bag slung over his shoulder, which holds all his belongings in the entire world. I wave to him so he sees me, and he waves back.

When he gets closer, the dark circles under his eyes are more visible, but at least he doesn't have any bruises on his face. I had been worried that something could happen in the last few days that might keep him from coming home, but nothing else has gone wrong.

"Brooke. Hi."

"Hi," I say.

When I visited him at the prison the last couple of months, we had to talk to each other through a wall of glass, using telephones mounted on the wall. We couldn't touch each other. Now there's nothing separating us, but we just stand there, smiling nervously. I don't know which one of us looks more anxious.

"Thanks for picking me up," he says.

"No problem." It's not like he has anyone else to do it for him—besides me, he's alone in the world. "How does it feel to be out?"

It's such a stupid question, and I feel silly for having asked it. But for the first time in a long time, the smile on his face looks genuine. "It feels amazing."

It won't be an easy transition back to regular life. Shane at least got his GED, but he had planned to go to college, and of course, that never happened. He has no money, and although he'll likely be completely cleared of all charges, it's hard to erase the fact that he spent the last decade of his life in prison. He can't just carry on like the last ten years never happened.

It's my fault, and I'm going to do whatever I can to help him.

I reach into my pocket and pull out a flip phone. I hold it out to Shane. "Here's a phone for you to use if you need it. It's got a bunch of prepaid minutes."

He takes it from me, turning it over in his hand. "Wow. At the prison, this would be major contraband. Thank you so much."

"It's not a big deal."

"I know, but I appreciate it."

I nod, my face suddenly hot. "Well," I say, "let's get on the road."

Shane throws his bag into the trunk of my car, and then he climbs into the passenger seat beside me. "I've *got* to get my driver's license back."

"I don't mind being your chauffeur in the meantime," I tell him.

"Thanks, Brooke."

"Want to grab some fast food on the way back?"

His mouth practically starts watering. "Jesus, you read my mind."

It turns out that taking a guy who's been in prison for the last ten years to a fast-food restaurant is even better than taking a kid to a candy store. Shane stares at the menu for, like, ten minutes, his eyes huge, and he ends up ordering more food than I've ever seen him eat in one sitting. After he orders, he digs out this envelope full of cash from his pocket, but I make him put it back. He has practically no money—the least I can do is treat him to this meal.

When he finally takes a bite of that greasy fast-food burger, he looks like he's going to die from happiness. "Holy shit, this is a fantastic burger."

I look at my own burger, with its rubbery patty and limp lettuce. "I guess."

He stuffs, like, eight french fries into his mouth all at once and then takes a long sip from his vanilla milkshake. "I'm sorry. You don't know what I've been eating for the last ten years."

"Was it that bad?"

He cringes. "I don't want to talk about it. But yes."

For a moment, I imagine Tim sitting at one of the long tables in the prison dining hall, staring down at a tray of mystery meat and waterlogged vegetables. It's what he deserves. It's *better* than he deserves.

"So," Shane says, "when does Josh get home?"

As much as he is enjoying this fast-food meal, it's become clear from the conversations I've had with Shane in the last several weeks that what he is really looking forward to is meeting his son. He was adamant that I couldn't bring Josh to see him at the penitentiary. *I don't want him to see me like this.*

"The bus usually arrives at our house at a quarter after three," I say.

He nods. "So…"

We're not entirely sure how the best way to handle this situation is. It's not the kind of thing you can easily look up online. *How do you introduce your son to his father who has been in jail for murder for ten years?* It's tricky. All I have told Josh so far is that an old friend of mine would be staying with us for a bit.

"I'm just going to say you're my friend," I tell him. "We're agreed on that, right?"

Shane nods. "I just want to meet him. We can tell him the truth when the time is right."

"Exactly."

"I was thinking…" He takes another bite of his burger. "Maybe on the way back, we could stop off, and I could buy him a present, you know? What sort of thing do you think he would like?"

"He loves baseball, but it's too cold to play now." I think for a minute. "Honestly, these days, he mostly likes his Nintendo."

"I could buy him a game?"

"They're so expensive though."

Shane flinches. "Well, maybe I could—"

"Shane." I reach for his hand, but at the last minute, I pull away. "Just relax. All you have to do is talk to him and maybe play some Nintendo with him. He's an easy kid. He'll like you."

He smiles sheepishly. "Okay. Sorry. This is just really important to me."

"I know. But trust me—it will be fine."

Josh *is* an easy kid, and I'm sure he'll like Shane. The hard part is going to be explaining to him who this man really is and why we have kept it from him for so long. How much of the truth can we tell him? I don't want to lie to him, but he's ten years old. I don't know if he can handle the entire truth.

I guess we'll play it by ear.

CHAPTER 45

After we get back to my house, the first thing Shane wants to do is take a shower. When I give him the go-ahead, he makes a beeline for the upstairs bathroom, and then he's in there for over half an hour. He comes out looking like he just spent the day at a spa.

"That was the best shower I've had in ten years," he announces. "I got to make the water any temperature I wanted. I could spend as long as I wanted in there. And I wasn't naked next to five other guys."

"Sounds great," I laugh.

He looks down at his watch. "So the bus should be here soon, right?"

"Pretty soon." I took the day off from work and gave Margie the afternoon off as well. "It probably will come in the next ten minutes."

"Okay." He rakes a shaky hand through his damp hair, then looks down at his blue jeans. "Do you think what I'm wearing is okay?"

He is so adorably nervous. I walk over to him and place my hands on his shoulders. It's the first time I have touched him since he walked out of the prison, but it feels right. "Don't be nervous. He's going to like you. I *promise*."

"How do you know?"

"Because." I grin at him. "You're a likable guy."

Our eyes meet, and one corner of his lips quirks up. Now that he's cleaned up and is out of his prison jumpsuit, he looks so different. I had forgotten quite how sexy Shane could be. And I have to admit, he has upped his game in the last ten years. Even the scar on his forehead that I stitched up myself is sexy.

It also occurs to me he has not been with a woman in over a decade. And tonight, he'll be sleeping in the bedroom right next to mine.

The quiet moment between us is interrupted by the sound of the doorbell ringing. It's Josh. The school bus has arrived.

Shane leaps away from me, staring at the door while tugging at his shirt collar. I rush over and unlock the door, and there is Josh, standing at the entrance with his backpack slung over one shoulder like this is any ordinary day and not the day he's about to meet his father for the first time.

"Hi, Mom," he says. "I'm hungry."

"Josh." I glance back at Shane, who is wringing his hands together. "We have a visitor here. This is Shane."

"Hi, Josh," Shane says. "It's really nice to meet you."

Josh ignores Shane and drops his backpack right in the center of the foyer. He's supposed to put it on the side, but he always manages to put it in the exact right spot for somebody to trip over. "I didn't even have lunch," he whines. "They had ravioli for lunch, and they only gave me, like, five ravioli. Five, Mom!"

I look over at Shane again, worried he's offended that Josh mostly just seems interested in having a snack, but he doesn't look upset. He's just smiling and staring at Josh like he can't quite get over it.

"Fine," I say. "What do you want for a snack?"

"I don't know. What do we have?"

"You know what we have!" Oh my God, this kid can try my patience sometimes.

"When I was a kid," Shane speaks up, "I used to love peanut butter on Ritz crackers. My mom used to make that for me all the time."

Josh looks up at Shane, considering his suggestion. The two of them look so much alike, it gives me chills. I wonder if Josh notices. I'm sure Shane does.

"Okay," Josh says. "I'll have that."

Thankfully, we have both Ritz crackers and peanut butter in the pantry—I think Margie uses them for snacks. Josh goes to play Nintendo while Shane helps me construct the snack in the kitchen. I put the crackers on the plate, and he covers them in peanut butter. It's not exactly a two-person job, but it gives us a chance to talk.

"I'm sorry he was kind of rude," I say.

"No way." Shane beams at me. "He liked my suggestion. That was great. Also..." He lowers his voice. "He reminds me a lot of myself at that age."

"I know. He looks a lot like you."

"Not just that." He casts a glance over his shoulder. "There's something about him. His personality. He just... it makes me think of what I used to be like at that age."

I don't want to disagree with Shane, but internally, I am shaking my head. Josh is *not* like Shane. I didn't know Shane that well before we started dating, but everyone knew Shane Nelson was wild. Josh isn't that way at all. He's shy and sweet and has never once started trouble at school.

"Why don't you go play Nintendo with him?" I suggest.

Shane's eyes light up. "Yeah?"

"Sure. Why not?"

"I used to play at friends' houses when I was a kid." Of course, the Nelsons could not afford a Nintendo. They could barely afford to keep the lights on. "You think he would want me to?"

"He definitely would."

I finish making the Ritz crackers snack myself while Shane goes into the living room to join Josh. I can just barely see them, and I can't hear anything they're saying, but it looks like it's going well. Shane leans over to Josh, talking to him. Then he settles down on the couch next to him.

After ten years, Josh is finally spending time with his father. I can't wait to tell him the truth.

CHAPTER 46

While Shane and Josh are playing Nintendo, my phone rings with a number I don't recognize.

When Tim was first arrested, I learned not to answer the phone if I didn't recognize the number. Mostly, it was reporters on the other line, desperate for a firsthand account of my experience both eleven years ago and over the last few months. They offered me mind-boggling amounts of cash to tell my story, but I always refused. It's bad enough I'll have to testify at Tim's trial—I have no desire to relive it with a reporter and then see my story smeared all over the news and the internet. Not to mention it would increase the chances of Josh finding out the truth.

And then there were the haters who used to call me. People who were furious with me for sending an innocent man to jail. For falling in love with a man who turned out to be a killer. I had to change my email address because my inbox was flooded every day with angry messages and even threats. I changed my phone number too, but it didn't help. If someone truly wants to reach you, there's always a way.

But it's been long enough. There have been, like, a hundred other news stories since Tim's arrest, and the public has a short memory. Reporters aren't interested in my story anymore. I'm yesterday's news, and that's the way I prefer it.

So it's safe to answer the phone.

I click the green button to accept the call as I settle down at the kitchen table. "Hello?"

"Brooke?"

It's a woman's voice. She sounds older, about the same age my mother would have been, but I don't recognize her.

"Yes…" I say.

"Brooke, this is Barbara Reese."

I cringe, wishing I hadn't taken the call. Barbara Reese left several messages on my voicemail way back when Tim was first arrested, but I never returned any of them. She was desperate to talk to me, which isn't surprising, considering I'll be testifying against her only son at his trial. And that's all the more reason I can't talk to her.

"Mrs. Reese," I begin, "I can't—"

"Please don't hang up, Brooke." Her voice breaks on the words. As hard as the last couple of months have been on me, I'm sure they were even worse for her. "Please. I need to talk to you."

I want to hang up the phone, but I can't do it to Mrs. Reese. The truth is I really liked her when I was a kid. I spent about half my childhood at Tim's house, and Mrs.

Reese was way nicer than my own mother. She always had better snacks than at my house, she and her husband made the best burgers on the grill, and she always had kind words to say to me. Not to mention when my mother caught Tim and me in a lip-lock that time when we were in middle school (practicing!), she did her best to smooth things out with my hysterical mother. I always envied Tim for his mother.

"I'm sorry," I say, "but we don't have anything to talk about."

I pull the phone away from my ear, but I'm stopped by the sound of Mrs. Reese crying out, "Please don't hang up, Brooke! Please just hear me out!"

I let out a long breath. "There's nothing to talk about. I…I saw a dead body in his basement. I'm sorry. I know it's hard to hear that. I never would've thought Tim would do that either."

"He wouldn't!" Mrs. Reese has lost her composure. "Brooke, you knew him better than anyone. Do you really believe he would kill that girl?"

"The body was *in his basement*."

"So someone else must have put it there!"

I feel a rush of sadness. She doesn't believe it because she wasn't stuck down in that wine cellar where a dead girl was wrapped in a tarp, rotting on the basement floor. She didn't see the panic on Tim's face when he realized the police were going down to the basement. It would have taken a lot to convince me that my former best friend was a serial killer, but that night made me a believer.

At that moment, Shane comes into the kitchen with his empty glass of water. He starts to fill it up, but when he notices I'm on the phone and catches the expression on my face, he raises an eyebrow at me. He mouths the words, *Who is it?*

"Please talk to Tim," Mrs. Reese whimpers. "If you talk to him and you still believe that he did those horrible things—"

"I'm not going to visit Tim in jail." That is absolutely out of the question. "I'm sorry, Mrs. Reese."

Shane's other eyebrow shoots up at the name *Mrs. Reese*. He stands there, clutching his water glass in one hand, listening to my end of the conversation.

"You have to, Brooke!" Mrs. Reese cries. "This is all happening because of you. Don't you understand? Give Tim a chance to explain. You have to—"

Before Mrs. Reese can complete her sentence, Shane snatches the phone right out of my hand. He presses it to his ear, listens for a second, then clears his throat loudly.

"Mrs. Reese," he says in a firm voice, "this is Shane Nelson. You need to leave Brooke alone. Don't call this number ever again." With those words, Shane jabs at the red button on the phone, then tosses it on the kitchen counter. "Some nerve of her," he mutters.

"To be fair…" I look up at him. "Your mother called me when you were on trial and said almost the exact same things."

"Right, but I was innocent."

"I'm sure Tim's mother thinks he's innocent."

"Oh, please." Now that I'm off the phone, he fills up his glass with water, right to the brim. "She knows the truth. How could she *not* know? She raised him after all." He takes a drink. "Don't you think if Josh were a killer, you would know it?"

It's funny because when I believed Josh's father was

a murderer, I was always watching my son for sociopathic tendencies. If he had shown any at all, I would've jumped all over it—but Josh was a good boy. Still, kids change after they grow up. Will I know him when he's thirty as well as I know him at age ten?

"I don't know," I finally say.

He rolls his eyes. "Don't be naive, Brooke. Tim's mother isn't looking for the truth. She's just looking to get her son off the hook. You can't let that happen."

He's right, of course. Mrs. Reese will do whatever it takes to get her son acquitted. But it's going to take a lot more than convincing me.

CHAPTER 47

After the stressful day I have had, I can't even contemplate cooking dinner. Instead, we order a pizza. There's a cute moment when Shane and Josh discover they both love pepperoni on a pizza, and I swear, Shane looks like he's going to tear up.

The conversation at dinner flows easily. I had forgotten how naturally charismatic Shane could be, and even though he's trying a bit too hard, Josh doesn't seem to notice. Josh has been a bit down ever since Tim was arrested, and this is one of the nicest dinners we've had since that night.

After Josh goes upstairs to finish his homework, Shane remains at the kitchen table, smiling to himself.

"What?" I say.

"He's a nice kid," he says.

"Yes. He is."

"He seems smart too." He cocks his head. "Good at sports?"

"*Really* good. You should see him hit a baseball."

His eyes widen. "Could I?"

"Well, not now. But when the weather gets better. And Little League starts up in the spring. You can go to his games—I'm sure he'd love that."

I've never seen anyone's entire face light up at the prospect of attending a kids' softball game, which are admittedly pretty boring. "Thank you, Brooke," he says.

"For what?"

"For doing such a good job raising our son."

I take a quick glance at the stairwell. "Careful what you say. The walls are thin around here."

"Right. Sorry." He clears his throat. "Anyway, I just wanted to tell you that I appreciate you putting me up here. I'll be out of your hair soon."

I blink at him. "What are you talking about?"

"Oh." He lifts a shoulder. "I forgot to mention. I heard from my lawyer, and apparently, my mom left me the farmhouse in her will. So after I get that place cleaned up, I can live there. I figure I'll head over tomorrow."

The farmhouse. The place where it all happened. The *massacre*.

"How could you want to live there?" I say. "After everything that happened."

His eyebrows inch upward. "That was my *home* for eighteen years, Brooke. And honestly, it's not like I have a lot of options."

"You can stay here as long as you want."

"I don't want to impose."

"You won't be."

He looks down at the plate in front of him, stained

with pizza grease. "I appreciate your generosity, but this is not my home. I need my own place. You get that, right?"

I get it, but I don't like it. That farmhouse only appears in my nightmares these days. I can't imagine how he could possibly want to live there. The thought of going anywhere near it makes me physically ill.

"If that's what you want," I finally say.

Just don't ask me to visit.

We get everything cleaned up from dinner, and I go upstairs with Shane to collect some bedding for the guest bedroom. I grab him an extra blanket too, because it's started snowing, and the room seems a bit chilly. He insists he can make his own bed, so I leave him to it while I say good night to Josh.

Josh is done with his homework and is quietly reading in bed. He puts down his book when he sees me walk in.

"I brushed my teeth," he tells me.

I settle down on the edge of his bed. For the first five years of Josh's life, the two of us shared a bed out of necessity. (It was excellent for my love life.) And now the kid has his own room. "Good job. All the homework is done?"

"Yep." He hesitates. "Mom?"

"Yes?"

"Why is that guy Shane staying with us?"

"He's an old friend." The lie is getting easier and easier. "He's just going to be staying a few nights. Why?"

Josh shrugs his skinny shoulders. "No reason."

"Don't you like him?"

He hesitates, and my stomach sinks. Josh likes *everyone*. Although I thought it was possible he and Shane might not be the best of friends immediately, it never even slightly occurred to me that Josh wouldn't like him.

"He's okay," Josh says carefully.

"Was he mean to you?"

"No."

"Is there something you don't like about him?"

"No." But again, there's that hesitation. There's something he's not telling me, and it gets me frustrated that I can't get it out of him.

I don't know what Shane could have done wrong though. I have had my eyes on them practically the entire time since Josh has been home. Shane has been great with him, considering he has zero experience with kids. I mean, Tim was a teacher. That was what he did for a living. Obviously, he was better at making friends with a ten-year-old boy than a guy who spent the last ten years of his life in prison.

"How long is he staying?" Josh asks.

"Like I said, not that long. Maybe a few nights."

Is it my imagination, or does Josh look relieved?

I don't know what Josh has against Shane, but I'm not going to let on to Shane about any of this. He would be completely crushed. I have to pretend Josh thought he was great.

When I get into the guest bedroom, Shane has just finished putting the new sheets on the bed. He's shaking out the blanket, but he lays it down when he sees me. "Hey," he says.

"Hey."

"So..." He rubs the scar on his forehead. "Did Josh say anything about me?"

I can't tell him that Josh seemed happy at the idea he wouldn't be staying long. "He likes you."

It was the right thing to say. A smile stretches across Shane's lips. "That's awesome. You know, I was thinking, maybe until I get a job, I could be here when Josh gets home from school every day and keep an eye on him for you."

"Oh." I avert my eyes. "Well, the thing is, we already have somebody who is here every day. So..."

"But this would save you money. And I'd get to spend time with him."

"Let me think about it," I say, even though I won't. There's no way I'm getting rid of Margie, especially when Josh doesn't even seem to like Shane that much. "Listen, there's some clothing you could wear in the top drawer over there."

Shane opens the top drawer of the dresser by the bed. He pulls out a men's T-shirt, which I now realize has the word *Syracuse* on the front of it. It's where Tim went to college, and from the look on Shane's face, he knows it. "Is this *Tim's* clothing?"

"Yes," I admit. "It was in the house so..."

Shane drops the T-shirt in disgust. "Great."

"I'm sorry." It hits me now how inappropriate this was. It didn't seem like a bad idea before though. I mean, it's just clothes. "I'll get you something else to wear tomorrow."

He lets out a sigh and drops onto the edge of the bed. "No, it's fine. I can't be picky. And it's all just clothes."

"I washed it," I say weakly.

He looks down at his lap. "It's my fault you were even in this position. If I had protected you better from him that night..."

"You tried to warn me."

"I did." He raises his eyes. "It kills me that he's been

taking advantage of you since you came here. I'll never forgive myself for letting it happen."

I settle down beside him on the bed. "It wasn't your fault. You were in *prison*. Anyway, it worked out in the end." I gently place a hand on his. "I'm glad you're out now."

He chuckles. "Me too."

He looks down at my hand on his, and then his eyes rake over me. The longing on his face is unmistakable. I suppose I shouldn't be surprised. The man has been in prison for a decade. He hasn't even *touched* a woman in all that time.

And Shane is still *very* attractive. I used to swoon when I watched him running across the football field, and he's even sexier now that he's older. He's more muscular than he was in high school—he must have worked out a lot in prison. He's hard to resist.

But I can't do this. And I better take my hand off his. Now.

When he notices I have withdrawn from him, he looks away. "Shit, I'm sorry."

I try to keep my voice even. "It's okay."

"I don't want to make you uncomfortable at all," he says. "I'm not going to lie—when I look at you, I want to…but anyway, that's my problem. Not yours. I promise you, I'm going to be a perfect gentleman while I'm staying here."

"Thank you." I smile at him. "And you shouldn't have any problems in the romance department. You're pretty hot."

He laughs. "Am I? That's good to know."

"I'm just saying. I don't think you're going to have

much trouble finding a woman to make up for lost time with."

"Hey, I don't want some random woman at a bar that I don't care about." He chews on his lower lip. "I mean, yeah, it's been a long time. But I still want it to be with someone I care about. Someone important to me."

"Shane..."

"Like the mother of my son."

His words stir something inside me. *The mother of my son.* Shane is something to me that nobody else can be. He is Josh's biological father. After all these years, he is the only man who can make this family whole. He wants to be here with me, and our son will never be second best to him like I feared he would be to any other man I chose to marry.

"Brooke?" he says. His eyes are filled with unmistakable lust.

"You should get to have that," I tell him. "You shouldn't settle. You should have that special connection."

When he leans forward and kisses me, I don't stop him.

CHAPTER 48

I wake up covered in a cold sweat.

Shane and I ended up having sex last night. I didn't quite mean for it to go all the way, but I could tell it was what he wanted very badly, and I couldn't bring myself to say no. After all, he had been deprived of this for ten years. You can't say no to giving a glass of water to a guy who has been lost in the desert for ten years.

Okay, I realize it's not the same thing. Still.

It was over quickly, and afterward, I felt strangely empty. Shane drifted off to sleep almost instantly, so we didn't have a chance to talk, which was for the best. I slipped out of the guest bedroom and back into my own room, where I tossed and turned for over an hour before finally drifting off into a restless sleep.

And of course, that sleep was filled with nightmares.

It was the same nightmare I always had. I was back at the farmhouse, in the black living room with the storm raging outside. And that snowflake necklace was tightening around my neck. The bolt of thunder shook the farmhouse, and a link on the necklace snapped.

And that's when I woke up at three in the morning, my nightshirt drenched.

I lie in bed shaking. It wasn't so much a nightmare as it was reliving what happened that night. Tim choking me with that necklace. And then the bolt of thunder. And then…

Something else.

I heard something else just as the thunder erupted. I'm sure of it. But I can't remember what it was. The memory claws at the outskirts of my subconscious, and I squeeze my eyes shut in frustration.

Well, if I haven't been able to remember for ten years, I won't remember now.

I realize that a sound had woken me up from sleep. Something from outside. There's still a snowstorm outside, so it was hard to make out, but it almost sounds like…

A car engine. Right outside my window. And something else:

The garage door opening.

I climb out of bed, my head spinning. I navigate through the dark to the window that overlooks the front of my house. It's pretty dark out there, with just the dim light from one streetlamp, but I can tell my garage door is closed. And…

Are those tire tracks in the snow?

I squint down at the front of my garage door, trying to decide if I should go check it out. Am I losing my mind here? Why would somebody be using my car? The garage door is locked. Nobody is getting in there except from the inside. And the only other person in the house is Shane, and he doesn't even have a valid driver's license. Not that he isn't capable of driving, but…

My heart is pounding too loudly to even attempt to get back to sleep right now. I shove my feet into my fuzzy slippers and creep down the hallway to the guest bedroom, where Shane was sound asleep the last time I saw him. And presumably, he still is.

The door to the guest bedroom is shut. There isn't any sign that Shane has been outside the bedroom. I press my ear against the door, and I can almost make out the sound of him breathing deeply. I don't want to knock or burst in on him. He looked like he could use a good night's sleep.

I'm being paranoid. Nobody was using my car. Nobody is out there. The garage door is closed.

Of course, there's one way to verify this for sure. I could go down to the garage and see if there's snow on my Toyota. If there is, somebody has been driving it very recently.

Except the more I think about it, the crazier it all seems. I don't think I heard a car engine. It must've been part of my dream.

I need to calm down and go back to sleep.

—

By the time I get out of bed in the morning, I feel truly horrible. My eyelids feel like they're glued together, and I almost have to pry them open with my fingers. Before I even shower, I stumble down to the living room to grab a cup of coffee.

Shane is already wide awake and in the kitchen. He's doing something at the stove while he hums to himself. I rub my eyes, watching him for a moment until he finally notices me.

"Good morning!" he says cheerfully.

"Morning." I yawn loudly. "Sorry. I didn't sleep well."

"I slept *great*." When he turns to look at me, the dark circles under his eyes are almost gone. I feel stupid for thinking he was wandering around town in my Toyota in the middle of the night—he was clearly getting the night of sleep I wish I had. "That bed is *so* comfortable."

It's really not. But I know how awful the mattresses are at the prison.

"I'm used to waking up early," he explains. "So I made some breakfast, if that's okay. I also brewed coffee if you want some."

I pour a cup of coffee from the machine. Usually, I put in cream and sugar, but this time, I drink it black. "What are you making?"

"Pancakes."

"Josh loves pancakes. Especially if you throw in a few chocolate chips."

"Will do."

I glance over at the pantry. "I thought we were out of pancake mix."

"I made them from scratch, actually."

"Really?" I didn't even entirely know you could do that. "I'm impressed."

"My mom and I used to make pancakes every Sunday morning," he says. "I'm making a ton of them if you want to wake Josh up and let him know."

He says that last part somewhat shyly. He wants more time with Josh. I get it, but he can't force this.

"After breakfast," he says, "I'll go out and shovel the driveway, okay?"

"That would be great." The snow stopped somewhere during the early hours of the morning, leaving a thick blanket all over the driveway and the street outside the house. I've been shoveling it myself—one of the many responsibilities that fall squarely on me as the only adult in the household. It's nice for Shane to step it up.

"And after," he adds, "I thought we could drive out to the farmhouse. See how bad it looks and maybe clean up a little."

I had a mouthful of coffee in my mouth, and I almost spit it out. "Drive out to the farmhouse? *Today*?"

He flips a pancake, which is now golden brown. "Why not? It's going to take a while to get it ready for me to move in there. And it's Saturday. May as well get started."

"Yes, but..." A cold sweat breaks out on the back of my neck. "I don't know if it's a good idea. It's probably really dirty and maybe even dangerous. It's been sitting empty for a long time."

He purses his lips. "Right, and that's why I need to check it out. It's not going to get any cleaner just sitting there."

My hands are trembling. I place the cup of coffee down on the kitchen table before I drop it. "I just don't feel comfortable driving out there. After everything that happened, you know?"

He looks at me in surprise. "Really? It was eleven years ago."

We did, in fact, just pass the eleven-year anniversary of that horrible night. "Yes, *really*."

He lays down the spatula he has been using to flip the pancakes. "Well, I don't know what I'm going to do then. I don't have a driver's license, so how am I supposed to get out there?"

"I..."

He frowns. "Could you at least give me a ride? You don't have to stay or go inside. Just drop me off."

I hesitate.

"Please, Brooke?"

I feel a stab of guilt. The poor guy doesn't even have a driver's license, much less a vehicle. All he wants to do is go back to his childhood home so he can get it back to inhabitable conditions.

"Fine," I say.

But even as the words are coming out of my mouth, I know I will live to regret them.

CHAPTER 49

Shane scores big points with his pancakes. Josh eats about eight of them and, with a full mouth, declares them to be "the best pancakes ever." Shane could not possibly look happier when he says that.

"Can I grab some cleaning supplies to take out to the farmhouse?" he asks as he's clearing away the food from the table.

"Sure." I don't want to tell him that I had been hoping he might change his mind.

"Thanks so much for doing this, Brooke."

He rests a hand on my shoulder and gives it a squeeze. I squirm, since Josh is still at the table. Yes, we slept together last night, but doesn't he understand that we have to be careful what information gets fed to our ten-year-old son?

Sure enough, Josh's eyes widen slightly at the sight of Shane's hand lingering on my shoulder. But he doesn't say anything.

"So," Shane says, "when can we get going?"

"Going where?" Josh pipes up.

Shane slides back into one of the seats at the kitchen table. "Your mom and I are going to this really cool farmhouse at the other end of town. I used to live there a long time ago."

"Oh," Josh says. "Cool."

"Do you want to come?" Shane asks.

I suck in a breath. I had been thinking Josh would stay behind while I drove Shane out to the farmhouse. But to my surprise, Josh bobs his head enthusiastically. "Yeah!"

"Oh, honey," I say quickly. "You don't have to come with us. It's going to be really boring. We're not even going to go inside."

"But I want to go," Josh pouts.

I guess this is going to be a family trip.

Shane heads outside to shovel the driveway, and I gather cleaning supplies from the house. I don't know what to bring, and I'm worried that the entire house will be filthy beyond words. There isn't carpeting, so I don't bother with the vacuum. I bring the mop and bucket, lots of cleaning fluid, some rags, and two rolls of paper towels. Shane is going to have his work cut out for him.

After I've got all the supplies, I go to grab my car keys to throw everything into the trunk. I keep my keys on the bookcase right next to the entrance to the house, on the fourth shelf from the top, right in front of a copy of *Webster's Dictionary*. Except when I go to reach for them, they're not there.

Where are my keys?

A split second later, I spot the keys on the third shelf. In the same spot where I usually put them, except one shelf higher. I snatch them up in my hand, looking at the key ring as if for a clue.

I'm sure I put the keys on the fourth shelf. I put them there every single day when I get home from the store or work or wherever. It's automatic. I do it without even thinking about it. So while I don't remember putting the keys on that shelf, I'm sure I must've done it.

Of course, when I got home yesterday, a lot was going on. I was bringing home the father of my son, a man who had been locked away in prison for the last decade. I had a lot on my mind. If there's ever a time when I might have put the keys in the wrong spot, it was yesterday.

Still, it makes me uneasy. Last night when I woke up in the middle of the night, I was certain I heard a car engine right outside my window. And now my keys are in a different place than where I left them.

I wish I had checked my car last night. If somebody had been using it, there would've been snow on it. But now it's too late. Any snow would have melted.

The front door swings open, and Shane bursts into the house, his gloves caked with snow. He rests the shovel in the corner by the door where he found it and smiles at me. "You got everything we need?"

This is silly. I must've just put the keys in the wrong place. I have a lot on my mind. I shouldn't drive myself nuts overanalyzing this. And anyway, what if Shane *did* take the car somewhere last night? Would that really be the worst thing that ever was? Maybe he just wanted to know what it was like to be behind the wheel again after all that time. I couldn't blame him.

"Yes," I say. "I got it all."

Fifteen minutes later, we have loaded up the Toyota with the cleaning supplies, and I get on the road with Shane in the passenger seat and Josh in the back. I have this awful sick feeling as I pull onto the road, but I promised Shane I would do this. I can't back out.

"You know how to get there?" he asks.

"Yes," I snap.

He's quiet for a moment. "Are you okay?"

No, I'm not okay. We are driving out to the house where I was almost murdered eleven years ago. There's nothing about this that is okay. But I can't exactly say all that in front of my son. "I'm fine."

"I appreciate you doing this."

"Yep."

Shane seems to realize that I don't want to talk about this anymore, so he shuts up and leans back in his seat. The roads have been mostly cleared out in the morning, so even though I don't have all-wheel drive, it's not too bad navigating around Raker. It isn't until I turn onto the smaller road to get to the farmhouse that it gets a little slippery. The road has been plowed but minimally, and because it's below freezing temperature, a lot of the remaining snow has turned into ice.

"Jesus," Shane comments as the car skids off to the side. "Be careful, Brooke. Don't you know how to drive in the snow?"

Not very well. I didn't have a car back in Queens—I just took the bus where I needed to go. This Toyota is the first car I have ever owned, and this is my first winter dealing with serious snow.

"Maybe you could give me some tips sometime," I say.

"Yeah, maybe."

I drive slowly for the rest of the mile stretch out to the farmhouse. I must be going less than ten miles an hour. After a few minutes, the house comes into sight.

It looked bad eleven years ago, and if possible, it looks even worse now. The red paint has nearly completely worn off, except for a few little patches, and the steps to the front door have almost completely crumbled away. The roof is covered with snow, and it seems to at least be holding up, but I bet there's plenty of damage there as well. This house is a little more than a fixer-upper.

Shane is staring at his old home, his hands clutching his knees. I can't quite read his thoughts until he bursts out, "Look! It's my old Chevy!"

Sure enough, Shane's old car is still parked out by the house, covered in a healthy layer of snow but still recognizable. I'm sure the car will need as much work as the house to get it into usable condition. I pull over next to the Chevy, hoping I can still get my car out after this. The Toyota is not good at backing out of snowy areas.

"That's where I used to live, Josh," Shane tells him.

"It's like a haunted house," Josh comments.

Shane winks at me. "It might be."

I wouldn't entirely be surprised. After all, three people died here. It feels like Shane isn't quite feeling the gravity of that. He actually seems *happy* to be here.

"Hey," Shane says to Josh, "you want to see inside?"

"Sure!"

I open my mouth to protest, but Shane and Josh are already climbing out of the car. I'm so angry at Shane right now, I want to scream. We had an *agreement*. I told him I would drop him off here and then leave. But if my son is going into the house, I obviously can't leave. So I have no choice but to hurry after them.

I start to yell at Shane to be careful about the steps, but without having to be told, Shane helps Josh up the four stairs to the front door, making sure he doesn't slip or fall. I follow behind, gripping the handrail to keep from sliding off the icy stairs myself. Shane digs around in his pocket for a key, which he fits into the front door. As he's unlocking the door, I feel a sick sense of déjà vu, from back when Shane and I were dating and he brought me back to his house a few times.

"Shane…" I say.

"Let's just take a quick look around," he says.

He struggles a little to get the door open, between the wood being splintered and rotten and the entire front of the house being frozen. He has to put all his weight against the door, but it finally pops open. And then, against my better judgment, we step inside.

The inside of the house is just as cold as the outside. There's no power, but since it's daytime, it's not as dark as it was that night eleven years ago. There are cobwebs stuck to the ceiling, and all the furniture is coated in a thick layer of dust. The smell of frost and mildew permeates the air.

But at least it's better than sandalwood.

"Geez." Shane looks around. "This place has sure seen better days."

My gaze strays to the area in front of the stairwell. That's where it happened. That's where Tim tried to strangle me with my own necklace.

Josh runs a finger along the sofa. He holds up his fingertip, which is now coated in black. "Look, Mom!"

"Yes, it's dirty."

"The sofa is a lost cause," Shane says. "But I could clean up the floor. And the kitchen…"

He's looking at me hopefully. He wants my help. He *needs* my help. It's going to take him the rest of his life to get this place cleaned up on his own. And now that I'm inside and I'm not actively having a panic attack, maybe this won't be as bad as I think it's going to be. Maybe I'll finally get over what happened here that night.

Maybe it will help me heal.

"Okay, we can stay here a couple of hours," I say. "And that's it."

Shane nods eagerly. "Thanks so much, Brooke."

"All right," I say. "Let's go get the cleaning supplies."

CHAPTER 50

The three of us clean as a family.

Even Josh gets into it. He hates cleaning his room, but this is more of a cleaning *adventure*. You have no idea what disgusting nugget you're going to find around every corner. For example, in an empty garbage can in the kitchen, we find a frozen rat. It's the most disgusting thing I've ever seen, but Josh gets a real kick out of it. And Shane gets a kick out of him getting a kick out of it.

"Please get rid of that rat," I mutter to Shane. "I don't want him trying to take it home to show his friends."

Shane laughs. "You definitely understand the mindset of the ten-year-old boy."

Unfortunately, after about two hours of cleaning, we have released a fair amount of dust into the air, and Josh can't stop sneezing. His nose turns red, and his eyes are watering.

"I think you need to go outside," I tell him. "Get some fresh air."

"Actually," Shane says, "we could take a walk. The woods right around here are really cool during the winter. We could even build a snowman. What do you say, Josh?"

"Sure," Josh agrees.

I shake my head. "It's too cold. I don't want to wander around in the woods."

Shane glances over at Josh and then looks back at me. "Well, I could take him myself if you want to stay behind."

An alarm bell goes off in my head. *Don't let him do this.* "I don't know if it's a good idea."

Shane looks at me for a moment, his eyes darkening. "Why not?"

"Because it's not safe."

"It's perfectly safe." He frowns. "I used to go through these woods all the time when I was his age. By *myself.* And I'll be with him—I'll look out for him."

"I know but—"

"I'll keep him safe." Shane's face turns slightly pink. "Don't you trust me?"

Do I?

I was the one who made sure Shane got released from prison. I invited him back into our lives. He's my son's father. He's our chance at being a family again, and if I can't trust him, I have much bigger problems than the two of them taking a walk together in broad daylight.

Josh tugs on my arm. "I want to go, Mom."

Even Josh wants to go. The two of them are finally bonding. It would be cruel to keep it from happening.

Shane reaches into his pocket and pulls out his flip phone I bought him. He shakes it in the air. "I've got my phone. You can reach me if you need to. And I've got your number if I need you."

"Fine," I say. "Just be careful."

Shane lays a hand on his chest. "I swear, I will protect him with my life."

I believe him.

I make sure Josh puts on his hat and gloves, and Shane does the same. I walk them to the door and watch them step into the small wooded area next to the farmhouse. At one point, Josh slips on a patch of ice, but Shane reaches out and steadies him.

It will be fine. Shane is Josh's father. He won't let anything happen to him.

I go back into the farmhouse, closing the door behind me. It is getting cold out there, definitely below freezing. I bet that after ten minutes, Josh will start complaining and want to go back inside. Although he isn't as bothered by the cold as I am. I always have had to struggle to get him to put his coat on for school, as if there's any chance I would let him go to school in just a sweatshirt when it's twenty degrees out. I wonder if Shane was the same way when he was a kid.

My back aches slightly from all the cleaning, so I take a minute to sit on one of the chairs we cleaned off. I dig my phone out of my coat pocket—it's just barely getting a signal. One bar for the cell service, but I guess that's enough. I bring up the internet browser and hesitate for a moment before typing "Timothy Reese."

I don't know why I keep looking him up. Nothing changes day to day now that it's been two months since his arrest. Right after, his name was plastered in every single newspaper. It was a big story—a mild-mannered assistant principal who killed a former girlfriend and might have been responsible for multiple murders years earlier.

Tim has had the gall to plead innocent—I almost feel like he's doing it to torture me. A woman's body was found in his basement. Does he really think there's any chance he is walking out of prison after something like that? I've already been told that I will be testifying at his trial. I'm dreading it, but that's what I have to do. It's my fault he didn't go to prison ten years earlier. He had me completely fooled.

I'm not going to waste any more time thinking about him. I delete his name from my search engine.

Instead, I bring up the local news site on my phone. I'll browse a few stories while I'm waiting for Shane and Josh to build their snowman or for Josh to get cold and want to come back, whichever comes first. It takes forever for the news site to load up. The text pops up first, with the pictures still loading on the screen. This is probably going to drain my battery. While I'm waiting, I look at the first story:

LOCAL PRISON GUARD FOUND MURDERED

I stare at the headline, my heart sinking into my stomach. It couldn't be. It *couldn't*.

I try to click on the headline. Nothing happens. Why does the internet have to be so bad out here? The picture next to the headline is filling in practically pixel by pixel. The beginning of a bald skull materializes on the screen.

It can't be Marcus Hunt. It *can't*.

And then the picture fills in a bit more. Just enough so that I can see his eyes.

Oh God. It's him. It's Hunt. He was found dead—possibly today. I tap on the article again, but the screen has completely frozen. I'm not going to get to read this story. I don't know when this happened or how, but somehow, Marcus Hunt has been murdered.

This is breaking news. Which means they must have just found him recently. Was he killed overnight? I have no idea.

But I do know that this morning, my car keys were in a different place than I left them when I came home yesterday. And I also know that after everything that happened at Raker Penitentiary, Shane must despise Marcus Hunt with a burning passion.

My head is spinning. I jump out of the chair, pacing around the room as if it might give me some clue about what went on last night. But of course, the room is completely silent. No clues. Just a lot of dust.

I freeze when I get to the foot of the stairs. I rest my hand briefly on the banister. Like everything else, it's dusty.

This is exactly where I was standing when Tim tried to strangle me. I had just come down the stairs, running out of Chelsea's room because, for some reason, I got it in my head that she might have stabbed Brandon and Kayla. Little did I know, she would be dead herself soon after, and my decision to leave the room cost my best friend her life.

I close my eyes, trying not to think about that night, but that only seems to make it worse. The more I try not to think about it, the more vivid it all seems. In the last few years, the memories had almost faded. But now that I'm standing in this farmhouse again, it seems like it all happened yesterday.

I ran out of Shane's bedroom. I raced down the stairs as quickly as I could, then I tripped. And then quick as a flash, Tim was on top of me, tightening that necklace around my neck as the smell of sandalwood filled my nostrils. Then there was a crack of thunder, masking another sound I couldn't quite make out.

I can almost feel the weight of his body crushing me. The air being cut off from my lungs. And I try to scream:

Shane, no!

My eyes fly open again. I back away from the stairwell, my heart pounding in my chest. As the years went by, I started to doubt myself. I never saw his face, so it could've been anyone that night. Except it *wasn't* anyone. I knew who it was that night. And I know who it was now.

It was Shane.

I had been dating him for months. I knew his body. I knew it was him on top of me. It wasn't Tim, who was skinnier and lankier. It was Shane. Shane was the one who tried to strangle me, and he was probably the one who murdered Hunt last night. How could I have ever deluded myself otherwise?

Hunt was right. Shane *is* manipulative. He really made me believe…

My whole body is trembling. I can almost feel that crack of thunder that shook the house all those years ago. And the sound that it almost masked. The missing piece of the puzzle. I can almost hear it. It was…

A muffled scream.

While Shane was strangling me on the floor of the living room, Chelsea was screaming in the upstairs bedroom. She wasn't screaming because she saw what Shane was doing to me though—because the door to the bedroom was closed. She was screaming because somebody was coming at her with a knife.

Except it wasn't Shane. It couldn't have been.

There was another killer in the house that night. Out of the three survivors, there was only one other person it could have been.

Oh my God.

Tim and Shane did it together.

CHAPTER 51

It makes such perfect sense. I can't believe I never saw it until now.

The night it happened, Shane dropped me off almost right in front of Tim's house. He *never* used to do that. And Tim just happened to be outside, in his yard. They must have figured I would invite him along. And if I hadn't, Tim would have finagled an invitation.

As soon as we got to the farmhouse, even though they claimed to hate each other, the two of them were suddenly deep in quiet conversation. I remember the way they kept looking at each other throughout the evening. I thought it was because they hated each other, but in retrospect, it was more than that.

Shane was the only one who somehow knew Tim had dated Tracy Gifford. We were all shocked he knew about it. But of course he knew. They probably killed her together. She was their practice run for that night.

And then after we found Brandon dead, Chelsea and I

left Shane and Tim alone in the living room. It was almost too perfect for them. Shane went outside, giving Tim a chance to slip up to Kayla's room and finish her off.

And the second Chelsea and I split up, Shane tried to strangle me in the living room. I had believed I tripped over Tim's body in the living room, but it was so dark—I must have tripped on something else while Tim was lurking in the shadows. And while my windpipe was being crushed, Tim went up to Shane's bedroom to simultaneously take care of Chelsea—the sound of thunder almost masked the sound of her screams. I never quite understood when the killer had time to get rid of Chelsea, but now it all makes sense.

When they realized I escaped the house, they must have done some quick thinking. It was obvious the tiny stab wound in Tim's belly was not meant to kill him. It was meant to make it look like he was a victim. Same deal with the bump on Shane's scalp. They were just pretending to be unconscious. Maybe the plan was to hope I never saw the face of the person who choked me, blame the entire massacre on a drifter, and claim the footprints had been washed away.

But then when I blamed it all on Shane, Tim flipped. He turned on Shane, going along with my story in order to save his own ass. It must've driven Shane wild but what could he do? If he told the truth, it would be admitting he was a murderer.

Lucky for Shane, Tim couldn't keep from killing again.

My knees buckle beneath me, and I barely make it to the chair before I collapse. Shane is dangerous. He tried to kill me that night—I have no doubt it was him anymore. And now he is out in the woods with my son.

Our son.

My hands are shaking almost too badly to get my phone out of my coat pocket. I've got to get Shane and Josh back here, and I can't let Shane know that I know what he did. As soon as we get back into town, I'll go straight to the police. I'll tell them everything I know.

The phone rings a gut-clenching five times before Shane's voice comes on the other line: "Hi, Brooke."

He sounds so normal. He doesn't sound like a murderer. I can't let on what I know. "Hey. Are you guys heading back soon?"

"Pretty soon," Shane says vaguely. "We're having a lot of fun out here building that snowman."

"That's great." I try to keep my voice steady and normal. How does my voice usually sound? I can't even remember. "But it's getting late. You should head back."

"Late? It's barely midafternoon."

"It's just…it's cold out. I don't want Josh to get sick."

"He's fine. He's all bundled up."

"Still. I think it's better if you head back pretty soon. You know?"

There's a long pause on the other line. "No, I *don't* know. I'm just trying to spend a little time with my *son*, Brooke. You know, the one I haven't seen in ten years and I didn't even know existed."

"Shane," I breathe. "Listen—"

"No, you listen, Brooke." His tone is clipped—I have destroyed any advantage I had. "I missed ten years. Ten *years*. You didn't even *tell* me."

"I'm sorry," I say softly.

"A little late for that, isn't it?" He snorts. "But don't worry. Now that I'm here, we're going to be making up for some lost time. And maybe *you'll* see what it's like to miss out."

"Shane..." I stand up from the chair, my heart pounding. I hurry in the direction of the door to the farmhouse. "What are you talking about?"

"I think you know, Brooke."

I get outside the front door of the farmhouse. I squint into the woods, in the direction Shane and Josh disappeared. I can't see anything—just blinding white. Where did they go?

"Could we please talk about this at home?" I beg him. "I understand how you're feeling, but we can work this out. I just want to be a family again." I reach into my coat pocket for the keys to my Toyota. "Tell me where you are, and I'll come pick you guys up."

I'm going to drive along the road until I see them. I'm going to find them if it's the last thing I do.

Except where are my keys?

"I think it will be hard for you to pick us up," Shane says, "since I have the keys to the Toyota."

"But..." I keep checking my pockets, certain he's got to be wrong. All I can find are balled-up tissues. "Why?"

"You know why."

This can't be happening. I can't be the one responsible for having unleashed this monster and letting him wander into the woods with my son. This is going to be another one of those dreams that I'll wake up from in a cold sweat.

Wake up, Brooke!

I race down the steps from the front door and slip on the last one. My legs slide out from under me, and a sharp pain jabs my right ankle. My phone has fallen out of my hands and is lying beside me in the snow. I snatch it up.

"Shane," I gasp, "please…let's talk about this."

"Oh, don't worry," he says. "I'll be back eventually." Before I have a second to feel relieved, he adds, "After all, I need to make sure you suffer for what you did."

"Shane…"

"I wonder," he says, "if you'll scream louder than Tracy Gifford did."

My mouth drops open. I try to speak, but no words come out.

"Goodbye, Brooke." I can almost hear him smiling on the other line. "Or should I say, see you later."

Through the phone, I can hear my son's voice. His laughter. I might never hear him laugh again.

"Shane!" I cry. "Please—"

But it's too late. The line is dead.

I try calling him back, but it immediately goes to voicemail. Shane isn't bringing Josh back. I don't know where he is, but he knows I have figured out his game. I have lost my advantage. And even if he comes back eventually to try to hurt me, he'll be smart about it. He's going to wait a long time—until the heat is off.

For some reason, the thought of facing off against Shane doesn't scare me. What scares me is what's going to happen to my son. I can't let that monster get away with this.

I grab onto the railing of the stairs to haul myself to my feet. The second I try to put weight on my right ankle, it screams in pain. It's definitely sprained, possibly broken. I'm afraid to pull off my boots to assess the damage, and it won't do any good anyway. It won't help me find Shane and Josh.

I type 911 into my phone with shaking fingers. He

won't get away with taking Josh. There will be an Amber Alert, they will find him, and Shane will go back to prison. He doesn't even have a car—he may have taken my keys, but the Toyota is still right here. The police will find them. I'm sure of it.

Except when I try to connect the call, it won't go through. I squint down at the screen of my phone.

No service.

It's almost too much of a coincidence that my service cut off just when Shane hung up with me. Does he have some sort of blocker to prevent cell phones from working? Is that what he and Tim did that night eleven years ago to ensure none of us could call for help?

What am I going to do? If I have no cell service and no vehicle, my best bet is to walk to the main road. But I'm not sure I can even put weight on my ankle.

I have no choice though. Even if I'm walking on a broken ankle, it doesn't matter. I have to do this for Josh. I can't let that monster steal him and do God knows what to him.

I put some weight on my right ankle. The pain is almost blinding, but I push through it. For Josh. I'm doing this for Josh.

I limp down the road, every step like a knife stabbing me in the ankle. I don't know how, but I'm going to do this. I'm not going to stop moving until I get to the main road, and then I'm going to flag down a car.

But to my shock and relief, I see a car coming down the road, right toward me. It's a green SUV, like the one Margie drives. Oh, thank God. I don't have to keep walking on my possibly broken ankle. I wave my hands in the air like I did that night eleven years ago. The SUV skids to a halt.

"Help me!" I scream. "My son has been kidnapped! Please help! Please!"

The driver's-side door opens up. To my utter shock, Margie gets out of the car, her gray eyebrows knitted together. "Brooke!" she cries. "Are you okay?"

What a strange coincidence that Margie would happen to be coming down this road right now. But I can't dwell on that. There's no time.

"Josh has been kidnapped!" I manage as I limp toward her. "He's in the woods somewhere. We need to call the police. He's in terrible danger."

Margie's eyes drop to my feet. "What happened? You're limping."

"I slipped on the snow." I am mildly irritated that I need to explain this to her when there is something so urgent happening. "I'm not getting any service. Can you see if your phone works so we can call the police?"

"Of course!" Margie reaches into the car and pulls out her giant purse. She rifles around until she finds her phone. "Oh fudge, there's no service."

I expected that. "Fine, then we'll have to drive to the police station. Let's go—now."

Margie swivels her head to look out at the woods. "Are you sure he's in danger? I mean, he's with his father. I'm sure he's fine."

"Margie—" I start to say, but then I stop myself.

I never told Margie that Shane was Josh's father. I never even told her I was with Shane. And I certainly never told her where I was today. Even though she doesn't look the slightest bit surprised to see me here.

"Margie?" I say.

Her lips curl slightly. "That's not actually my name.

We have met before, and you do know me by my real name, but I doubt you would remember it. Of course you wouldn't." She titters. "In fact, I'll tell you what, Brooke. If you can tell me my real first name, I'll take you right to Shane and Josh."

I stare at her wrinkled face, trying desperately to place her. While I'm trying to figure it out, she sifts around in her purse again. But this time, instead of her phone, she pulls out a gun.

And she points it right at me.

CHAPTER 52

I don't understand what's happening here. Why does Margie have a gun? What is she doing here? How does she know Shane is Josh's dad? I'm sure I never told her that. I never told anyone except Tim—and he wouldn't have told her.

"Margie," I gasp. "Why...why are you doing this? I thought we were friends."

"Friends!" Margie throws back her head and laughs until her jowls shake. "No. We weren't *friends*. I only *tolerated* you so that I could spend time with my grandson. That's the only reason I didn't spit in your face."

My mouth falls open. "Your..."

"Josh *is* a very sweet boy," she muses. "Not as sweet as *my* boy, but of course, he was raised by *you*, not me. All those years, your witch of a mother wouldn't even tell us he *existed*. Can you believe that?"

I can only shake my head. "I don't understand. What about your daughters? What about your grandchildren?"

She grits her teeth, her knuckles whitening as she clasps the gun tighter. "I don't have any daughters. I have *one son*, and I have watched him rot in prison for the last ten years. And I have one grandson that I didn't even know existed until a year ago."

"You're Shane's mother," I gasp.

"I didn't expect you to remember me." She shrugs. "We only met a few times, and it was a long time ago. And it wasn't like I meant anything to you."

It's not just that. Pamela Nelson looks very different from the way she did a decade ago. I remember her as having dark hair and a curvy figure, but the woman I hired to take care of Josh was gray-haired and pleasantly plump. She entirely changed her appearance over the last decade. I didn't have a chance.

"Mrs. Nelson..." I've got to appeal to her. I know she cares about Josh, and he adores her—she *was* much better with him than my mother ever was. Maybe she doesn't realize what kind of monster her son is. Of course, she's holding a gun, so I'm guessing she must understand *something*. "Look, I know you love Shane, but he has done some terrible things. I was wrong about that night eleven years ago. It wasn't Tim. I mean, it was, but he was working together with Shane. The two of them killed three people that night."

Mrs. Nelson sneers at me. "Oh please. Is that really what you think?"

"Yes! It's the truth. Tim and Shane were working together. While Shane was strangling me in the living room, Tim was upstairs, and he...he stabbed my best friend."

"No," she says. "He didn't."

"You don't know that!"

"Yes, I do." She shakes the gun at me. "Because I'm the one who stabbed Chelsea."

My whole body goes numb. *What?*

"You really think that Goody Two-Shoes Tim Reese would have done that?" She snorts. "He was just our patsy, starting with that girl he dated...Tracy Gifford. The plan Shane and I came up with for that night was to let him live so the police would blame it all on him. And if you hadn't gotten away, it would've worked."

I can't believe what I'm hearing. This doesn't make sense. I know what I saw in Tim's basement. "What about that woman, Kelli Underwood?"

She licks her chapped lips. "I had to get my son out of jail. I knew you were going over to Tim's house that weekend, so I got everything ready. I even called in the anonymous tip to the police. And it was *so* helpful that the two of you exchanged keys so I could get into his basement."

I stare at the barrel of the gun. This woman is out of her mind. How did I never see it? I even called up a reference, and they raved about her. I can't imagine who I was talking to—the reference was obviously fake.

"It disgusted me to watch you dating that man." She sneers at me. "Watching him treating *my* grandson like his own child. But I had to encourage you to stay with him. It was the only way to clear Shane's name. And oh my Lord, you should have seen your face when he gave you that necklace I sold him at the flea market over the summer. I found it on the floor of my house after you ran out, and I thought it might come in handy someday."

My face burns. I should have known. I always

believed Tim Reese was a good man. I should've trusted my gut.

"Why would you do it?" My ankle throbs, but I barely feel it. I need to keep her talking, keep her from pulling the trigger while I figure out a way out of this. "Why would you and Shane kill a bunch of innocent teenagers?"

"Killing the other three was unfortunate," Mrs. Nelson says in a voice that doesn't sound like she cares much at all. "*You* were the target, my dear. A lesson had to be taught."

"Me...?"

She brushes a strand of gray hair from her face. "Did you ever wonder why your parents were so adamant that you couldn't date Shane? You probably just thought it was because he was white trash. They never told you the real reason, did they? Because if they did, you would've stayed away from him instead of dating him behind their backs."

I shake my head wordlessly.

"When Shane was five years old, I fell in love with your father." Her voice cracks slightly. "We were together for almost a year. He was supposed to leave your mother for me. He told me he would. He was supposed to save us—me and Shane. But then he decided he couldn't do it. He couldn't leave your mother, and he couldn't leave you. So he left us instead. You got to live the life that Shane and I should have had."

"I...I had no idea..."

"Of course you didn't!" She tightens her grip on the gun. "You were too busy living your charmed life. You had no *idea* what your father did to us. And your mother knew all about it, and she wouldn't give us a red cent. My son had to work all through high school just to help pay the mortgage here." She pauses. "Those two deserved to die. I would have done it anyway—even if I didn't have to do it to get you to come back here."

I clasp a hand over my mouth. My parents' accident. I had thought it was an act of God, but apparently not. This woman killed them. She's even crazier than I gave her credit for.

I hadn't been close to my parents. I never forgave them for the way they shunned me after I decided to have Shane's baby. Although now I understand it a little better. I understand why they never wanted me to come back to Raker and hid my pregnancy from everyone they knew. It wasn't because they were ashamed of me—they didn't want Shane's mother to find out she had a grandson.

"I told Shane what they did to me," she says, "and we planned the whole thing together. It was all his idea. He is *such* a good son. He would do anything for his mother. *Anything*."

"I'm sorry about what my parents did to you," I say carefully. I've got to remain calm. For Josh's sake.

"They could have at least told me about my grandchild!" she bursts out. "They took so much from me. I deserved to know about Josh. I deserved to be part of his life—not just the last six months!"

There are tears in Mrs. Nelson's eyes. Maybe there's a way to persuade her to put the gun down. Maybe I can reason with her. She does love Josh after all. Despite how dangerous she is, she has a good side. She couldn't fake the way she was with him.

"Mrs. Nelson," I say slowly, "Josh adores you. And you've been like part of the family these last few months.

Can't we find a way to work it out? To be a family together?"

For a moment, she almost seems to be considering it. She lowers the gun ever so slightly, her features softening. I take a tentative step forward, but then the gun goes right back up. "We can't work it out."

"Margie, please..." I say, even though it's not her real name.

"No." Her voice is firm. "We can't trust you. You'll betray us, just like your father did. The only way Josh, Shane, and I can be a family is if you're out of the picture."

"Please." My knees tremble beneath me. "*Please*. You don't have to do this."

"I didn't do it." A smile creeps across her lips. "A drifter driving by did it. While Shane and Josh were in the woods, he shot you in the head and stole all your money. *Very* sad. Lucky thing Josh's father is around to step it up."

"Please."

She's going to kill me. Shane and Josh are going to come back from their outing in the woods, and they're going to find me lying dead in the snow. Josh has always wanted to meet his father, but he needs *me*—his mother. He can't grow up without me. I can't let this happen. I can't let these two maniacs raise him.

But I don't know how to stop it.

Then a resounding thump echoes through the wind, coming from somewhere out in the woods. Mrs. Nelson jerks her head to the side at the sound, and now I see my chance. My only chance.

So I lunge at her, grabbing for her right wrist with everything I've got.

CHAPTER 53

The gun went off, but it didn't hit me. It must have fired off into the distance. I struggle against Mrs. Nelson. She's a lot stronger than I would have thought for a woman her age, but I'm in good shape too. Of course, I've got that twisted ankle, but I don't even notice it anymore. I've got to overpower Mrs. Nelson. It's my only chance. I've got to do this for Josh.

And then the gun goes off again.

This time, Mrs. Nelson goes limp against me. The gun clatters to the snow beneath me, which I now see has a spreading stain of red. She's been shot.

I snatch the gun up from the snow as Mrs. Nelson collapses beside me. She's got a hand on her light-brown coat, and the fabric is slowly turning dark. She's been shot in the chest. The color drains from her face, her life trickling out into the snow in a growing circle of red around her body.

"Mrs. Nelson?" I whisper. "Margie?"

She opens her mouth, but no sound comes out. A little blood trickles out of the side of her lips. Lying there on the ground, disarmed, she doesn't look like the evil woman who was pointing a gun at my face. She looks like the kindly grandmother who cooked fresh, home-baked meals for my son every single night and was always on time so he never came home to an empty house.

Bile rises in my throat. I didn't mean to do this. I didn't mean to shoot her. She might *die* because of this. But it wasn't my fault. I had to do it. It was her or me.

Somehow that doesn't make it easier.

I close my eyes for a moment and take a deep breath. I don't have time to freak out about Mrs. Nelson. I have to keep moving. She might not be a danger to me anymore, but my son is still with that maniac.

I've got to save him.

Hang in there, Josh!

I limp around the side of the car, clutching the gun in my right hand. I feel comforted that I have it, but Shane may have one too. And truth be told, I don't know how to fire this thing. I understand that you pull the trigger, but that's about the extent of it. I certainly can't aim worth a damn.

But as I start into the woods, a small figure emerges from between the trees. It takes a second to recognize that it's Josh. He's all alone, and he's sobbing hysterically. But he looks unharmed.

"Mom!" he manages. "Mommy!"

I shove the gun into my coat pocket so he doesn't see it. He races into my arms and clings to my body for dear life. "Josh, what did he do to you?"

"Mom!" He raises his face, which is streaked with tears. "There was an accident! I think Shane is hurt!"

What?

"A snowdrift fell on him from a tree!" Josh hiccups. "He's over there!"

My ankle is screaming in pain, but I allow Josh to tug me deeper into the woods. Just when I can't stand it another second, I spot the snowman in the distance—the one Shane and Josh had been building together. Josh tightens his grip on my arm. "That's where he is!"

I don't want to keep walking, and it has nothing to do with the fact that my ankle is killing me. Eleven years ago, Shane Nelson tried to kill me. Five minutes ago, his mother tried to kill me. Even if he is temporally incapacitated, there's no telling what he might do to me out here, with no witnesses aside from a scared little boy.

What if this is a trick? What if he is lying in wait, and the second I get over there, he's going to jump up and wrap his fingers around my neck?

"Mom!" Josh is tugging on my arm. "You have to come help him!"

I reach into my pocket and wrap my fingers around the gun. If he tries to attack me, I'm going to be ready for him. I shot his mother. I can shoot him too.

I push on for the last ten yards, my hand gripping the pistol. Just past the snowman, there's a figure lying in the snow. The figure appears completely still.

And not just that, but there are droplets of crimson around his head, marring the perfect white of the snow.

"Is he okay, Mom?" Josh wipes his nose with the back of his hand. "The ice from that tree over there just all fell on him at once!"

The trees are all covered in frozen icicles that hang down like ornaments on a Christmas tree. It's actually very beautiful. My hand is shaking around the gun as I tentatively step closer to get a better look at Shane, lying in the snow. His body is half-covered with snow and ice, and his face is bloody. There's a gash on his forehead much bigger than the one I sewed up all those months ago.

And his eyes are open and not blinking.

"You need to call an ambulance!" Josh tugs on my sleeve again. "He needs to go to the hospital!"

I can't bear to tell him the truth. I hated this man, but Josh doesn't know that. He doesn't know that the icicles from the tree may have saved his life. He doesn't know that the man lying in front of us in the snow is his father—the one he has been desperate to meet all these years.

He doesn't even know Shane is dead.

CHAPTER 54

ONE MONTH LATER

"I saw Tim today."

Josh drops that little nugget on me at the dinner table. I'm in the middle of chewing a bite of macaroni and cheese. And I'm not talking about gourmet macaroni and cheese made with four different varieties of cheese, with a layer of crispy, buttery bread crumbs on top like Margie (sorry, I mean *Pamela Nelson*) used to make. I'm talking about macaroni and cheese from the box. It came in a six-pack that cost three dollars. It's flavored with powdered cheese that is labeled cheese number forty-two.

I don't know what happened to the other forty-one cheeses. I don't want to know.

"You did?" I ask, wanting desperately to hear the story but not really wanting to hear it at all.

"Yep." Josh smacks his lips on the *p*, which has become an annoying habit of his. "When I went to the corner to mail that letter for you. He was also mailing a letter."

A million questions are running through my head. *How did he look? Is he okay? Did he mention me? Does he hate my guts?* "Did he say anything?"

"He said hi."

"And what did you say?"

"I said hi back."

This could be the most uninteresting story Josh has ever told me, yet I'm hanging on his every word. "And then what?"

Josh lifts a skinny shoulder. "I went back home."

The suspenseful story of Josh running into Tim for the first time since he got home from jail appears to now be over, and Josh goes back to shoving macaroni in his mouth. I saw the Oldsmobile in the driveway of the Reese house a few days ago, and I deduced that Tim's parents had returned to Raker to pick him up and help him put his life back together after all the murder charges ended up being dropped.

As it turned out, Pamela Nelson survived the gunshot wound, and it was a good thing she did. She ended up confessing to everything, which is more than Shane was ever willing to do. After she found out her son was dead, she didn't really care anymore. She told the police everything—the whole shocking story.

For example, she told them how she helped cover up Tracy Gifford's murder eleven years ago, when Shane had come to her in a panic, Tracy's blood on his hands, and told her what he had done. But getting away with Tracy's murder made them cocky. She told the police how she and Shane planned to kill me that night at the farmhouse to get revenge on my father for not leaving his wife and daughter for her. She even told the police how she had lured Kelli Underwood to Tim's house one night when she knew he was spending the night with me, sending her a text message supposedly from Tim. Then once Kelli was inside, Pamela Nelson pretended to be Tim's housekeeper and offered her a drink laced with sedatives, saying Tim would be home "any minute." After the drink knocked her out, Pamela rolled her body down the stairs into the basement—the fall broke her neck, but it was Pamela slitting her throat that killed her.

The big mistake I made? Social media. My parents always warned me to keep my likeness off the internet, but I had no idea that the family Christmas party thrown by the company I worked for in Queens had plastered pictures of the event all over their Facebook page. That's how Pamela Nelson found out about Josh. And that's why she murdered my parents—to punish them for keeping the secret from her…and also to get me to come back to Raker. She even ensured I would end up working at the prison by calling every medical practice in the area to complain about my shoddy medical care.

And of course, Shane did his part too. He got rid of my predecessor Elise by ratting her out for distributing drugs to prisoners. Not that she was really doing it—she was exonerated as well.

Once DNA evidence confirmed that Shane and Pamela Nelson had been the masterminds behind all these murders, the DA dropped all the charges against Tim. But justice is slow, and he only got out of jail a few days earlier.

Not surprisingly, he hasn't stopped by to say hello.

"Maybe Tim can come over," Josh suggests. "He could fix that string that came off the light in the closet."

The string that turns on the lightbulb in our hall closet popped free in my hand a week ago. Since that time, I have been groping for my coat in the dark every day. I would love to get it fixed. But I have a feeling if I stop by the Reese house, Tim won't be jumping at the chance to do home repairs for me. I'll be lucky if he doesn't slam the door in my face.

"I don't think it's a good idea," I say carefully.

"Why not?"

"I think Tim might be mad at me."

"Why?"

I don't know quite how to explain to Josh everything that has happened in the last few months, so I haven't. He's only ten. I took him to a few therapy sessions after the poor kid saw his father killed right in front of him in a freak accident. Of course, Josh didn't know Shane was his father. He still doesn't. I'm hoping it will stay that way.

Anyway, Josh seems fine now. He misses Margie though. I ended up pulling him out of school for a couple of weeks when everything exploded online, just to minimize the chances of him finding out what his beloved babysitter had done.

Or that she was really his grandmother.

"You should ask Tim to come over, Mom," Josh says.

"I should?"

"Yeah! I miss him."

That tugs at my heartstrings. Josh has lost so much, some of which he doesn't even know about. In the last year, he lost his father, a grandfather, and two grandmothers. All he's got left now is me.

Maybe Tim will never forgive me, but if he could be there for Josh, that's better than nothing.

—

After we finish dinner, Josh stays behind to do his homework while I tug on my coat and boots. I could take Josh along with me to Tim's house, but just in case we get a frosty welcome, I don't want my son around. I fully expect that Tim won't ever forgive me for this. And either way, this won't be a pleasant conversation.

There are still a couple of inches of dusty snow on the ground as I walk the familiar path between my house and Tim's. How many times had I made this journey as a child? Too many to count. Every time I left the house, it felt like the last words out of my mouth were, *Going to Tim's house! Be back later!*

I should have trusted him. I should've known he would never do anything that horrible. Shane had me completely brainwashed. Not that it's any excuse, but I wanted so badly to believe that my son's father wasn't a monster.

I was wrong.

I stand on Tim's front porch, hugging myself, working up the courage to ring the doorbell. It takes me at least a minute or two, and then before I can second-guess myself, I reach out and push my index finger into the bell.

I stand there for close to another minute. There's a very real chance they might not open the door for me.

That I might have to trudge back to my house without even getting to talk to Tim, much less tell him how sorry I am and have him slam the door in my face.

But then the locks turn. I plaster a smile on my face just in time for the door to swing open. But it's not Tim at the door. It's Barbara Reese.

I haven't seen Mrs. Reese in over a decade, but she looks at least two decades older—the same as my mother did before Pamela Nelson killed her. The last time I saw her, her hair was the same maple color as Tim's, but now it's gone all white.

"Hi!" I wring my hands together. "Mrs. Reese, it's me—Brooke."

"Yes," she muses. "I know."

Of course she knows. She hasn't been living on another planet for the last three months.

"I…" I dart my gaze around—I'm having trouble looking her in the eyes. "I was wondering if…if Tim is around?"

"Yes," she says, "he is."

She is *not* going to make this easy for me. It's what I deserve though.

"Could I talk to him?" I ask.

Barbara Reese gives me a long look. I square my shoulders, trying to measure up, even though I already feel defeated. Who am I kidding? I blew it with Tim, not just for me but for Josh as well.

"I'll go get him," Mrs. Reese finally says.

I feel a rush of gratitude. "Thank you. Thank you so much."

She cocks her head thoughtfully. "You look good, Brooke. I can see why he liked you so much."

With that slightly baffling statement, Mrs. Reese disappears from the doorway, closing the door part of the way behind her. I stand there, shivering slightly in a jacket that isn't warm enough for the amount of time I've been out on this porch. I hear raised voices inside the house—Tim and his mother arguing. I can only imagine what they're saying to each other. He doesn't want to see me. That much is clear.

After what feels like an eternity, the door swings open again. And there he is. Tim Reese. The boy next door. The guy I thought I was falling in love with before I *temporarily* sent him to prison for murder.

Oh boy.

He doesn't look great. I remember how I swooned a bit when I saw him standing outside the elementary school on Josh's first day of school. But now he looks tired and pale and about fifteen pounds thinner.

And pissed off as hell.

"Brooke." His eyes are like daggers. "What are you doing here?"

He doesn't invite me in. He doesn't even budge from the doorway.

"Um." I wish I had planned something to say. I could have written down a little speech. Why oh why didn't I write out a speech? "I wanted to say hi."

His eyebrows shoot up. "*Hi*?"

"And welcome home," I add.

There isn't even a hint of a smile on Tim's lips. "No thanks to you."

"Look..." I squirm on the porch. "This hasn't been easy for me either, you know—"

"I was in *prison*, Brooke."

"Yeah, well." I raise my eyes to meet his. "Josh's dad tried to *kill* me. So, you know, it hasn't been any picnic."

"No kidding." Tim folds his arms across his chest. He's wearing just a sweater, and I'm cold in my coat, so he's got to be freezing, but he doesn't look it. "I'd been telling you all along that Shane was dangerous. Didn't I tell you? Didn't I warn you *repeatedly*?"

I hang my head. He absolutely did.

"The guy stabbed me in the gut." His fingers go to the area on his abdomen where he still has that scar. "I was practically bleeding to death, barely conscious, and I dragged myself off the floor when I saw you make a run for it. I grabbed that baseball bat off the floor and hit Shane as hard as I could so he wouldn't come after you. I didn't even know I had it in me, but I knew if I didn't do it..."

I swallow a lump in my throat. I know what he did for me that night. And how did I repay him? I refused to believe him when he was framed for murder. "I'm sorry," I croak. "You have no idea how sorry I am that I didn't believe you."

He blinks at me. "I don't know what to say. It's a little late for that."

"I know you hate me." I wring my hands together. "I get it. But look, don't take it out on Josh. He's lost everyone but me. And he really likes you. At least...at least spend some time with him. It would mean so much to him. I could clear out of the house if you wanted, or I could send him over here or..."

I'm having a lot of trouble reading the expression on Tim's face. But the syllable he utters makes my heart drop. "No," he says.

"Please, Tim." I hate to beg, but I'll do it if I have to. For my son. "Just once or twice even. I know you care about him."

Tim shakes his head. "No," he says. "That's not what I meant. I meant, *no*, I…I don't hate you."

What?

"I mean…" His eyebrows scrunch together slightly like he's surprised by this revelation as well. "I'm mad at you. I'm *really* mad. I thought after everything we went through together, you trusted me more than that. But… Christ, Brooke. I've known you since we were in *diapers*. You were my best friend for my entire life. You were the first girl that I ever…well, you know. And that night at the farmhouse when I told Shane he better treat you right, I meant it. Because you deserve the best." His Adam's apple bobs. "So no. I don't hate you. I could never…"

He doesn't hate me. Tim Reese doesn't hate me. I almost cry with happiness.

"Josh keeps talking about this drawstring for the lightbulb in the closet that came apart," I say. "He wants to fix it with you. If you're free…"

Tim is quiet for a long time. Finally, he nods. "I'll come by this weekend. Take a look."

"Thank you."

"Don't mention it."

I offer a tiny smile. "I'll see you then."

As he closes the door on me, I catch it. It was so quick, if I had looked away for a second, I would have missed it. But it was unmistakable—the corner of his lips quirking up in a smile of his own.

He doesn't hate me. That is a good start. Friendships have been built on less.

EPILOGUE

THREE MONTHS LATER

JOSH

Today was a really good day, because I had a math test at school, and I got a perfect score. I got every single question right. I even got the bonus question right, and I was the only kid in the class who did!

Tim was really proud of me. He and Mom were really mad at each other for a while, but now he's started coming over again, and he helped me study for my math test. And then after I went to bed last night, he and Mom stayed in the kitchen talking. Also, when I got up to use the bathroom at six in the morning, he was coming out of my mom's bedroom in his bare feet. He held up his finger to his lips to let me know I shouldn't mention to Mom that I saw him.

Tim is nice. I like him, and I'm glad he's been hanging around the house more again. I know he's not my real dad, but I would be okay if my mom wanted to marry him or something. Anyway, whoever my real dad is, it seems like he doesn't really want to meet me.

Also, I'm glad Tim is around more because I don't like the new babysitter Mom got for me. I liked Margie. She was really nice, and she cooked better than anyone else, even my mom. And she would always let me help and give me the funnest jobs. Margie used to say things to me like, "You're my favorite person in the whole world. Do you know that?"

But then Mom said Margie did some bad things and she couldn't come over anymore. I saw Margie on TV right after she stopped coming over. But they were calling her a different name. Pamela Nelson. And then Mom caught me watching and shut the TV off.

Anyway, it's nice having Tim around again. He makes my mom really happy. And he's smart too. Like, when he says stuff, I always listen.

For example, a long time ago, at the beginning of the school year when I first moved here, Tim and I were sitting together on the couch, and Mom had gone out somewhere. And he said to me, "There's something really important I need to tell you, Josh."

"What?" I said. I put on a serious face so that he could tell I was old enough to hear something important.

"You need to know," Tim said, "there's a man named Shane Nelson who might contact you someday and want to hurt your mom. This man, Shane Nelson—he's a really bad man. *Really* bad. So if you ever see him or hear from him, you need to know that he's dangerous."

I nodded very seriously. I was glad Tim trusted me enough to tell me that. Even though I didn't really expect to ever meet a man named Shane Nelson.

So I was super surprised when Mom brought home that houseguest named Shane Nelson. He seemed nice enough, but I kept thinking about what Tim told me. That Shane wanted to hurt my mom. Tim said it was really important.

And I trusted Tim.

So when Shane took me out into the woods to make that snowman, I noticed that all the trees had a lot of icicles. They looked really heavy and pointy. Shane was a lot bigger than me, so I figured if I wanted to protect my mom, this was my only chance.

I waited until Shane was standing under one of the branches. I reached up and shook the branches, and all the ice fell on him.

It was a lot of snow and ice. It was enough to make him fall down. I walked over to see if it had knocked him out, like in Little League last year when Jaden threw that ball at Oliver's head (accidentally). But it didn't knock Shane out. He was on the ground, rubbing his head, but he was still fine.

That was when I saw the icicle on the ground.

It was huge—about the same size as the bat in Little League, where I'm the best hitter on the whole team. So I picked it up with my gloved hands, and I swung it—the way Tim showed me when we practiced in the fall. And I swung it again. And again. And again.

I thought it might break, but the ice was pretty strong. It didn't break. It held together really well.

The first time the icicle hit Shane's head, he shouted. But not the second time. Or the third. Eventually, Shane stopped moving at all. I can't remember how many times it took before that happened.

When I do something bad, Mom always tells me to say I'm sorry. But I'm not sorry I hit Shane in the head with that icicle. I had to do it. Tim said he was dangerous and that he was going to hurt my mom. And I could hear when he was talking on his phone that he wasn't being nice to her. Tim was right.

I had to do what I did.

After all, I would do anything for my mom.

READING GROUP GUIDE

1. Why did Brooke apply to the prison when she was so certain that her connection to Shane would be exposed and disqualify her? In the first part of the book, did she seem more worried or excited by the idea of running into him?

2. Brooke struggles to get anything beyond the most basic patient care approved by her supervisor. What is Dorothy's reasoning? Why isn't there room in the budget for treatments that would ensure inmates are not suffering unnecessarily? In real prisons, do you think there are more budget-conscious Dorothys or patient-advocate Brookes?

3. Why was Tim so insistent that Shane was dangerous when they were in high school? Why did Brooke ignore his repeated warnings?

4. How would you describe Officer Hunt? Do you know anyone like him? How does he think about his own behavior?

5. What prevented Brooke's parents from accepting Josh? How did Brooke feel about giving up her relationship with them to care for her son?

6. Tim claims that he's never been able to seriously date because he's been hung up on Brooke since they were children. Is it romantic to hear that someone has never moved on from you or uncomfortably obsessive?

7. Who did you think called the authorities the night Brooke found Kelli's body in Tim's basement? If the police hadn't arrived when they did, how would Brooke's conversation with Tim have gone differently?

8. How much influence did Shane's mother have on him? Do you think he was a willing participant in her first attempt on Brooke's life? Do you think anything changed while he was in jail?

9. Why do you think the author chose to end on Josh's perspective? What do you think the rest of his childhood will be like?

ACKNOWLEDGMENTS

My husband just caught me writing this.

I admitted to him that writing the acknowledgments can be the hardest part of the book. I save it until the bitter end—as close as possible to release as I can get without risking forgetting about it entirely. I am always scared of thanking people inadequately.

"Do you have to write an acknowledgment for *every* book?" he asked.

"*Yes.*"

"But why?"

"Are you asking me why I have to thank the people who helped me? Are you asking me why that's important to do? Is this a serious question?"

"Okay fine," he said. "Hey, do you ever thank *me* in your acknowledgments?"

"Yes, sometimes," I said thoughtfully. "I mean, I thank my family. You're *in* my family."

"Hey, I'm helpful! I give *great* suggestions. It's *your* fault if you don't take them."

"…"

"Conjoined twin. I'm telling you."

On that note, I want to say thanks to my mother for reading this book repeatedly and in the face of eye struggles and for repeatedly nagging me to change the font on the cover. Thanks to Jen for the amazingly thorough critique as always. Thanks to Kate for the great suggestions. Thank you to Avery for the excellent beta critique and for cover advice. Thanks to Rhona for looking at a bazillion covers. Thank you to Val for your eagle eyes. Thank you to Emilie for the awesome beta read.

I want to say a huge thank-you to all my readers out there. I wanted to highlight a few, but there are so many incredible reader friends I have made that I would surely leave someone out. A special shout-out to *all* my McFans! If you're not a McFan, then you must ★spooky voice★ join us…

And as always, thank you to the rest of my family, especially Mr. McFadden. If there's ever a conjoined twin in one of my books, that's all him.

ABOUT THE AUTHOR

#1 *New York Times*, *USA Today*, *Publishers Weekly*, and *Sunday Times* internationally bestselling author Freida McFadden is a practicing physician specializing in brain injury. Freida is the winner of both the International Thriller Writer Award for Best Paperback Original and the Goodreads Choice Award for Best Thriller. Her novels have been translated into more than thirty languages. Freida lives with her family and black cat in a centuries-old three-story home overlooking the ocean.